THE CORNISH WIDOW

Jacqueline Beard

The Constance Maxwell Dream Walker Mysteries are published by Dornica Press

The author can be contacted on her website https://jacquelinebeardwriter.com/

While there, why not sign up for her FREE newsletter.

ISBN: 1-83-829552-6

ISBN: 978-1-83-829552-3

First Printing 2021

Dornica Press

Coming Soon

The Constance Maxwell Dream Walker Mysteries

The Croydon Enigma

Also, by this author:

Lawrence Harpham Murder Mysteries:

The Fressingfield Witch
The Ripper Deception
The Scole Confession
The Felsham Affair
The Moving Stone

Short Stories featuring Lawrence Harpham:

The Montpellier Mystery

Box Set containing
The Fressingfield Witch, The Ripper Deception & The Scole Confession

Novels:

Vote for Murder

The Cornish Widow

PROLOGUE

I wake with a start. The window has unlatched in the night and is slamming against the stone walls of our cottage. It is dark outside, and I reach for my stick, feeling its comforting weight in my hands before I limp towards the window. A bolt of lightning flashes through the sky as I fumble for the latch, and I place my hand on the windowsill, not noticing the pool of rainwater until it is too late. Then I stand on my tiptoes and catch the buffeting frame, almost losing my balance as I close it. I wipe my wet hands on my nightdress and shiver. How long was the window open? I can't tell because I don't know how long I have been sleeping. I've been dreaming again. Another dream so vivid that I cannot separate it from reality.

I sit on the end of my bed, wondering whether to light a candle. I don't know the time, and I haven't got a clock in my bedroom. It would serve no purpose. I rarely have appointments, and my condition leaves me unable to travel alone. A timepiece is no use to someone like me.

My thoughts return to the dream. It was lucid, real, but then they usually are. And I always remember them. I started keeping a journal of my dreams, but as I so rarely forget, the journaling seemed redundant in the end, and I abandoned it. Tonight's dream was unusually unnerving. I found myself in a house somewhere up north. Well, anywhere is north of here, but this was a good distance away. Two middle-aged ladies occupied the property, and the younger of the two was fast asleep when I arrived. I stood beside the bed, watching for a moment as her chest rose and fell. Then a muffled noise came from outside, and I passed through the wall and onto the landing just in time to see the older woman creep downstairs. I followed behind, confident that she wouldn't see me. They never do. She opened a door, and I waited for her to light a candle, but she reached for a wall switch instead, and the room lit up in seconds. They must have been wealthy as the house had electricity, which is unusual in a terraced property. Where I live, there is a limited electricity supply at the nearby hotel, but our little cottage runs on gas lamps, and I can't see Mrs Ponsonby changing things. She would disapprove.

I watched the woman as she fussed around the kitchen. She approached a cupboard, opened it, and started pushing things around as if she were looking for something. She didn't find what she was searching for and quietly closed the doors, muttering under her breath. Then she opened another door to a nearby room and removed two clothing items from a coat hanger before laying them over the table. I couldn't see much of the second outfit, but the first was a knee-length skirt with a fitted jacket. They must have different styles up north as the clothing was a world apart from the simple, feminine fashions I know. All my skirts are long, of course, to hide my leg. My friend Mary wears a calf-length dress, and she looks every inch the fashionable lady. But this tailored outfit was very modern in appearance.

Once the older woman had moved the clothes, she opened a second cupboard behind the door and rummaged inside, feeling for an object. A relieved half-smile spread across her face as she located it. She walked towards the sink and placed a brown bottle on the surface before easing the stopper free with her thumbs. Then she washed the dust off her hands and sniffed the contents, recoiling at the smell. There was a drawing on the label that I couldn't quite see, and I drifted towards it for a closer look. The bottle was the old-fashioned kind, and I remember seeing a similar one in Mr Pennigan's shop when I was much younger. The object on the dog-eared label was all that remained of a skull and crossbones – poison.

The woman put her hand into her dressing gown pocket and removed a second bottle. This one was slim and made of blue glass, and someone had fastened a dropper to it with an elastic band. She took the dropper, placed it in the neck of the brown bottle, squeezed the bulb, and transferred a few drops of liquid. Then she rinsed the dropper under the tap and wiped it dry. Finally, she replaced the top and vigorously shook it.

I knew what she was doing. It was obvious. There was no need to follow her up the stairs and watch her put the doctored medicine bottle by the younger woman. But I did it anyway. I tried everything to warn the sleeping woman. I touched her, prodded her, and I even tugged her bedclothes. Then I tried to scream, but it was noiseless. There was nothing I could do. I would have waited, but the storm woke me up, and she had gone. And although it's happened before, I cannot will myself back into a dream state. I am powerless to help her. But of course, it is just a dream – lifelike and lucid, but existing only in my imagination. I press my cheek into my pillow and listen to the sound of waves crashing against the shore, then thank God that I haven't just witnessed a murder.

CHAPTER ONE

Constance

Thursday, November 13, 1930

I wake bleary-eyed to a new day. I couldn't get back to sleep last night and lay awake until dawn, fighting the urge to go downstairs and make better use of my time. I have nearly finished my book, *Women in Love* by D.H. Lawrence, which I hid in the bottom drawer of the bureau as my guardian, Mrs Ponsonby, would have kittens if she saw it. She hasn't forgotten Lawrence's last scandalous book, and though this one doesn't come close in content, it is not worth the aggravation of her seeing it.

I am twenty-five years old – an adult – yet still living under the guardianship of a woman I know little about. Mrs Ponsonby doesn't like me. She never has. I am nothing more than a responsibility, a duty. She might be a groomsman taking care of a horse for all the affection she shows me.

Our cottage is small and basic, but we do not lack creature comforts. I eat well and can always call upon Elys for help. She is our housemaid and lives in, attending to Mrs Ponsonby's every whim. If I want something, I ask for it, and it usually arrives. I can go outside within reason, although Mrs Ponsonby frowns on any travel beyond Newquay, at least without her permission. We don't have a telephone, but the hotel staff let me make or take calls. I only need to ask Dolly, the receptionist, if I want to speak to someone, which because of my situation, is infrequent. The local people are friendly, and the omnibus is reliable, although I may not travel alone. All in all, I cannot complain about the physical aspects of my life.

Someone unknown pays for my upkeep. Mrs Ponsonby dresses smartly and enjoys all the trappings that a woman her age could want. But I don't know who funds our home, and she won't tell me. I've often asked her and sometimes begged her, but she says that no good would come of it. Mrs Ponsonby occupies the largest bedroom, inside which is a walk-in cupboard. She always keeps the door locked, and I know because I've often tried to open it over the years. She wears the key on a chain around her neck and is never without it. Mrs Ponsonby fell down the stairs one night and severely sprained her ankle. They took her straight to the hospital, and I thought my luck was in. But despite her pain, she remembered the key and passed it to Elys for safekeeping. I tried to persuade Elys to lend it to me, but she refused and wouldn't budge on the matter. "It's more than my job's worth," she said. So, my benefactor remains a mystery, as do my origins.

My life started when I was about five or six years old. No. I should re-phrase that. My memories begin from then. I know I wasn't born in Cornwall, but I cannot remember anything before arriving here. As hard as I try, anything further back is dark and hazy. No other words can adequately describe the terrible void. I used to think there was something wrong with my head. But that was before Doctor Maltravers arrived. He replaced stuffy old Doctor Kimbrell, who was older than his years and set in Victorian ways. It wouldn't have surprised me if he'd produced a jar of leeches from his bag instead of medicine, although he never did. Doctor Maltravers is quite the opposite. He trained in London and took a particular interest in psychiatry. He says that most people suffer from childhood amnesia, but my case is extreme. He thinks it's my brain's response to childhood trauma. He might be right, for all I know, but with no relatives to hand, I can neither confirm nor deny his theory. It makes sense, though. My scarred left leg with its wasted muscles is shorter than my right, and Doctor Maltravers thinks this might have happened from lack of use. He asked if I had a bath chair when I was younger, and of course, I couldn't tell him because I don't know. It is embarrassing, and I feel naïve and stupid to know so little about my early life.

I rise, get dressed and hook my stick over my arm, leaning heavily on the bannister as I go downstairs. It's Tuesday, and book changing day at the hotel. I want to return three of my four books, though not the hidden one, of course. Elys is setting the breakfast table and calls me over.

"Do you want some porridge, Connie?"

Mrs Ponsonby flashes a glare from the chair in the opposite room. She thinks Elys is too familiar for a domestic servant. It's 1930, for heaven's sake and about time she came off her high horse.

"No thanks," I say, walking towards the coat stand. "I'm going for a walk."

"Where?" asks Mrs Ponsonby curtly.

"To the beach and then the hotel," I answer, waiting for her response with a prepared one of my own. It's a conversation we have almost every day, and the content rarely varies.

"Well, don't go too far," she continues as if I could go any distance without a chair or transport.

"Only to the Lizard and back," I say facetiously. She scowls, and I leave, pausing only to share a knowing smile with Elys. Poor Elys. I don't know how she does it. I get out whenever I can, which isn't often, but it's more than Elys does.

I fasten the top button of my coat as I leave the cottage and head towards the beach. Our home is immediately behind the hotel, and both buildings are elevated, which makes for a steep walk. If it were up to Mrs Ponsonby, I would never go outside. She doesn't like me walking anywhere, much less to the beach. She says it will do untold damage if I fall over, but I won't get any stronger if I sit around all day indoors. I know the limits of my endurance. If the weather is mild and the tide is out, I can manage a walk to each end of the bay, which works out to about half a mile. We live in a hamlet with a scattering of houses, and the hotel, of course. The nearest village is Trevarrian, but I can't get there under my own steam because it's too hilly. As for Newquay, there is a walk across the cliffs for those lucky souls with functioning limbs. But it is beyond my capability without help.

The wind whips my scarf from the top of my coat as I approach the ramp towards the beach. The path is steep, but one of the odd-job men at the hotel erected a wooden fence a few years ago, and it helps to have something to hold on to, especially if it's wet. Today is dry, the tide is out, and the expansive beach is a joy to behold. I walk towards the water where the sand is firmer, and before long, I turn around to see stick marks peppering the once-pristine sand. I inhale the salty sea air and watch the seagulls shrieking overhead. There is not a soul on the shore – unusual for this time of day. Mostly, the holidaymakers can't keep away. But it's cold, and I expect they have sensibly huddled around the fire back at the hotel.

I will join them soon enough, but first, I head towards my favourite cave. I know it's an extravagance to have a choice, and I don't take my residence by the seaside for granted. There are about half a dozen small caves within a few hundred yards, and one is more spacious than the others. Last year I dragged a wooden chair to the cave and left it there, half expecting someone to take it away over the summer. But instead, the holidaymakers treated it as their own, adding a wooden packing crate and a small but hardy pot plant. A month or two later I discovered a small suitcase. Someone had put half a dozen books inside, to which others were subsequently added.

I can see the cave ahead of me now, every detail of its entrance as familiar as my home. I walk inside and head towards the chair.

It is damp but not enough to seep through my coat. I turn it around to face the sea and sit with my stick across my legs, watching the waves ebb and flow. It is peaceful and soporific, and despite the cold, my eyes grow heavy. But I must not fall asleep here. It's hard enough to keep control of my dreams from the relative safety of my bed. So, I take a quick inventory of the cave's contents; everything is still there, with nothing new added. Satisfied, I prepare to walk back.

My route back to the hotel takes longer, of course. I tire quickly, and my limp gets worse the longer I stay on my feet. I start my daily walk with a straight back, but a lack of concentration leaves me hunching again. I stop, look forward and straighten my shoulders. It is easy to fall into bad habits, and I have enough medical problems without adding to them. I trudge back, doing my best to ignore the pain in my hip and brace myself for the climb up the ramp. Some days, it brings me close to tears. Moving on the flat or a slight downward incline is not onerous, but a slope is usually painful no matter how shallow. It's because my legs are different lengths. The cobbler has always made my boots and builds the left heel taller than the right, but it is never enough, and I often feel unbalanced. I grit my teeth and begin the climb, with the lyrics to 'It Had To Be You', looping in my head as a distraction. It works, and I find myself at the top of the ramp and head towards the hotel's entrance with little exertion. I open the door and go inside.

CHAPTER TWO

Porth Tregoryan

The Porth Tregoryan hotel perches high on the cliffs just feet from the shore and facing towards Newquay. It is a handsome stone building with a gothic feel, yet far from being ancient, it is only a little older than I am. But there is something about the hotel that evokes caution, as though if not currently occupied by ghosts, they could arrive at any moment. Despite this, it is a welcoming place, and for several years the owners have extended their hospitality to the locals. This generosity includes access to the hotel library, although I am the only one who takes advantage. Their loss is my gain and provides me with a haven in which neither Mrs Ponsonby nor any of her informants can bother me.

I visit the library most days, but always on a Thursday when the reading room truck arrives from Newquay. Quite how a private hotel has arrived at this arrangement with a subscription library, I don't know. But I expect it involves the exchange of money or the acquisition of new books. I must ask Peter when I see him. And no sooner does the thought pop into my head than Peter is walking down the corridor. I am about to follow him when a head pops up from behind the counter.

"Morning, Miss Connie," says Dolly, the receptionist. She is sporting the hotel's grey and white uniform and is looking immaculate. I don't know how old Dolly is. She could be in her late twenties or perhaps early forties, but it's impossible to tell. Dolly is slender, almost skinny, which amplifies the problem in assessing her age. I could ask her, but it might seem bad-mannered, so I have held my tongue up to now. Dolly lives in the upper rooms of the hotel and stays in Porth Tregoryan all year long. Hotel work is seasonal, and most of her friends go home when the summer is over, but after three years of loyal service, Dolly is part of the scenery. I count her as one of my close friends and can barely remember the hotel without her.

Dolly smiles at me, revealing crooked teeth and a slight overbite. It is a shame as she has a pretty face and melting brown eyes with the longest eyelashes I have ever seen.

I return the smile. "Good morning to you too. And how are you today?"

"Very well," she says, beaming. Dolly is always smiling and would still perform her duties with good humour if the hotel fell off the cliff. She is a perfect employee, spreading happiness and calm around her. If I had to stand at the reception desk all day, I would bite people. Not that I could stay on my feet for half an hour, much less eight.

"It's busy today," says Dolly, stifling a cough.

I frown. "Oh dear," I say. Some people like people, but I like books, and I prefer to read them quietly. Occasionally it is nice to see a friendly face in the library and exchange a few pleasantries, but only if I'm left alone to read once I have done my bit.

"You've just missed Peter," she continues, and for one moment, I think I see her wink. But it must be my imagination. Peter Tremayne is five years my junior, and if I had a brother, then my feelings towards him would be the same. There is not a flicker of romantic interest between us, and I'm not sure Peter even likes girls. But he is an interesting young man, and we get on very well, all things considered.

"I'll look for him," I say, lifting my stick as I carefully step up. I have missed that step too often, ending up on the floor on my hands and knees. It's a stupid place to put one, but despite the indignity of frequent falls, I still forget. I limp up the hallway towards the rear of the hotel, where the large reading room overlooks the sea. Dolly was right. The room is full of people, and I ignore them and search for Peter. I see him swapping books at the end of the room. He spies me and waves.

"What have you bought?" I ask eagerly, forgoing the usual small talk. I have read most of the books in the hotel library and am dreading the awful prospect of having nothing to read.

"You like Agatha Christie, don't you?"

"You know I do," I say eagerly.

"Here. Take this before someone else does," says Peter, placing a book on the table. "You'll be the first to read it."

I pick up the book and reverently open the cover. "But where's Poirot?" I ask disappointedly.

"Not here," he says. "This book features a new character called Miss Marple. One of a series, I believe. It's hot off the press and only arrived last week. You will love it."

I look at the title page – *Murder at the Vicarage* – and I know he is right. I want everyone to leave the room so that I can read it in peace. Failing that, I'll take it home and devour it in front of the fire, and a thrill of excitement courses through me as I anticipate the twists and turns of a new story.

"What else?" I ask excitedly.

Peter waves a hand towards the shelf, and I rifle through his treasures while he finishes his chores. There are about two dozen new books, which should be enough to keep me going for a while. E.M. Forster, F. Scott Fitzgerald, and a non-fiction book by someone called Sigmund Freud. I recognise one or two of the covers, but most are new to me. I pore over the books and finally select two with the most exciting descriptions. Then I find Peter, who is now sitting in the corner nursing a cup of tea. He stands up as I arrive, waiting until I am sitting comfortably with my stick safely tucked to one side before resuming his seat. For a young man, he has excellent manners.

"How are you?" he asks.

"Tolerably well," I say.

"I see you've been beachcombing." He points to my stick and the grains of sand liberally scattered across the hotel carpet.

"Oh, dear. I usually remember to clean it," I say, annoyed that Peter has mentioned the mess in public. I look around, but nobody is listening – they are all preoccupied with their books. One man is writing in the corner with his head bowed in concentration.

"What have you been up to then?" Peter asks.

"The usual," I say. "Reading, avoiding Mrs P, my daily constitutional and yet more reading. How about you?"

"Much of the same," he says. "I say, have you seen today's paper?"

"No. You know Mrs Ponsonby doesn't like them and won't have them in the house."

"She's a funny old stick," says Peter.

"There's nothing amusing about my captor," I say darkly.

"Still lacking the maternal spark?"

"Not a suitable subject for levity," I say, crossing my arms. "I have come to terms with my parents abandoning me, but why they thought it was a good idea to leave me with her, I will never know. It's unforgivable."

"You're still alive," says Peter, and for the first time in my life, I want to hit him.

"That's enough," I say.

"No, seriously. I know you don't like Mrs Ponsonby but think about it and then tell me three good things about her."

"It will take all day."

"You're not trying. I promise it will make you feel better."

I sigh. It is all I can do to stop myself from leaving, but I suppose I ought to humour Peter. He is generally good to me and must see some value in this seemingly pointless exercise. "She keeps me fed and clothed," I say.

"Good. We'll count that as one. Next?"

"She doesn't beat me."

"I'm not accepting that. Try harder."

"She's brave. Billy Baxter's dog tried to bite me when I was younger, and she chased it down the road with a stick. Everyone else was terrified, but not Mrs Ponsonby. Actually, there's an odd-looking sword in the outhouse. I bet it's hers."

"Excellent. Last one."

"She's got a sense of humour when she's not being mean and checking up on me. She listens to the radio sometimes and laughs. But if I walk in, she stops and re-sets her miserable face."

"So, she's nurturing, brave and funny," says Peter.

"No," I snap. "You're putting words in my mouth."

"You said them. My mother likes her."

"She would," I say, not embellishing on the subject. I like Peter's mother, but if he's going to bring her into it, then I'm not playing.

Peter raises an eyebrow. "You don't like Mrs Ponsonby because she's strict," he says. "But it's because she cares, not because she doesn't."

"You don't have to live with her." I glower. "Change the subject, or I'm going."

"You haven't asked me about the newspaper."

"I forgot," I say when what I really mean is that I don't care.

"There's an interesting death notice inside. A woman called Alice Thomas died in Plymouth hospital."

"I should think it happens a lot," I say, wondering whether it would be rude to start reading my books now.

"Yes. But there's going to be an inquest next week," says Peter, "and Malcolm's asked if I'd like to go."

I shrug. "Why would you? And anyway, I thought you didn't like him?" Malcolm is Peter's much older cousin. He is a reporter with the Cornish Advertiser, not an especially well-regarded paper, but well suited to Malcolm, who enjoys digging up dirt.

"I don't," says Peter, honestly. "But I've never been to an inquest before, and I expect it will be interesting."

"I'm sure you're right," I agree.

"Still, nothing may come of it, but I'll let you know what he says."

"Good. Please do."

"Anyway, I've got to go now. It's drama club tonight."

I shake my head and smile, watching Peter's eyes sparkle. He is in thrall to Oliver and Felicity Grenville, a pair of actors trying to fund a Newquay drama group. The unofficial throng meets at their house every second Thursday, and it is the highlight of Peter's week.

"Off you go," I say. "Will I see you this time next week?"

"Before then, I expect," says Peter. "I'll be back in the next few days, and I'll come and find you."

"Enjoy yourself, won't you?" I watch as Peter walks from the room, sandy hair flopping over his glasses. He strolls casually with his hands in his pockets, nodding as he passes the hotel guests. They smile back, and I can almost hear them thinking, 'what a nice young man.'. They are right. He is.

I sit back and look around the room. It is quieter now. Some residents have left, and one is stirring a cup of coffee while she reads. The bald man by the window is still scribbling in his journal. He hasn't stopped and is writing with a sense of urgency. I cannot help but stare. A few moments pass, and he looks up. Our eyes meet, and I blush and turn away, pretending to pick a hair from my jacket. I enjoy watching people, but I hate getting caught. It always seems so intrusive.

#

I contemplate my pile of books and decide to take them home, then get distracted when I open the front cover of the Agatha Christie novel. Before I know it, I am halfway through the first chapter, and I force myself to stop, or I will sit here for the rest of the day. I stoop to pick up my stick as a shadow looms beside me, and a journal falls by my outstretched arm. I look up. The man writing by the window is standing next to me, and he is carrying an armful of books. He apologises and reaches towards the journal, which has toppled off the heap, but I get there first. I hand it to him, but not before a piece of printed paper falls out and flutters to the floor. I smile and pick it up, intending to pass it straight back to him, but I can't help noticing what it says. "Lucid Dreams by Sylvan Muldoon," I read. "I'm sorry. I didn't mean to be nosy. Here, take it."

The man reaches for the paper and folds it in two, inserting it back into the journal. "Thank you," he says.

"What are lucid dreams?" I blurt the words out without thinking.

"Now, there's a question," he says. "Do you really want to know?"

I nod.

"Can I join you?"

I nod again, torn between going home and hearing his answer.

"Oliver Fox," he says, offering his hand.

"Constance Maxwell," I reply, about to get to my feet.

"Please don't," he says and sits beside me, crossing his legs as he pushes the pile of books across the table. "Have you ever had a dream so lucid that you can remember and control the direction it takes?" he asks.

"Often," I say.

"Really? In my experience, it's rare."

"Not in mine," I say confidently.

"How do you know that you're in a dream?" he asks.

"It depends. Usually, when something happens that wouldn't be possible in reality."

"Such as?"

"Running," I say.

He opens his mouth to contradict me, but I stare pointedly at my stick and the penny drops.

"I see. That's fascinating, Miss Maxwell."

"Why?"

"Because one day I hope to write a book about lucid dreaming and astral projection."

"Are they the same thing?"

"No. Astral projection is a different phenomenon. The dreamer separates from their earthly body, often staying attached by a silver cord."

"I don't," I say, listening with interest.

"I'm not surprised. Astral travel is less common."

"I mean the silver cord. I don't feel any physical connection to my body and have little control away from it."

"Are you suggesting that you can travel independently from your body?"

"Well, yes. It seems that way, although I know it can't be true. But it feels so real and happens so regularly that I sometimes wonder."

"And can you remember what happened during your dreams when you wake the next day?"

"Yes, and a lot longer besides."

"Would you mind describing one of your dreams?"

I think about it for a moment. I won't mention last night's episode, which was strange even for me. Instead, I tell him about my latest foray over the cliff to Morgan Porth, a dream that happens frequently.

He cocks his head to one side and waits until I've finished talking. "What makes you think it was an out-of-body experience?" he asks.

"Because Connor Green carved a bench and left it near Beacon Cove," I say.

"And?"

"Well, I saw it in my dream and mentioned it to Elys."

"Elys?"

"Our housemaid, but never mind. She asked me how I knew because Connor had only just put it there. I can't walk far, and a clifftop jaunt is impossible. There wasn't time for anyone to tell me, yet I knew the bench was there and stupidly said so. It was hard work explaining myself to Elys and I lied because I didn't want to worry her. Nobody knows about my dreams. I've kept them secret for fear of what people would think of me if they knew."

"Don't be embarrassed, Constance. It's a remarkable ability," says Fox.

"Do you think so? I've kept it to myself for so long that I don't expect anyone to believe me now. It sounds ridiculous, after all. Besides, I'm never sure whether I'm dreaming or in a different kind of reality."

"Are you staying at the hotel?"

"No," I say, pleased that he thinks I could afford it. "I live in the cottage at the rear."

"But you come here often?"

"Almost daily," I say.

"Good. I'm staying here for a week," Fox says, offering me a card. I take it and note the unfamiliar name. "Hugh George Callaway," I read. "Who is he?"

"I am," he says. "I'm sure you will understand that not everybody is sympathetic to psychic research. Hugh Callaway is my proper name, but I use the alias of Oliver Fox. I am, in fact, an actor and writer."

"My goodness," I say, genuinely impressed. "How should I address you?"

"Oliver," he says. "Please call me Oliver. I feel sure we will meet again."

He rises, nods, and walks away, leaving me with his calling card. I wait for a moment, contemplating what has passed between us, then set off for an afternoon of reading.

#

Disappointment washes over me as I turn the last page of *Murder at the Vicarage.* I am not dissatisfied with the plot or the denouement and certainly not with Miss Marple, who I already adore. I am disappointed because I was so desperate to finish that I couldn't bring myself to take my time over the book and savour it. I sigh and put it back on my dressing table, wondering whether it is too soon to reread it. No doubt the book will be just as good, even without the element of surprise.

My stomach rumbles. I glance outside and see the night sky. I should have finished my supper, but I wasn't hungry then, and now I am paying the price. It must be well after ten o'clock, perhaps even later. I get into bed and huddle under the bedspread, trying to ignore the thought of the steak and kidney pie I left on my plate, much to Mrs Ponsonby's disgust. She said nothing but raised an eyebrow and stared down her nose as her top lip trembled, no doubt with the effort of trying to hold her tongue. Mrs Ponsonby hates waste of any kind. After spending long hours queuing for food during the war, she has nothing but contempt for what she calls fads. She does not understand my fluctuating appetite and thinks that I should force down what Elys gives me whether or not I'm hungry. I disagree and refuse to make myself sick trying to please her. She seems to think she was the only one who suffered during the war, but Elys and I both grew up with it, and she doesn't own the discomfort.

But tonight, it appears Mrs Ponsonby was right. I didn't eat enough, and I am now ravenous. I don't think I can wait until breakfast. Elys will have put the pie in the pantry with a bit of luck unless she has eaten it herself. She wouldn't dare throw it out for fear of upsetting Mrs Ponsonby, who is so set against waste that she will scrape the mould off week-old bread and eat it.

I climb out of bed and reach for my stick before opening the bedroom door, listening for sounds of snoring from Mrs Ponsonby's room. I hear only silence. She's closed the door, and I can't tell whether she's in bed or downstairs, but now that hunger has infiltrated my thoughts, I can't resist the delights lurking in the pantry. I must be cautious so that Mrs Ponsonby doesn't catch me in the act. The only thing worse than her frown of disapproval would be her smug 'I told you so' smile.

I grab my dressing gown and tie it around my waist, then set off downstairs. Darkness surrounds me as I reach the bottom step, which is a good sign and should mean that both Mrs Ponsonby and Elys are safely in bed. I tiptoe down the corridor as quietly as one can while carrying a walking stick, then I pull a spill from the jar on the bureau and light a candle. The flame flickers as I open the kitchen door to a waft of cold air, and I cross the room and open the pantry door before placing the candle on the marble slab. I shut the door behind me in case of late-night wanderers and smile at the brace of pheasants hanging from the hook. Pheasant casserole is one of my favourite meals, and I look forward to the upcoming week's menu for a brief few seconds. Then I open the fish kettle and meet the gaze of a dozen pilchards that Jory Clark must have given to Elys on his earlier visit. I wish he wouldn't. I love most fish, but there's something about pilchards that I can't abide. Apart from tasting foul, I don't appreciate their lifeless accusatory eyes, especially when Elys arranges them in a stargazy pie. Worse still, Elys thinks I like it. I can't imagine why – it is all I can do to force a small slice down, and I'm amazed she hasn't noticed. When Elys makes stargazy pie, she announces it as 'my favourite', and I haven't got the heart to tell her the truth. Thank goodness for Mr Moggins, resident household cat and Mrs Ponsonby's familiar, without whom I would have to eat the disgusting things myself. For a moment, I contemplate disposing of the pilchards before morning but decide it's too risky. As soon as Elys missed them, she'd tell Mrs Ponsonby, and I would be the obvious suspect. I replace the lid and try to forget them, hoping that some calamity will prevent their inevitable appearance on tomorrow's dinner table.

After a close examination of the remaining food in the pantry, I find the pie has gone. My stomach rumbles again, and I explore other options. I lift a cake tin from the window shelf, which feels suitably weighty, and am rewarded with the sweet smell of gingerbread when I open the lid. I cut two slices, search for a plate, and balance the candle on my illicit late-night supper tray while manoeuvring towards the kitchen table. Then, I sit down and eat gingerbread by candlelight, wondering what I will do to make tomorrow pass quickly. As usual, I settle on a walk followed by a trip to the hotel library. I am just mopping up the last few crumbs of cake when I hear a soft thud, and Mr Moggins appears from the garden room. He slinks towards me, purring and rubbing his head against my leg. I reach down and tickle his ears, then run my hand over his smoky grey fur. His purr rumbles like a tiny generator, and my heart swells with love. I can take or leave people, but animals are all dear to me. Except for pilchards, of course, if you can count them as such. I have my limits.

Feast over, I contemplate returning to my room before an idea pops into my head, and I giggle like a naughty schoolgirl at the thought. I wonder if I dare go ahead, but it's too irresistible to ignore. 'Are you hungry, Mr Moggins?' I ask, rhetorically, picking him up and walking into the pantry. I open the fish kettle, place the cat on the shelf, then unlatch the side window. Mr Moggins stares at the pilchards and then at me as if he can't believe his luck. I smile and nod, then turn away and close the door before collecting my stick and the candle.

Once back in the hallway, I pass the bureau, remembering the D.H. Lawrence book, which I still haven't finished reading. It should keep me entertained until my fuller stomach makes sleep more likely. I slide the drawer open, retrieve the book, then notice a sliver of light coming from the parlour. I creep to the door and listen but hear nothing. I wait for a moment to be on the safe side, but if Mrs Ponsonby is in there, she must be fast asleep. I hold my breath and turn the handle as quietly as I can, and the door opens with a gentle squeak. I breathe a sigh of relief at the empty room and shake my head smugly when I realise that Mrs Ponsonby has gone to bed, leaving a lit candle in the wall sconce. It is most unlike her, and if I had done the same, she would scold me about it for a week. I extinguish the candle and turn to the window to draw the curtains, which she has also left open.

As I place my hand on the windowsill, I see a pale form standing under the gas lamp at the rear of the hotel. I squint at the male figure and wonder why he's there. A glance at the clock on the mantlepiece tells me it's almost one o'clock in the morning and a strange time to be up and about. I peer at the man. His form is familiar – I know him but from where? And then it comes to me. The figure is Oliver Fox, the man I met earlier today, and he is staring blankly towards the hills behind our cottage as if he cannot see them.

I wave towards him, but he ignores me, and I try again, both hands signalling semaphore-like to attract his attention. He doesn't react, and I suppose he cannot see me in the unlit room. Fox is so pale and out of sorts that I consider opening the door to check he is safe and well, but I am in my nightclothes, and I wouldn't want to embarrass him. I look away briefly as I think about what to do, and by the time I check back, he has gone. I rub my eyes, wondering how he slipped away so quickly. He was there one moment and gone the next, yet I didn't see him walk away – he vanished like smoke in the wind. But then it occurs to me that he might have used the back entrance into the hotel, and I shrug my shoulders and limp away, closing the door behind me. I ascend the stairs to go to bed. My midnight foray has sapped my energy, and my legs are weary. I pause halfway up the stairs to catch my breath, and I hear Mrs Ponsonby moving around in her room. She could emerge at any moment, and the knowledge gives me the impetus for a speedier climb. As I close the door and get into bed, I listen again, hearing nothing untoward. I smile, confident that my expedition to the kitchen will remain a secret, and I settle down to read.

About an hour later, I extinguish my light. I am sleepy now, and the book, though adequate, lacks the charm of the Agatha Christie novel that I read earlier. I lie still in my bed, waiting for sleep to come, and eventually, it does, but not for long. Time passes, at least an hour, possibly two, then all hell breaks loose downstairs as a clatter of pans and a yowl from the kitchen wakes the household. Elys rises first, swiftly followed by Mrs Ponsonby. I lay in my bed feigning sleep. Mr Moggins has had his fill of the pilchards, and the kettle is now on the pantry floor minus its contents. There will be no pilchard pie for tea after all. I smile to myself, and this time I fall asleep until morning.

CHAPTER THREE

Meeting Oliver Fox

Friday, November 14, 1930

I wake, dress, and go downstairs to find Mrs Ponsonby and Elys deep in discussion over a forthcoming gathering at Mrs Potts' house in Tregurrian. Mrs Ponsonby said she would bring a cake, and they are trying to decide what to bake. She has intimated that she expects me to join her and will no doubt push me into the orbit of Edgar Sutton, a family friend who has been staying with the Pottses for some months. I don't know why she is so insistent. I have only met Edgar once, and he was condescending and aloof. There is no possibility of a romantic attachment, and I have all the friends I need. So far, I have resisted her attempts to force me to go, but I fear I'm losing the battle.

"Good morning," says Mrs Ponsonby dryly.

"Would you like some breakfast, Connie?" asks Elys.

"A boiled egg would be nice."

"I'll see to it right away."

"But we haven't settled on the cake yet," says Mrs Ponsonby, frowning.

"How about a nice Hevva cake?" asks Elys.

"I don't think so," says Mrs Ponsonby, wrinkling her nose as if Elys has said something thoroughly inappropriate.

"It's traditional," says Elys.

"Plum cake or Madeira?" asks Mrs Ponsonby. "Your choice."

"As you wish," says Elys, leaving the room with a swish of her apron. I can't see her eyes, but I bet they are looking heavenward.

"The cat got into the pantry last night," says Mrs Ponsonby.

"Oh dear," I answer, stifling a grin.

"Elys must have left the window open," she continues. "It's not good enough."

"How do you know it was Elys?" I ask, feeling guilty.

"Who else could it have been. I hope you aren't suggesting that it was me."

"Not at all," I say. "But Jory came yesterday, and so did the coalman, and the butcher, for that matter."

"Yes, they did," said Mrs Ponsonby, softening. "Now, what are you doing today?"

"I'm off to the Lizard," I say.

Mrs Ponsonby turns towards me. I look into her eyes, and for one awful moment, I think they are welling up. But she blinks and looks away. "Are you going to the hotel?" she asks.

I nod. "Yes, why?"

"Can you give this to Dolly?" She holds out a copy of *Country Life*, and I raise an eyebrow, wondering why she thinks Dolly would want it.

"Page twenty-three," she says as if reading my mind. "Dolly will want to see the piece about beagles."

"Why?"

"Her parents keep one. Dolly misses Suki dreadfully."

"I didn't know," I say. "But I'll be sure to give it to her."

Elys returns with the boiled egg, and I devour it, keen to leave the dining room before the cake discussion resumes. I shrug into my coat and make my way to the hotel, avoiding the tradesman's entrance so I can be sure of seeing Dolly. But when I arrive in the lobby, she is noticeable by her absence. In her place is a young, slim woman I have never met before.

"Can I help?" she asks, looking up from the journal that she's scribbling in.

"I'm looking for Dolly," I say.

"She's not here."

"Evidently. Where is she?"

"Who are you?" she counters.

"Connie Maxwell."

"You're not a guest."

"I know. Where's Dolly?"

The woman sighs.

"What do you want with her? I'm in charge while she's unwell?"

"Dolly – unwell? She's never ill."

"Are you suggesting that I'm wrong?"

"No. Look. We seem to have got off on the wrong foot. I'm Connie Maxwell, a friend of Dolly's and a local resident. As you're new, you may not know that the hotel owners kindly allow us to use the library."

"I am fully aware," she says, peering at me as if she wished I would go away.

"Then perhaps you can let me know more about Dolly's condition. I have something for her."

"Give it to me," she says, "and I'll see that she gets it."

"I'd rather do it myself."

"That won't be possible," she replies.

"What won't be possible?" A deep voice booms behind me as Doctor Kit Maltravers approaches and places his medical bag on the reception desk. My heart skips a beat.

"Well, good morning, Miss Maxwell," he continues, flashing me a smile.

A rictus grin fixes itself to my face and lingers while I struggle to say something sensible.

"Good morning to you," I say feebly. "I was just asking Miss, er..." I peer at the receptionist, hoping to see some identifying name badge, and my words trail away as I fail.

"Miss Templeton," she says, with an unnecessary flick of her hair. "But you can call me Roxy".

Roxy? Surely to goodness, that can't be a real name, I think. If it is, her parents should be ashamed of themselves.

"Pleased to meet you," says Doctor Maltravers, pressing her hand. I scowl, then rearrange my features before he notices.

"Where's the patient, then?" he asks.

"Top floor, first room on the right," she says.

"Are you going to see Dolly?" I ask.

"Yes."

"Please, can you give her this?" I fish the magazine out of my bag.

"Of course," he says.

"And pass on my best wishes. Is it serious?"

"I doubt it," says the doctor. "Are you going to the library?"

"I nod."

"I can pop in and let you know how she is when I've finished."

"Yes, please," I say, a little too quickly.

He smiles and sets off towards the stairs.

Roxy Templeton turns her back on me as if I don't exist. I smile sweetly and follow the doctor to the rear of the hotel, watching as he ascends the stairs two at a time.

#

I linger by the stairwell until Doctor Maltravers is out of sight, then peer into the library. To my immense pleasure, it is empty. I make for the comfortable sofa by the fireplace, slide my stick out of sight and tuck my legs beneath me, hoping that nobody will come in. I reach into my pocket, remove *Women in Love* from my bag, uncurl the folded page, and begin. But my attention wanders, and I find myself at the bottom of the page with no memory of the words I have read. I sigh and stare into the fireplace, watching the flames flicker and dance. The proximity of Doctor Maltravers is putting me off. I don't know what it is about him, but I turn into a dithering wreck in his presence. He is unobtainable and happily engaged to Charlotte Napier, youngest daughter of Colonel and Mrs Napier of Briarwood. The Napiers are rich, and Briarwood nestles in a substantial estate on the west side of Newquay. Naturally, Charlotte is beautiful both inside and out. She dresses in the finest fashions while regularly performing charitable acts for the townsfolk. I cannot find anything to dislike about her except for her betrothal. But Doctor Maltravers is so far out of my reach that I must stop thinking of him in that context. I have had sharp words with myself about this on several recent occasions. Though I am resigned to his unavailability, my heart has been slow to obey.

I've stared at the flame for so long that orange shadows now linger in my eyes. I turn away, focusing instead on the library window, which looks out over the bay. The sky is a murky shade of blue, and the sea is choppy, so I decide to forgo my walk today, although what I will do instead, I don't know. My world is tiny, and my days long and impossible to fill.

I hear a click behind me and turn to see Oliver Fox walking through the library door. "Hello," I say, flashing a broad smile, my previous reluctance for company forgotten. "How are you?"

"Very well, indeed," he says, striding towards me. "May I join you for a few moments? I can't stay long – I must finish an article for *The Occult Review*."

"How interesting," I say. "What are you writing about?"

"Dream travel," he says.

"Like we talked about yesterday?"

"More or less. I promised I would deliver my article next week, and it's only half done."

"Well, I won't keep you," I say. "You have a lot to do, and I expect you're exhausted after last night."

He raises an eyebrow. "Not particularly? Why?"

I smile conspiratorially. "I saw you on your midnight stroll."

Oliver Fox blinks and stares at me with his mouth open. "You saw me?"

"Well, yes. I was hungry and went downstairs for a late-night snack. I noticed you while I was drawing the curtains."

"You saw me?"

"Yes, I did."

"Last night?"

I nod.

"What time?"

"Gosh, I don't know. I don't have a clock in my bedroom. It must have been after midnight, but how long after, I can't say."

Fox continues to stare at me, then rests his chin on his hands. "What did I look like?"

"As you do now, except that you were very pale," I say. "I thought you looked ill, and I nearly came outside to check on you. I would have done if I were more suitably clothed."

Fox sits quietly, staring at the table for several moments until I don't know how to respond. He drums his fingers and frowns. Finally, he licks his lips and looks up again. "You didn't see me," he says.

"Oh, I'm sorry. The figure looked like you. My mistake."

"No. That's not what I meant. You didn't see my earthly body because I was asleep. It was my astral being that you noticed."

"Oh. I see what you mean. Were you dream walking?"

"I was," he says. "I passed through the pineal door last night and attempted to explore my surroundings."

"I don't understand."

"I'll help you with that another time," he says. "It's a complicated process which I have perfected, and I can now enter the dream state at will."

"You are lucky," I say. "I find myself thrust into it, whether or not I want to be there."

"If you have the basic ability, you can train yourself," he says. "And I believe that you have an inherent gift."

"Why?"

"Because you saw me. Generally, I am invisible to people. I can enter a restaurant and talk to a waiter, but he won't hear me. I can pass through a man, and he may experience a disquieting feeling, but he won't know why. It is a good thing, for the moment I lose concentration, my body draws me back in a flash. My wanderings are always of limited duration because it is difficult to stay in the trance state. But your experiences may be different to mine. Tell me again, what technique do you use to separate from your body?"

I close my eyes in concentration as I consider his question. "I fall asleep and think I'm awake, but I'm not."

"Ah, the false awakening," he murmurs.

"Whatever you say. But as soon as I realise that I'm neither asleep nor properly awake, I leave my bed and go for a walk."

"Do you always follow the same path?"

"Almost always. Though I found myself in an unknown location recently."

"And how often do you travel?"

"Frequently," I say.

"Can you control it?"

"No. I can choose where I go most of the time, but not when I travel. It just happens."

"Would you like to take part in an experiment?"

"It depends. What kind?"

"A meeting," he says.

"Where?"

"Here. In this hotel, at midnight tonight."

"You mean by dream travel?"

He nods.

"I told you, I can't simply summon it."

"Have you tried?"

"Well, no. Sometimes I dream walk, and sometimes I don't. I've learned to live with it and haven't thought about forcing the matter."

"Why don't you try?" he asks.

"How?"

"I'll tell you what works for me. It may not have the same effect on you, but there's no harm in trying, is there?"

"I suppose not."

"I lie down," he says, "and half close my eyes. When I am fully relaxed, I see a series of small misty blue vibrating circles, like frogs' spawn. I concentrate, and eventually, if I stare hard enough, I find myself in a trance-like state. Once there, I imagine my astral body is rising, and it does. Failing that, I find staring at a candle to be equally effective."

"Or a fire," I say.

"Yes, a fire will do nicely as long as you are lying down and comfortable. As I said, this technique may not work for you, but it would interest me to know. Don't expect too much the first few times," he continues. "But let's set a goal to meet here tonight, and if that is not possible, then the following night. I will come here at midnight every day until I leave."

"Alright," I say, happy to humour him. Waking dreams are a fact of life for me, but I'm not sure I want to encourage them. Still, he's a nice man and very enthusiastic, so I agree and will make a determined effort to do as he asks.

"Good. Then I'll leave you to it," Fox says as he turns and makes his way to the table underneath the window. He smiles towards me as he settles down and writes.

I pick up my book again, but I'm too distracted now and decide to leave before remembering that Doctor Maltravers is still in the building. I wait for five minutes, and the door opens again. There he is, all six feet of him, standing tall and slender in the door frame.

"How is Dolly?" I ask.

He walks towards me. "Not as well as I hoped," he answers, furrowing his brow.

"What's wrong with her?"

"She has a respiratory infection," he replies.

"She seemed fine yesterday," I say before remembering that she'd coughed more than once.

"She hasn't had it for long," he says. "But the coughing is getting worse, and this morning she had a high temperature and was vomiting, so they sent for me. Quite right, too. I must keep a close eye on her."

"Can I see her?"

"Not today," he says, shaking his head. "We'll see how she is tomorrow. I'll send word when she's up to receiving visitors."

I grin, pleased at the idea. "Thank you."

"My pleasure," he replies, acknowledging Oliver Fox's presence as he leaves the room.

I stow my book the moment he closes the door and prepare to leave.

"I'll see you tonight," says Oliver Fox as I take my stick and ready myself to go, suddenly filled with an uncharacteristic foreboding.

CHAPTER FOUR

A Rare Day Out

"Miss Connie. I'm glad to see you. Do you fancy a trip?" asks Elys as I hang my coat on the hall stand.

"A trip? Where to?" I ask, surprised. There was no mention of a trip earlier in the frosty atmosphere of the dining room.

"Newquay," says Elys. "Mrs Ponsonby has settled on a plum cake, and we've run out of almonds." She smiles as if the lack of an essential ingredient has made her day. I expect it has. Elys rarely escapes our cottage prison.

"But how…?" I ask. Elys interrupts me.

"Jory has offered to take us," she says. "They're not fishing today, and his father needs supplies from the chandlery. He's borrowing the pony and trap."

"Mrs Ponsonby won't like it," I say.

"She's already agreed," says Elys, beaming. "She had a word with me while you were out and asked if I let the cat get in the pantry. Mrs Ponsonby didn't scold me and was nice about it. But I was so distracted trying to convince her of my innocence that I pricked my finger while darning and dripped blood all over my apron. I felt sick and nearly passed out. Then, when she asked me to go into town, I said I would if someone went with me. Mrs Ponsonby said having Jory ought to be enough, but I said he had his own business to attend to. She almost suggested taking you, then checked herself. So, I took full advantage and asked anyway, leaving her with no choice."

"You clever thing," I say. "I would love to join you. An errand for you is an adventure for me. How exciting."

"Do you want to change?" she asks. "Jory will be here in ten minutes."

I shake my head. I'm tired already and worry that I might flag if I take an unnecessary trip upstairs.

"Oh, we've run out of time anyway," Elys says over her shoulder as she rushes down the corridor. "He's already here."

I walk into the parlour and stare outside. Jory has parked his trap in front of the cottage, and a bay horse is nervously pawing the ground. I look at the sky. The trap is open, and the clouds are heavy with rain. I am amazed that Mrs Ponsonby has allowed this expedition. Then Elys runs up the hallway carrying a bundle of blankets and two large umbrellas.

"Come quickly," she says. "Mrs Ponsonby is on the verge of changing her mind.

As soon as he sees me, Jory jumps from the cart, lowers the footrest, and holds my hand while Elys unceremoniously shoves me into the seat.

"Take this," she commands, thrusting the blanket towards me. I spread it over my legs while she clambers up the other side.

"Thanks, Jory," she says, smiling at him.

He winks as he lifts the reins and the horse trots away.

I recline in the seat, breathe in the sea air, and relax, feeling free of my bonds as I look forward to the trip. And as we pull away, I see Mrs Ponsonby peering anxiously behind the curtains. I wave at her, willing to forgive anything today.

The journey to Newquay passes in a flash. I sit in contemplative silence while Elys and Jory chat and soon realise that a budding romance is developing between them. I am thrilled at her evident joy, but my own loveless situation provokes feelings of jealousy. Sometimes, I consider the prospect of marrying and having a family. There is no reason why I shouldn't, although I appreciate that my condition is limiting. A future husband must love me enough to accept my lameness and the challenges it brings. On my rare darker days, I wonder if I will live the rest of my life as a spinster. Perhaps I will never marry and instead fill my days imagining what it might have been like to have a husband and children. But life is what you make it, and I will endeavour to get what I want, starting with an escape from Mrs Ponsonby's clutches. As we pass Porth and round the headland into Newquay, my thoughts turn to the opportunity at hand. I must make the most of my distance from Mrs Ponsonby as soon as Elys has finished buying almonds.

"How long have we got?" I ask as the carriage draws to a halt.

"Not long," says Elys. "I promised we'd be there and back as soon as possible."

"I'll be with the chandler for at least an hour," says Jory.

"I know," says Elys. "But then we must return right away if Connie is to come again."

Jory shrugs as if he doesn't care one way or the other. No doubt he wants Elys to himself.

"I'll meet you here at three fifteen," says Jory, allocating himself an extra fifteen minutes, which is fine by me. I have a plan that nicely fills the unexpected additional time.

"As you like," says Elys, checking her watch. "See you then."

Jory pulls away. The chandlery is by the docks, and he has left us in the centre of town. We walk down Bank Street, and Elys enters the grocers to make her purchase. I prefer to wait outside and find a low wall by the printers and perch there, watching the world go by. The threatened rain has not materialised, and the clouds have lifted. Though far from pleasant, the icy wind is bearable while I am clad in a winter coat, yet something troubles me as I gaze across the street. Something that has lapped at the periphery of my thoughts for some time and has suddenly breached my defences. The only women dressed in full-length skirts are also wearing aprons. They are, without exception, housemaids, and even the older women are sporting ankle-length dresses. I gaze at my outfit in horror. I look positively Victorian compared to everyone else. I consider the women in Porth Tregoryan who are less concerned with high fashion. But aside from the servants and anyone over the age of fifty, their clothes are markedly different from mine. I can't imagine how I have never noticed this before, but now I've realised, I stare at my clothes in embarrassment, hardly daring to stand for fear of ridicule.

I am sitting with my head in my hands when Elys finds me.

"Got them," she says, then sees my ashen face as I lower my arms. "What's wrong with you?"

"What do you wear on your half-day off?" I ask, wishing I was more observant.

"A day dress," says Elys.

"Long or short?"

"Calf length. Why?"

"I have nothing modern in my wardrobe," I say.

"That be your doing," says Elys, slipping into her childhood Cornish accent. She tries hard to speak like Mrs Ponsonby, who has no accent at all. I don't know why. The Cornish way of speaking is delightful, and I find it pleasant, although I have never picked up the accent myself.

"It's Mrs Ponsonby's fault," I correct her.

"No. It's yours," Elys repeats firmly. "Mrs Ponsonby has frequently offered to buy you new clothes. You always refuse, and she understands why. So do I, although your fears are groundless."

"My leg looks dreadful in stockings and boots," I mutter.

"But not in coloured stockings and a carefully constructed shoe," says Elys.

"I look so old-fashioned," I say. My lip wobbles and I dig my nails into my palm, trying not to cry.

"Then let's go and buy you an outfit," says Elys.

"I don't have any money, and I wanted to drop in on Peter," I say.

"Well, you can't be that bothered," she replies unsympathetically.

"Anyway, I'd die of embarrassment," I say, shuddering at the thought of a dress fitting while exposing my leg to someone I don't know.

"Connie, why don't you let me make you a dress?" offers Elys.

"Really? You can do that?"

She nods. "I'm an excellent seamstress, and you've got a lovely figure."

I smile at her kind words. Though disadvantaged in the leg department, I have a tiny waist and shapely hips. "Yes, please," I say. "What do I need to do?"

"Nothing," she says. "Do you still want to see Peter?"

I nod.

"I'll walk you to the reading room," she says, "then I'll buy some material and a pattern from the haberdasher with the housekeeping allowance. Mrs Ponsonby won't mind at all. She'll be pleased."

"Thank you," I say, grateful for her efforts. "There's no need to walk me to the reading rooms, though. It's only around the corner."

"I'm going to," says Elys. "Please don't try to stop me. I promised Mrs Ponsonby that I'd watch over you and even leaving you with Peter is a breach of trust. But I'll do it as long as you cooperate."

I sigh and mutter my agreement while feeling aggrieved and frustrated. Elys is my junior. I am a grown woman yet treated like a child, and their attention is cloying and unnatural. I know I can't walk far, but I am completely normal in all other regards. Sometimes I worry they think I'm half-witted, but I know I am not – quite the opposite. I did well at my studies and wanted to extend my education or get a job, neither of which passed the Ponsonby safety test. She refused point-blank to entertain the idea.

I resist making a scene and sweetly smile as Elys escorts me down the street and into a nearby alleyway.

#

Elys opens the door of the reading room and strides inside, leaving me in her wake. "Look who I've brought," she says as she spies Peter by the open window. He is disposing of a dead spider and examines the withered corpse in disgust.

He turns towards me. "What are you doing here?" he asks, wearing a puzzled expression.

"Nice to see you too," I say, taken aback.

"Of course, it's good to see you, but I can't remember the last time you were in Newquay, let alone here."

"July," I say, hardly believing how long it's been since I was last in town. "Except for a trip in the autumn with Mrs Ponsonby which doesn't count," I continue.

"Right. I'll be off," says Elys. "You'll be here for a while longer, Peter?"

He nods. "At least until five o'clock."

"Good. I'll collect Connie in half an hour."

I glare at her retreating form. "It's too much, Peter," I say, feeling my hackles rise again. "I don't think I have ever felt so trapped and undermined as I do today. It's suffocating."

"What is?" he asks as he closes the window and takes a seat behind his desk. "Sit down, Connie, dear."

"No, I won't sit down," I explode. "Don't you start. If I can walk half a mile, then I can stand unsupported for a few moments. What's wrong with everybody?"

Peter gazes at me, blue eyes creased in concern. "I was only trying to be polite," he says. "And I'd offer a chair to anyone, male or female." My anger disappears in a flash, and I inwardly curse my bad-tempered outburst. "I'm sorry," I say. "I shouldn't have shouted. You've been a good friend."

"Tell me what's wrong," he says. "It might help."

I sigh, and despite my previous objection, I lower myself into the chair. I'm already tired. I want to share my frustrations with Peter, but I don't know where to start. "Life is passing me by," I murmur.

"Why? What has changed since last week? You've always seemed perfectly content."

"I know. Up to now, it's been enough to potter around and fill my days with reading. It's all I've ever known. But I feel increasingly trapped. My world is tiny, Peter, and look at me – look at this dress."

He doesn't argue and chews his lip in contemplation.

"You knew, didn't you? Do people talk about me?"

"Everyone I know is fond of you. They sympathise and understand."

"Understand what? I'm twenty-five, Peter, and they've made me into an overgrown child. Why? Stephen Pemberton only has one leg, and he lives alone and works for a living. And what's more, he's two years younger than me."

"It's not you, Connie," says Peter. "Mrs Ponsonby is very protective. She always has been, but there's nothing sinister about it. She only wants what's best for you."

"I'm her prisoner," I say, and my face crumples. Salty tears spill down my face and drip into my lap. If I weren't so upset, I'd be mortified at my lack of self-control, but now the tears have started, I can't stop them.

"You poor thing," says Peter, producing a handkerchief from his trouser pocket and passing it over. "I didn't realise you felt this way."

"I don't know how to make it stop," I say, finally confronting my unspoken fears. "I know I can lead a normal life, and I am usually optimistic about my prospects, but today has been a shock. I'm a child in a woman's body with barely any control over my life, and unless something changes, I will never escape it. No wonder my dreams are so peculiar."

Peter reaches for my hand, and I hope he will ignore my talk of dreams. He is the one person I have told, and he thinks it's all in my imagination.

"Can't you talk to Mrs Ponsonby?" he says.

"I have – endlessly. She refuses virtually any request that takes me away from her prying eyes. She nearly changed her mind today."

"What would you have her do?"

"Give me my freedom," I say. "Let me come into Newquay alone or allow me to travel on a train."

"Could you manage alone?"

I shrug my shoulders. "Not with luggage," I say, eventually.

"What would you do if you ran into trouble?"

"You win. I need a companion. But Elys could come along."

"She needs to keep house. Would Mrs Ponsonby go with you?"

"In my worst dreams. She wouldn't let me do anything worth doing."

Peter picks up a pencil and chews the end while tapping on the table with his other hand. He doesn't speak for a moment.

"Do you know Lewannick?" he asks.

"No. What is it?"

"It's a little village not far from Bude."

"I've never been there."

"No reason why you should, but that's where Alice Thomas lived."

"So?"

"You remember I said I'm going to the inquest in Plymouth with Malcolm?"

"Yes."

"It's about her murder."

"Was she murdered?"

Peter frowned. "I told you that yesterday. Weren't you listening?"

"I don't think you mentioned murder. How remarkable."

"Isn't it?" he says, leaning forward. "Would you like to come?"

I stare at him and shake my head. "Haven't you understood a word that I've said? I can barely go to the bottom of the garden without permission from Mrs Ponsonby, much less attend a court in Plymouth of all places. I don't think I've ever ventured that far."

"What if my mother took us?"

"Why would she?"

"Because when I told her that Malcolm invited me to join him, she suggested we go together. Her sister, my aunt Veronica, lives in Plymouth and will put us up."

"She doesn't know me, and neither does Malcolm for that matter. Why would he tolerate my presence?"

"Don't worry about that. It's a public inquest, and Malcolm won't care one way or the other. It's more a matter of whether my mother can persuade Mrs Ponsonby that you will be safe in her care."

"I doubt it," I say, but my mind is already whirring. Peter's mother, Isla Tremayne, is a regular attendee at church and secretary of the Newquay Women's Institute. Mrs Ponsonby is also on the committee and holds her in high regard.

"Shall I ask her?" he says, registering my unspoken interest.

I nod. "Do you think she will go along with it?" I ask.

"Yes. Mother feels, well – she will want to help."

"You were about to say that she feels sorry for me."

"She understands," says Peter. "It's likely to be the week after next," he continues.

I look heavenwards and pretend to think. "I have no engagements that week," I say, allowing a flicker of hope to ignite. Tell me a little more about this inquest, just in case your mother can perform miracles."

"I know little about it," Peter admits. "Most of what I've heard is hearsay. Malcolm knows a lot of policemen and has more information than he ought to. I saw him earlier, and he says something interesting is about to come out, and I should keep an eye on the newspapers. That reminds me, I've got a couple put aside," he continues, eyeing his watch.

"You've got plenty of time until the shops shut," I say. "And Elys won't be back for a while. Tell me what you know."

#

"Alice Thomas was a farmer's wife," says Peter, leaning back in his chair. "She married a chap called William – quite a dour character, as I understand it. Anyway, they lived in Lewannick in a place called…" Peter breaks from the conversation, opens his desk drawer and removes a jotter which he flips open. "Trenhorne Farm," he says triumphantly.

"You've taken notes," I say. "I didn't know you were that interested."

"I've always found crime fascinating," says Peter. "Anyway, Mr and Mrs Thomas were friendly with a woman called Annie Hearn. She lived in Trenhorne House with her aunt and her sister until both women died, and she found herself alone. Mr and Mrs Thomas befriended Annie, hoping to ease her loneliness. They often visited and took her for occasional trips and treats. William's mother stayed at the farm the week before Alice fell ill, and the couple made plans to drive her back to her home in Bude. They invited Annie along for the ride. She accepted, and they dropped the mother off and called into Bude to look around. The two women went shopping while William visited the barber for a haircut, and at five o'clock, they met in Littlejohns Tea Rooms."

"Very nice," I say, thinking about my stomach. I would give a lot for a nice cup of tea and a cream cake right now. Supper time seems a long way away.

"It was," says Peter. "William Thomas ordered tea, cakes and bread and butter. Annie contributed a packet of salmon sandwiches and some chocolate cake that she'd made earlier."

"Quite a feast," I say.

Peter ignores me. "After tea, they parted company again," he continues. "William went to the Globe hotel and started feeling nauseous, but after a tot of whisky, his sickness vanished. Alice was not so fortunate. She suddenly felt unwell and complained about a sickly-sweet taste in her mouth. Alice bore the discomfort until they met up again, then asked for some fruit to take the peculiar taste away. William found a shop and bought her some bananas, but it didn't help. The drive back was eventful. Alice was so poorly that William had to stop the car several times so she could vomit at the roadside. Unfortunately for Alice, William had a business appointment near Launceston on the way back. While he was busy, poor Alice was sick in the public toilets with a concerned Annie helping her afflicted friend."

"How awful," I say. "Did they get back to Lewannick?"

"Yes, eventually. Annie helped Alice to bed, and William Thomas immediately sent for the doctor, who assumed that she had food poisoning. Annie stayed at the farmhouse for a few days to help her friend. Alice recovered briefly, and then her symptoms returned with a vengeance. She was so ill that the doctor arranged for her immediate admission to Plymouth hospital, where she died. And that is when they diagnosed arsenic poisoning," says Peter, closing his notebook and slamming it on the desk for effect.

"Poor Alice," I say, staring into the distance. I know little about science, but I can imagine how painful it must be to die from poison. And knowing that someone thought her life expendable is too dreadful to contemplate. Did Alice spend her dying days agonising over who wanted to end her life? I shudder and shake the thoughts away before turning to Peter. "How do they know it was murder?" I ask.

"She couldn't have taken arsenic by accident," says Peter. "And her symptoms came on suddenly. Logic dictates that the poison entered her system the same day, and she'd only kept company with Annie, William, and William's mother."

"Which of them did it?" I ask, now genuinely interested.

"That's the question, isn't it?" says Peter. "My money is on Annie Hearn."

"And mine is on the mother-in-law."

"Don't be silly," he says. What reason could she have to harm Alice? It's either William or Annie. I don't see how it could be anyone else."

"It would be the butler in an Agatha Christie novel," I say. "And there would be a decent cast of suspects. I'm extremely interested, Peter, but I would like more choice for a murderer."

"It's not a game," he says. "So have I whetted your appetite?"

I nod, dreading the disappointment I will undoubtedly feel if Mrs Ponsonby says no, which is highly likely.

"Right. Well, let me speak to my mother, and we'll see what we can do. In the meantime, give some serious thought to our suspects."

CHAPTER FIVE

Escape Plan

Saturday, November 15, 1930

I wake up later than usual, having benefited from a good night's sleep. The tide is high as I make my way to the beach, and I spend a brief five minutes walking across the sand before a sudden gust of rain hits. I haven't even had time to reach the cave and didn't go there yesterday either. I stand for a moment, debating whether to persevere despite the rain. Leaving the cave unsupervised for this long makes me feel out of control. I cast an eye at the greying sky, sombre and thick with clouds, and decide that the weather is unlikely to improve. I can't move quickly, and I'll get soaked to the skin if I carry on. If there is the slightest chance of Isla Tremayne convincing Mrs Ponsonby to let me go to Plymouth, I can't ruin my chances by catching a cold. Reluctantly, I turn my back on the sea and make my way to the library to finish *Women in Love*.

Miss Templeton, whose full Christian name I have since learned, thanks to Elys, is actually Roxanne, is still guarding the reception desk. She hears me approach, raises her head and sighs. She is so loud and delivers the sigh with such purpose that I know it can't be a product of my overactive imagination. I wonder what I have done to provoke such obvious dislike. I hesitate as I walk past, about to ask her how Dolly is keeping, but I am put off by her hostility and decide to find another way. Instead, I proceed to the library without comment, feeling her eyes jabbing into my back as I walk down the passage.

As I push open the library door, I nearly fall over when someone wrenches the handle from the other side. I stumble and almost topple into the arms of Oliver Fox, who is trying to leave the room.

"Ah, Miss Maxwell. How are you today?"

"Very well," I say, steadying myself.

"A shame our little experiment didn't work," he says. "Still, we can try another day."

"Experiment?" I ask, then I remember yesterday's conversation. "Oh, dear. I fell asleep," I say, crossing my fingers at the little white lie, which was only a slight variation on the truth. In reality, I was so excited about the murder case that I forgot all about it. Once home, I'd waited for Mrs Ponsonby to settle in the parlour, then proceeded to the kitchen before tracking down Elys. I'd made her promise to buy me a daily newspaper so I could keep an eye on the case. Elys refused at first, but a little gentle persuasion did the trick. She'd agreed as long as I didn't tell Mrs P. And by the time I'd got to bed, so much had happened that I'd forgotten Mr Fox's astral travel experiment altogether. "I was tired," I explain, trying to sound convincing.

"I quite understand," he says. "Please don't feel in any way obliged. I mean, it's fascinating to me, but esoteric matters are not everybody's cup of tea. Of course, your abilities are extraordinary, but I appreciate how difficult it is to control them."

"I want to help," I say, watching him intently. Oliver Fox must be in his mid-forties, but his hair has already receded, elongating his face. With sagging cheeks and a down-turned mouth, his appearance is not dissimilar to Samuel Potts' bloodhound, Piper. Fox always looks sad and a little disappointed in life, and I fear I have added to his melancholy. "I'll try again tonight, I promise. Sleep won't get the better of me this time," I say.

The corner of his mouth twitches, and he nods. "Only if you are sure," he says.

"I'm sure."

"Then please excuse me." He gives an odd little bow and leaves the library.

I sprawl on the sofa, feeling guilty. My life is not so busy that I can't spare a few moments exploring an ability that I have always taken for granted and mostly considered a nuisance. It's delightful dreaming my way across the cliffs to Tregurrian, but I've never yet seen them in daylight. Not that I've ever tried. At last, someone is offering to help me harness this gift, or perhaps this curse. Who knows? Well, I won't find out if I don't try, so tonight I will make an effort.

I read my book, turning page after page until I reach the end. It was worth it. Not the best I have ever read, but by no means the worst, and I rise and make my way back to the cottage. Not a single soul disturbed me in the library. It was bliss.

I arrive at the cottage to find two things of interest. A parked car is outside and can only mean a visitor. But before I have time to find out who it is, I see a letter addressed to me propped up on the side table in the hallway. I pick it up and turn it over. The back of the envelope is blank, and the postmark blurry. I stare for a few moments, trying to remember the last time I received a letter. It must have been last year when Dolly travelled to Somerset and sent me a postcard from Minehead. I am almost reluctant to open it and spoil the surprise for fear of disappointment. But it is a handwritten letter and must be personal. Eventually, curiosity gets the better of me, and I tear it open and withdraw the contents with shaking fingers.

I read the letter greedily. It is from Mary Newson, a woman I met quite by chance on the beach a few years ago. She is an exceptionally talented painter who lives in an artist's colony near Penzance. Mary and I are close in age, but that is where the similarity ends. Mary travels abroad several times a year and has often exhibited her paintings, gaining quite a following of admirers, of which I am one. She is a liberated, uncompromising woman committed to her art. Mary is an impressionist painter, specialising in temperature and tones, but Mrs Ponsonby describes her work as pretentious nonsense. She thinks all artists should paint like the great masters. I disagree. There is an indescribable honesty about Mary that shines through her work.

I turn the pages of the letter and read about her recent journey to Tangier. Her words drip like honey from the page, and I can smell, taste, almost feel the warmth of the sun over the Moroccan souk that she describes. I clutch the letter to my chest, dropping my stick as I read, but I don't care. I yearn to travel and explore the world. There must be something out there for me. I crouch and fumble for my stick, hooking it over the door handle while I finish the letter. The last page is the best and contains excellent news. Mary is coming to Porth Tregoryan tomorrow to paint the cliffs. She doesn't need to, having plenty of access to seascapes of her own, where she lives on the coast at Bosula, but Mary says she wants a change. Porth Tregoryan inspired her so much last time she came that she hopes to emulate her success. But only if the weather holds. I approach the window and anxiously look outside. The rain is still tipping down. I say a brief prayer to the gods of the skies and hope they are listening. Mary has invited me to join her on the beach, followed by lunch at the hotel. Nothing must get in the way of this rare treat.

Elys walks through the hallway on her way to the dining room. "Mary's coming," I beam.

"Mary who?"

"Newson."

"Who?"

"You know. The painter."

"Oh yes. Your friend."

I smile at the thought. I've only met Mary a few times, mostly on the beach, and she sent me a postcard last year. Describing her as a friend is something of an exaggeration, but this is the second time Mary has sought my company, and she must see something in me.

"She's asked me for lunch," I say. "Tomorrow, as long as it doesn't rain."

Elys grimaces. "I don't like your chances, weatherwise," she says. "But at least Mrs Ponsonby approves of her. Anyway, the Tremaynes are here."

I gasp. "Peter's mother?"

"And Peter too."

"Oh, goodness. It's important business. Where are they?"

"In the garden. Mrs Ponsonby is introducing them to the girls."

"Why?" I curl my lip as I ask then rearrange my scowl. "Sorry, I don't mean to be rude, but the last thing I need is Mrs Ponsonby boring them to death with chicken stories."

Elys laughs. Mrs Ponsonby has little empathy for the human condition, but our chickens fascinate her, and she regularly adds to the flock. She has found a new powder for poultry mites and relentlessly eulogises its benefits to anyone who shows a passing interest.

"Why are you so concerned?" Elys asks.

"Didn't I tell you? Peter has invited me to Plymouth."

"No," she says. "You gave me chapter and verse about newspaper reports, but not a word about a trip."

"Do you think she'll let me go?"

Elys bites her lip.

"Oh, for goodness' sake. I'm not a child."

"She might, with the right approach," says Elys, sounding serious beyond her years.

"Peter thought so too. That's why he's asked his mother for help."

"It's your best chance," says Elys.

"Well, if she says no, I'm going anyway," I say, feeling a sudden surge of rage.

Elys doesn't speak, and she doesn't need to. She knows perfectly well that I can't make the journey without help. I scowl and mentally file away the idea of planning an assisted escape, but voices interrupt my musings as the back door opens.

"I'll make a pot of tea," says Elys, disappearing into the kitchen.

"There you are," says Mrs Ponsonby. "Look – we have visitors." She smiles as she gestures to Peter and his mother.

"Lovely to see you," I murmur, exchanging glances with Peter.

"Elys is fetching tea and cakes," says Mrs Ponsonby. "Won't you join us in the parlour?"

"Let them have a few moments to themselves," says Isla Tremayne. "There's something I'd like to ask you," she continues. "Give us ten minutes to talk among ourselves, Peter."

"Of course." Peter nods, and I direct him into the dining room while Mrs Ponsonby and his mother disappear into the parlour. As Mrs Tremayne shuts the door, she turns to Peter and smiles. My heart floods with affection for her. How I wish Mrs Ponsonby were capable of the same light-heartedness.

#

"It's now or never," I say, taking a seat at the dining table. Peter has already made himself comfortable and is reclining on the chair by the window, with a newspaper in front of him.

"My mother is remarkably persuasive," he says confidently.

"Elys doesn't share your faith," I say, feeling slightly nauseous. My heart lurches at the thought of them deciding my fate next door. I have already invested far too much hope.

"There's nothing we can do," says Peter sensibly. "But I've got something here that might take your mind off it." He opens the newspaper, locates an article, and folds it again.

"What's this?" I ask.

"You'll never guess?"

"They've arrested William Thomas?"

He shakes his head.

"Another murder?"

"Try again."

"Just tell me," I say, bored with the game.

"Annie Hearn has only absconded," he says.

"No!" I am shocked by this turn of events and immediately assume the worst. "Has he killed her?"

"By he, I presume you mean William Thomas?"

"Who else?" I say, mildly irritated. "I wasn't referring to the milkman, and there are precious few suspects."

Peter shakes his head. "I don't think so. They saw Annie Hearn leaving her home."

"Tell me more," I say.

Peter smooths the newspaper pages and summarises the report. "It starts with the usual guff, age, description, that sort of thing," he says.

"Don't gloss over it. I want to know everything about Annie," I say. Only the facts will interest Peter, but though I can take or leave people, they fascinate me.

"Very well. Annie Hearn is about forty years of age."

"Oh. I thought she'd be much older," I say, savouring this new piece of information. I had imagined the elderly Mrs Thomas to be in her nineties and her daughter, husband, and friend twenty years younger. It just goes to show the importance of detail.

Peter looks up. "Indeed," he says brusquely. "Anyway, Annie Hearn is the widow of a Sheffield doctor. She is" – he runs his finger down the column – "five feet two inches tall with dark hair and a sallow complexion."

"Charming," I say. There must be better ways to describe Annie's appearance. It is almost as if the reporter is using his words as a weapon. I wonder how they would write about me under similar circumstances. *Constance Maxwell, a spinster of Porth Tregoryan, committed murder today. She is five foot four inches when standing straight in a built-up boot and has windswept auburn hair. Prisoner of her guardian, the veritable Mrs Ponsonby, Miss Maxwell has expressed no remorse for her dreadful deeds.* At least they couldn't describe my skin as sallow. I spend far too much time on the beach.

"Are you listening?" asks Peter.

I nod. "Yes. Tell me more."

"She left her house on Tuesday with no luggage and only a small handbag. She was wearing a black and white coat, black shoes, stockings and a black hat," he continues. "And she commissioned a car."

"To drive or be driven?" I ask.

Peter squints at the paper. "It doesn't say. I can't see how it matters. The police have it on good authority that she's in Looe."

"She's probably visiting someone," I say, feeling deflated. "It means nothing."

"The police believe she is suffering from memory loss," says Peter.

I snort. "How convenient."

"I thought you didn't suspect her?"

"That's not what I mean. The most likely explanation is an extended trip. The implication that Annie has lost her memory is a good press story, isn't it?"

"You haven't got a very high opinion of reporters," says Peter.

I consider his cousin Malcolm and refrain from an honest answer.

"It's not that," I say. "But it's in their interests to make an entertaining story. It leaves their readers wanting more. Anything else?"

Peter inspects the newspaper again. "Only the conclusion that nursing Alice Thomas has had a detrimental effect on Annie's health. They think that overwork and sleepless nights together with the grief of losing a good friend have tipped her over the edge."

"It must be just as hard for Mr Thomas," I say. "And presumably he is still living in Lewannick?"

"As far as I know. Anyway, that's that for now. Fascinating, isn't it?"

"I can't tell you how much I want to be at the inquest," I say. I can see Annie Hearn in my mind's eye, pale and shivering in the dock as she faces a barrage of questions. No wonder she needs a few days away to forget about it. I almost feel protective of the frightened, grief-stricken widow.

The door opens, interrupting my thoughts, and Elys comes in, balancing a tray on her other arm. "Tea's ready," she says brightly.

We follow her into the parlour, where Mrs Ponsonby and Isla Tremayne sit in the two armchairs nearest the fire. Peter and I position ourselves on the sofa and try to decipher the unreadable expressions on their faces.

"Pour the tea, Elys, dear," says Mrs Ponsonby. Elys obliges, then offers a plate of toasted teacake halves that she has hastily gathered, having had no notice of the Tremaynes' visit.

I take one and nibble it nervously. "I hear you are going to the Pottses supper party tomorrow night, Connie," says Mrs Tremayne, blinking. For a moment, it looks as if she has something in her eye, and then I realise the blink was a subtle wink. I understand immediately.

"Yes. I'm looking forward to it," I say, hoping I haven't overplayed my hand.

The edges of Mrs Ponsonby's mouth lift slightly. She reaches for her teacup, takes a sip, and licks her lips. "I have some news, Connie. Mrs Tremayne has invited you to Plymouth for a few days. Would you like to go?"

"Oh, very much."

"I have agreed on the condition that you remain with her throughout your visit. No going off alone," she says. "Not even with Peter."

"Of course," I say. "Yes, anything. Thank you so much." I grin at Peter, and he smiles back all-knowingly. Peter never doubted his mother for a moment.

CHAPTER SIX

Experiments in Astral Travel

I retire to bed early, having borrowed the clock from the dining room mantelpiece. Tonight, I am mindful of my promise to Oliver Fox and determined not to let him down. I get into bed and start reading, but the clock is distracting, and I wonder how people sleep through the relentless beat. A few moments later, I blink my eyes open and understand the power of the hypnotic tick. I nearly fell asleep, and it is only ten o'clock. I get out of bed and limp to the window. Flinging it open, I push my head into the chilly night air. It is freezing tonight, and the wind is high. A short blast and I am shivering and wide awake. This time, I perch on the end of my bed and read a *Woman's Own* magazine belonging to Elys. It occupies me for a few brief minutes and reminds me why I rarely bother. The dull articles involve knitting and housekeeping, none of which appeal to me. I close the magazine and sigh, then wonder if I ought to prepare for the experiment sooner. The urgency vanishes as I fuss around the room, opening and closing drawers, tidying a bit of this and that. I look at the clock again. It is only half past ten, but I have assumed that I will fall easily into dream travel, which might not be the case. Relaxing into a trance could take much longer, and I haven't considered how it might work, let alone how

I ought to prepare. If I get inside my bedclothes, I will inevitably fall asleep, leaving the matter to chance. I'll need to think of another way.

I resolve the problem by lying on top of the bed. Then I gaze at the night light on my bedside table, but before long, I've cricked my neck, and I'm going cross-eyed. The candle is too close to watch comfortably. Sighing, I stand up and move it onto the nearest corner of my dressing table, then I adjust the window until it is fractionally open. I test my position on the bed again and eye the candle. The flame flickers to the rhythm of the draft, and I find myself drawn to the dancing light. I recline on my soft pillow and yawn, worrying that I'll fall asleep before I can give the experiment my best effort. And there's another problem. The draft from the open window is cold and distracting. I'll have to get into bed after all.

I lay unmoving under the eiderdown, pleasantly warm as I stare at the hypnotic flame. The light glows soft and orange while my eyes grow heavy. I relax and drift, numb and immobile, then a tingling starts in my little finger. Pins and needles, I assume, but it's a passing thought and barely registers. Then the feeling creeps up my arms, like an army of ants. It warms and chills, leaving me sleepy yet curiously alert. I'm not worried and yield to the sensation, and soon vibrations course through my body like static electricity. I am still lying prone on the bed, aware of my surroundings but not distracted by them. I am comfortable and safe.

My focus is on the candle when something penetrates the glowing light. A moth has flown through the open window and is circling, its gossamer wings flirting with the naked flame. I hope it will not succumb, but I cannot tear my eyes away. I need not worry. It glides towards me and settles on the eiderdown within a hair's breadth of my left hand. I move my little finger close enough to shoo it away, but it does not connect, and I realise the moth is further away than I thought. I try again and make a gentle flicking motion with my fingers. They pass right through the little creature.

I watch, bemused but not afraid, as I raise my hand and place it over the insect, fascinated to see the two things merging. I raise my head, sit up straight, and put a hesitant foot on the floor, followed by another. I lean over and put my hand on the floorboards where it rests for a moment, then I take a deep breath and push. My hand disappears up to the wrist, and I view my arm disinterestedly while acknowledging that something has indeed occurred. I stride towards the window, long confident steps, and smile at the easy, familiar movement. I turn and face the bed to see myself lying prone under the cover. I am free of my weak and useless body. The sensation of dream walking is more joyful knowing that I've conjured it myself. It is liberating to have control.

I remember my promise to Oliver Fox, and no sooner do I imagine the library than I feel pulled towards the outside of Pebble Cottage. I screw my eyes tight and fight the urge. I want to make every moment count and walk there unaided. I don't know how long I will stay in the dream state. It rarely lasts long and might end at any moment, so I want to take full advantage. I look at the clock and note that it is now five minutes to midnight. I reach for the door, and my arm passes through, followed by my body. I don't feel a thing. Then I walk downstairs, but my feet don't touch the steps. The sensation is hard to describe, and I miss hearing my footsteps on the hard wooden stair. I traverse the hallway, push through the front door, and I am outside, turning my face into the wind. It should be cold this late at night, and I can see from the shimmering treetops that it's windy, but it doesn't affect my skin. There's no chill air, no goosebumps. I can see and hear, but I've lost all sense of feeling, and I wonder if I can still smell.

I lift my skirts and run toward the hotel. Though only half prepared for this, I had the foresight to stay dressed. Our cottage is moments away, and I am only outside for a few seconds. As soon as I arrive at the hotel door, I allow myself to think of the library, and instantly I'm there, standing in front of the cold, unlit fire. It is dark, and I can see the leather chairs by the pale moonlight. It feels strange to be there at night. Apart from my most recent dream, all previous travel has been outdoors, and I don't know whether I can perform normal basic functions. I decide to sit on the couch and partly succeed. But it is an uneasy combination of being both in and on the sofa at the same time. I am neither comfortable nor uncomfortable without form or substance, and I'm unsure how to feel about it. I sprawl across the sofa, head on one arm, my feet on the other, but it does not help. I am immune to external sensation in this strange state and decide I might as well be upright for all the relief that sitting affords.

I pace the room, excitedly waiting for Mr Fox so he can acknowledge my success. But when I look at the clock, it is five minutes past midnight. He is late, and a wave of disappointment engulfs me. At least my emotions still work. I stand by the fireplace, staring towards the mirror, and immediately experience a surge of fear. Once again, an overwhelming sensation is pulling me away, and I know that it's trying to draw me back against my will. I concentrate and think of the candle, take deep breaths, and I am steady again. The idea of looking in the mirror and not seeing my reflection frightens me beyond reason, filling me with existential dread. I am here, but I am not. I exist, yet I don't. My mind is buzzing, but I imagine the library in the daytime with Peter and his books and soon feel calmer.

I can't face what I'll see if I look in the mirror and I banish the thought from my head. I walk towards the window and peer outside but stop in the certain knowledge that someone's behind me. I turn around. Oliver Fox has materialised through the door and is gliding my way. As I step forward, he sees me, and his jaw drops in shock as if he has confronted a ghost, which I suppose he has. But no sooner have I registered his presence than he's gone – vanished. Not in a puff of smoke, nor gentle evaporation, but there one moment and gone the next. It is an anti-climax, and I am left feeling deflated.

Duty over and still feeling strong, I return to the window and watch the sea crash over the bay. It is high tide, and the waves have stolen the beach, leaving only a narrow strip near the caves – my caves. My heart fills as I burst through the walls, down the slope and onto the beach, running with arms out, hair loose – free of my broken body, free of Mrs Ponsonby's rules, free of the constraints of my life. I am at my cave in no time – not tired or out of breath, but present in the moment. Yet, something is wrong. I can't taste the salty air or feel the dank oppressiveness of the cave. I miss the cold more than I ever thought possible. Freedom has come at the expense of humanity. My haven isn't the same without a book to curl up with and a blanket over my knees. I shouldn't have come.

I turn away and start back along the sand. Then the unexpected screech of an owl assails my ears, and I am pulled backwards with a sickening whoosh. I am in my body on my bed, shallow panting with a racing heart. I test my pulse. Its throb makes my fingers tingle. The room is chilly from the open window, and I shiver, but not with cold. I have dream walked many times before and accepted it as normal. But tonight, for the first time, I'm frightened. I snuggle under my eiderdown, glad to be alive and in no hurry to repeat the experience. Within moments, I am fast asleep.

CHAPTER SEVEN

Lunch and Other Distractions

Sunday, November 16, 1930

I wake late feeling exhausted, with memories of the previous night tumbling through my head like unruly children. The waking dream was so disturbing that I don't know whether to believe it. I take a few moments to marshal my thoughts and try to assemble the memories in the correct order. I recollect falling asleep, but everything else is blurry. I rise, pour cold water into the basin on the washstand, and splash my face. As I look up, my reflection greets me in the mirror, and the resulting stab of fear reminds me of last night's foray into the library. My memories flood back, and I feel a growing unease about the experiment. It wasn't worth it for the fleeting moments I spent with Oliver Fox. Still, I have done as he asked, and there is no need to repeat the experience if I don't want to. I gaze through the window, looking out to the rear of the hotel and glimpse the beach, reminding me of the soulless cave. No, I don't want to experiment again. I am prepared for the dreams to come to me, but I won't chase them.

I grab my stick and limp to the wardrobe. My limbs are as heavy and stiff as if I really did run along the sand last night. My lower back aches, and there's a nasty twinge in my hips. I sniff and blow my nose, wondering if I have caught a cold, then I look at the clock, noting that it is nearly half past eight. I could get used to having a timepiece. It is surprisingly helpful, and I don't know how I ever did without one. It won't be returning to its home in the dining room.

I sit on the bed and roll my woollen stockings over my legs, tempted to go back to bed. If I tell Mrs Ponsonby that I'm unwell, she won't make a fuss. But my presence at the Pottses' supper party matters to her, and I can't risk letting her down. If I do, the trip to Plymouth will disappear in a flash, no matter how justified my absence. By the time I finish dressing, brush my hair, and apply a little cold cream, I feel better and less concerned about last night's events. I'll speak to Mr Fox, then try to forget all about it. Cheered by this decision, I leave my room and prepare to go downstairs when I see myself in the mirror and reconsider my outfit. I haven't put a scrap of makeup on. I never do. My hair is straggly, and my dress shabby and old. I must speak to Elys today and ask her to measure me for the dress she promised. In the meantime, I'll try and change into something a little less old-fashioned.

Leaving my best dress for the supper party, I select a navy blue frock. It is long, slim-fitting, and passable. My hair needs a good cut, and the best that I can do is pin it tidily. It takes three attempts before I am satisfied. Finally, I open the top drawer of my dressing table and remove a few items of makeup that I've hardly used. I apply a little rouge and the barest trace of lipstick. It is not much, but the effect is pleasing and not too dramatic. I limp downstairs for some breakfast, but as I walk past the sideboard, I see a note addressed to me in Mary's handwriting. I hook my stick over my arm and slit the envelope open. It's good news – Mary is already here. She arrived early this morning and will have settled on the beach by now. My heart thuds with excitement. A friend of my age to talk to will provide more pleasure than I have had in a long time. I forgo a proper breakfast and cut the crust from the loaf on the table, butter it and hold it between my teeth while I don my coat. Then I slowly head off, eating as I go.

It is clement outside. The day is mild, and there is barely any wind. It is perfect weather for painting, and I am delighted for Mary, who has travelled a long way to capture the beauty of Porth Tregoryan. I look to the right, but the beach is empty; Mary is not by the caves, but I turn left and soon see her. Mary has thoughtfully positioned herself only a short distance from our cottage. She has set up her easel and is daubing paint onto the canvas with a palette knife, her jaw set in concentration. Mary hears my stick on the sand and looks up as I approach. "Connie," she exclaims, her face wreathed in smiles. She breaks from her work and walks towards me, linking her hand through mine and leaning into me.

"You're a sight for sore eyes," she says. "Let me look at you."

She steps backwards and peers into my face. "You look different, healthy," she says.

"Thank you," I reply, wishing I could say likewise. But something is wrong. Mary is pale and angular. She has lost weight, and her eyes lack their usual sparkle.

"It's lovely to see you," I offer instead. "It has been too long."

"I know. What with being away and everything…" Her words trail away, and I find myself momentarily tongue-tied.

"Look. I have brought you a seat," Mary says, pointing to a deckchair beside her easel. "It will be alright, won't it?"

"It's perfect," I say, lowering myself with the aid of my stick.

"Do use this, dear," she says, passing me a blanket. I don't need it. My coat is lovely and warm and the weather unseasonably mild, but I take it anyway in recognition of her thoughtfulness.

"What are you painting?" I ask, gazing at the canvas.

She points towards Newquay. "I want to capture that view," she says. "Or rather my interpretation of it."

"Lovely," I say, relaxing into the deckchair. "Now, Mary, you're looking very tanned. Have you been travelling?"

"Yes," she says. "Earlier this year. But I've been back for some time now. I'm surprised you can tell."

"I long to travel," I say, imagining the thrill of setting off on an adventure. "Where have you been? Tell me everything about your journey."

"Tangier," she says and describes the city and its people. She talks at length and in detail as she paints, knowing that I am unlikely to leave Cornwall, much less travel to North Africa. I am not envious and enjoy hearing her stories. Then, just as she starts describing her rooms at The Continental Hotel, she pauses and chews her lip.

"Somerset Maugham was staying too," she says, and I relish the precious titbit of information. I read Maugham and know that his protagonist Philip Carey has a club foot. It is unusual to read about an imperfect hero.

"He was there when the news arrived," Mary continues. "Mr Maugham was very kind to me."

"What news?" I ask.

"News about my brother," she whispers.

"Crawford?" I reply, then curse myself for the thoughtless question. Mary was one of three children, and her younger brother died many years ago. It could hardly have been anyone else but Crawford Newson.

She nods.

"What happened?"

Her eyes well, and she puts her brush down before gazing towards the sea. I stare at her profile, tracking the tear that trickles down her cheek. She closes her eyes, takes a breath, and turns towards me.

"He drowned."

"Mary, no," I say, reaching for her hand. She clasps mine and kneels on the sand beside me. "I am so sorry," I say, lost for words. I don't know how she's managed an hour of chat about Tangier without mentioning her brother. He must be at the forefront of her thoughts. "When did it happen?"

"In April, while I was away," she says.

"How awful. Couldn't your brother swim?" I ask.

"Very well," says Mary. "You never met him, did you?"

"No, but I have read reviews about his books. I hear he was a wonderful writer."

"Crawford led an interesting life," she says. "He travelled all over the world and was a real adventurer like the ones you read about in *Boy's Own*. To die in Salcombe harbour like that is unthinkable. Even now, I can hardly believe it."

"You poor thing," I say. "And his wife – it's a terrible thing to be a young widow."

"Laura is coping in her way," says Mary. "She would manage even better without the awful rumours."

"Rumours?"

"Yes. Silly stories invented by people who ought to know better."

I wait, unsure whether to ask more. I am dying to know the details, but further questions would be insensitive. Mary senses my reluctance, sighs, and continues.

"Crawford was staying on a yacht moored off Salcombe estuary," she says. "But on the Saturday night of Easter weekend, he went to a dance with his friends at the nearby hotel. They had a high old time by all accounts, and he left in the early hours of Sunday morning before boarding a collapsible dinghy to row back."

"How many sailed?" I ask, thinking how dangerous it would be with a large party aboard.

"Only three," says Mary. "My brother, his friend Harry Hollings, and a local doctor's daughter."

I raise an eyebrow and quickly lower it before Mary notices.

"The wind was up," she continues, "the tide was strong and the sea choppy. A sudden swell tossed the dinghy around, and it sank. Harry and the girl swam for the shore, but Crawford headed for the yacht. They both survived but never saw Crawford again."

"How far were they from the shore when the dinghy sank?"

"I'm not sure," says Mary. "But it's so unfair. The girl was wearing a fur coat, yet she made it back while my brother died."

"Do the rumours concern the doctor's daughter?" I ask, unable to help myself.

"Partly," Mary replies. "I mean, his friend was there, so he wasn't in a compromising situation, but even so..." Her words die away, and I squeeze her hand.

She tucks a curl of hair behind her ears with paint-stained fingers and continues. "They didn't find Crawford's body," she says. "And the rumours are unspeakably awful. They claim he didn't die but disappeared by choice."

"Why would he?" I ask, shocked.

"For family or financial reasons, they say," she replies.

"Were there any?"

"Not that I'm aware of. Crawford seemed perfectly happy with Laura, and she adored him. And if he had money troubles, we could have helped. You know how successful my father was, and I have an annuity as well as my earnings."

"I know," I say. Mary lives an idyllic life in an artist's colony in Bosula. Her widowed mother is wealthy, and so are several of the other residents. They would, no doubt, have been morally and financially supportive.

"Besides," she says. "Not only was Crawford a successful novelist, but his articles and poems were always in great demand. He didn't have financial problems, and I don't know why these rumours have persisted."

"Was he happy?" I ask.

Mary frowns. "Well, yes. I suppose so. Although the last few times I saw him, he was out of sorts – preoccupied, I suppose."

"In what way?"

"It's hard to say. One moment, Crawford would be larking around, telling stories and full of bonhomie. The next, he would be quieter and introspective. I left for Tangier in January and saw him at Christmas. He didn't live with us in the colony, and our last meeting was at his home. I arrived before the others and let myself in the back door. Crawford was in the study with the door open, and I went inside. He was scribbling away, hard at it, and couldn't have heard me. When I coughed, he started as if someone had let off a firework. I have never seen him so pale and shaken. He poured a drink before shooing me out of his study. But not before I saw the contents of his jotter."

"Was he writing?"

"No. Crawford was sketching – it was an odd sort of picture – ore like a symbol, but it meant nothing to me. Then Mother arrived, and he switched on the charm as usual."

"Do you think it had anything to do with his death?"

Mary shakes her head. "No. I'm only telling you because you asked me if he was happy, and it's the first time I've considered his state of mind since then. Anyway, this canvas won't paint itself."

Mary stands and eyes the seascape pensively. I watch as she chats and finishes her painting, but she is not quite the Mary I remember, and I am glad when it is time for lunch and other distractions.

#

Mary dismantles her easel and packs her painting in the car, then we make our way to the hotel and go inside. The attractive but sour-faced Roxy Templeton is still occupying the place where Dolly ought to be. I avoid her gaze and hope Dolly is feeling better. Mary advances confidently towards the desk and announces herself.

"I've booked a table for luncheon," she says, opening a silver case and depositing her card on the counter.

A shadow crosses Roxy's beaming face as Mary turns to speak to me. She realises we're together and quickly escorts Mary towards the dining room, knowing full well that I can't keep up. Mary hangs back, and by the time Roxy turns to show her into the room, we are still a considerable distance down the corridor. She flashes Mary an insincere smile as we finally reach her but does not apologise. "Roberto will take you to your table," Roxy says, beckoning to the dark-haired waiter who is balancing a tray of drinks on a silver salver.

"This way," he says, showing us to a table overlooking the seafront. He places the tray on a nearby empty table, pulls out two chairs and waits for us to sit, then passes the lunch menus. "One moment," he says before hurrying away to deliver the drinks. He soon returns, by which time Mary and I have already chosen lobster salads.

"What would you like to drink, madam?" the waiter asks

"Two glasses of wine," says Mary without consulting me.

I open my mouth to contradict her. I have limited experience of alcohol, more or less confined to Christmas Day. But something stops me from speaking out, and I nervously sip from the glass when it arrives, feeling rather decadent.

We watch the sea as we eat and talk. The wine lowers my inhibitions, and I tell Mary my frustrations at living in a hamlet without travel or adventure. She sighs. "I have the opposite problem," she says. "I love to travel and always arrive abroad with great expectations, in high spirits and eager to work. It doesn't last long. Within days I'm missing Cornwall dreadfully and desperately want to come home.

"Why do you travel if you don't enjoy it?"

"To gain inspiration," she says. "And I do enjoy it, but I miss home too."

"You are very independent," I say enviously, thinking of the shiny saloon car parked outside. "I wish I could drive?"

"Is it medically possible?" she asks.

I consider the matter. "Yes, in theory. I can't walk far, but I should be able to apply enough pressure to the pedals."

"Then why don't you?"

I laugh a hollow laugh. In telling Mary about my restricted life in Porth Tregoryan, I have glossed over the baleful influence of Mrs Ponsonby. Telling her would make me sound even less sophisticated than I already do. But I can't expand on my lack of freedom without revealing everything.

It spills out in a torrent of words, and Mary gazes at me, eyes soft with sympathy. "How can I help?" she asks.

I smile, grateful that she wants to try. "You can't," I say. "I have very little money, and I can't walk far. Mrs Ponsonby is my guardian, and I don't have any living relatives to turn to."

"It must be awful," she says.

"She doesn't ill-treat me," I add quickly, feeling uncharacteristically protective of my environment. "But I can't go anywhere."

"Freedom is so important," says Mary. "Look, why don't I teach you to drive?"

"Mrs Ponsonby will never allow it," I say.

"Come and stay with me. Then she won't know any better."

I tell Mary about my impending visit to Plymouth and how difficult it was to achieve. "Even now, I am afraid that Mrs Ponsonby will change her mind before I leave," I say.

"Yes, but now that she's given permission once, she'll find it harder to refuse in the future," says Mary.

She has a point. If we'd discussed this last month, I'd have told her the Plymouth trip was an impossibility.

"I know what to do," says Mary. "Come to Bosula for Christmas. You will love it."

"I can't," I say. "It's out of the question."

"Do try – you'll be doing me a favour. With Crawford gone and my mother only widowed four years ago, it will be quieter than usual, though we can spend time with the other artists. You will enjoy yourself, I promise, and it will be so nice to have company. While you're there, I can teach you how to drive."

I gaze towards the sea, feeling my forehead furrow as I consider the prospect. Mary is right. I can't think of anything more enjoyable than Christmas away from the confines of Pebble Cottage. To be around other people, singing carols and other yuletide jollities is appealing. But I don't know how to achieve it short of running away. And given my fastest speed is a brisk limp, then it is not to be. I shake my head. "I would love to," I say. "But I can't."

Mary takes my hand. "We will find a way," she says. "I'll send a formal invitation to Mrs Ponsonby in early December and see what happens. She might get carried away by the yuletide spirit."

I almost tell her not to bother. It is better not to hope for something so completely unattainable, but I don't want to throw Mary's kindness back in her face. I nod and smile instead.

"Anyway," Mary says, scrunching her napkin and tossing it on the table. "I must get back. It's been a great pleasure, and I have thoroughly enjoyed myself."

"Me too," I say. "Thank you for lunch. Are you sure I can't contribute?" I wait for her to reply. Paying my half would take every penny I have, but it's the least I can do and would be money well spent.

"Absolutely not," says Mary. "This was my treat. Shall I walk you home?"

"No, thank you," I say. I get to my feet, feeling woozy from the wine, and know that it will be a challenging walk back. I don't want Mary to witness my unsteadiness.

"Very well," she says, hugging me. "I'll see you at Christmas."

I watch as she walks towards the reception desk and pays the bill. She turns, waves, and then she's gone. I take my stick and walk towards the entrance, passing but not looking at Roxy Templeton, who will ignore me whether or not I speak. I am about to leave the foyer when I hear footsteps behind me, and a voice calls my name. I turn around to see Oliver Fox striding towards me. "Glad I caught you," he says, sounding breathless.

"How are you?" I ask politely, wishing he wasn't there.

"I am very well and excited. It worked."

I bite my lip. I don't want to have this conversation at all, much less in public.

"Can you spare a few moments?" he asks.

"I was on my way home." My voice, without its usual warmth, is matter of fact and disinterested.

His face falls, and he looks more like a bloodhound than ever. "Perhaps I could walk you to your cottage?" he asks.

I can hardly say no, so I agree, and he joins me, walking without a coat or hat. Even in this mild weather, he must be cold, but he does not complain.

"I could hardly believe my eyes when I saw you last night," he says.

For a moment, I contemplate pretending that I don't know what he means.

"You saw me too?" he asks, sensing my reluctance.

I cannot tell a lie and nod uncertainly. "Yes, I saw you."

"Then it worked. Was it difficult?"

"Not at all," I say, remembering how easily I had slipped into the waking dream.

"Marvellous." Oliver Fox clasps his hands, his face wreathed in smiles. "How wonderful. Were you in the dream state for long?"

"Yes. I walked on the beach after I saw you."

"I believe your inherent talent surpasses mine already," he says, and I can't help but smile. Fox is an odd little man, learned, old-fashioned, yet as excitable as a child. "So, what's next?" he asks. "Shall we try it again to be sure?"

I stop and lean on my stick. "I don't want to," I say, the words spilling out without thought.

I expect him to express his disappointment, but he is remarkably phlegmatic. "Can you at least tell me how it felt?" he asks. "I won't ask you to try again if you don't want to. I understand how you feel."

He has said the right thing, and a wave of guilt takes me by surprise. "Yes, but I need to sit down," I say.

"We can talk tomorrow, then."

"No. I'd rather deal with it today. I can rest here," I say, pointing to a flat rock I sometimes use to break my journey if I feel frail. I sit down, and he stands in front, watching me with concern.

"Are you sure?" he asks. "I am more than willing to wait."

"No, it's fine. What do you want to know?"

"Just start at the beginning," he says.

"I used your technique with the candle to make it happen," I reply. "I wasn't sure it had worked until I tried to swat a moth away, and my hand went through it."

"Did you experience any discomfort?"

"No, not at all."

"That's fortunate. In the early days, I found it difficult to pass through the pineal door without pain. It's much easier now."

"I don't understand what you mean."

Fox sighs. "I was going to teach you the nuances of dream walking, but there is no point now. Besides, you have a natural ability which might suffer from too much tuition."

He has raised my guilt levels again. His calm response to my lack of interest can't hide how much he would have enjoyed acting as a muse to a willing pupil. But I am not that person. I tell him more about my experience and pause when I recollect my arrival in the library. The image of the mirror looms large in my mind, and goosebumps prickle my skin. I shudder at the memory, and he notices.

"What happened next?" he asks.

"I saw you."

He shakes his head. "Before that," he says.

I close my eyes and try to find the words. My hands shake, and I can't stop them. The same fear that gripped me in the library last night slithers down my spine. My teeth chatter, and I can hardly speak. "It's a silly thing to be frightened of," I manage to say.

"What is?"

"The mirror." Saying the word brings no relief. If anything, it conjures an even greater terror.

"What about it?"

"I didn't dare look at it for fear of what I might see. I must sound ridiculous, but the sight of my reflection would have been almost as bad as seeing nothing. It brought the reality of being awake and asleep at the same time into sharp focus, and it was all I could do to stay in the room."

Oliver Fox leans over and pats my shoulder, eyes heavy with concern.

"But you remained there. The slightest distraction and I find myself back in my body. You have a magnificent gift. What you experienced, my dear, was an existential crisis. I have felt the same, but like anything else, you get used to it. Yes, you will drift by ghostlike and ethereal, your surroundings mysterious and uncertain. And there is much yet to learn about astral projection. It takes time to feel confident in an unknown environment."

"What would I have seen if I'd looked?" I ask. For some unfathomable reason, it is still preying on my mind.

"I don't know," he says simply. "I know what I see because I have tried. I see my reflection as I would in my normal state."

Relief washes over me. If Fox sees his reflection, then I should see mine. I don't know why this matters so much, but it does.

I relate the rest of the details, now more comfortable with the discussion, and finish by explaining my disappointment at not sensing the wind against my skin while running on the beach. Fox nods sagely.

"I am accustomed to it now," he says. "But it's an odd experience at first. Now, do you have any questions for me?"

"Only one," I say. I have been preparing for this moment. I don't want to ask, but I ought to know. "Is dream travel dangerous?"

Fox hesitates. "It is not without risk," he says, after some thought. "Attaining release from your body through dreams as you have done up to now brings little chance of danger. Last night was the first time you achieved it through self-induced trance. The way of dreams is generally more pleasant and carries the least risk. Not that you shouldn't try the self-induced approach, but I don't recommend it without supervision, at least not to start with."

"Why? What might happen?" I ask.

"I am not a medical expert," he says as if trying to avoid my question, but I persist.

"Please tell me?"

"I know some esoteric societies that engage in astral travel as part of their philosophy, and they know the pitfalls better. They could give a fuller answer to your question. I avoid these groups as a rule and suggest you do likewise. It's the secrecy and ritual that puts me off. They study other matters of a more sinister nature. I take a scientific approach to astral travel, and I have never personally encountered anything untoward," Fox says. "But others think it might harm anyone with a weak heart because dream travel involves separation of the soul from the body."

I stifle a giggle. We are not a religious household, and I haven't considered the prospect of having a soul, let alone one that detaches itself. I have always accepted dream walking as a matter of fact. It has never seemed ridiculous until now. This talk of souls makes me reluctant to speak of such things again. I thinly smile as if I understand, and he continues.

"A silver cord joins your body and soul," he says. "This cord must not become detached."

"I don't have one."

"You said you felt something pull you back last night."

"Yes."

"Well, there you are."

"I can't see or feel it."

"That doesn't mean it's not there," Fox says. "If you try this again..."

"I won't," I say.

"Just in case you do, be careful. That's all. Now, I hope our little experiment has not put you off your natural dream travels. Enjoy them as you did before."

Oliver Fox offers his hand and helps me to my feet. "Thank you for taking the time to speak to me today. Can I write about your experience if I keep the account anonymous?" he asks.

"Of course," I say. Oliver Fox deserves this much for the disappointment he undoubtedly feels.

"Do you still have my calling card?"

"Yes."

"I am here for a few more days, and you can contact me by telephone when I leave. My number is Wimbledon two five one," he says. "Call anytime."

Fox shakes my hand then returns to the hotel, waving towards me as he enters. He has been friendly to the last, but I doubt we'll speak again. And for once, I have better things to think about.

CHAPTER EIGHT

The Pottses' Supper Party

It is six o'clock, and I am wearing my least awful outfit, which until a few days ago, I would have thought perfectly adequate for the Pottses' long-dreaded supper party. Thankfully, it is slim-fitting, and although too long to be fashionable, it is not hideous, which is more than I can say for my boots. I slept for a few hours after returning from the hotel before Elys woke me at Mrs Ponsonby's request. She drew the curtains, passed me a cup of tea, and used the time to chat about her ideas for my new dress. I should have asked her to speak to the cobbler about new shoes, but I have only just thought of it. I lift my skirts and look at the built-up boot, feeling grateful that it's mostly hidden. I have made a reasonable effort in all other regards. Elys pinned up my hair and insisted on doing my makeup. The transformation is tolerable. Despite feeling self-conscious about my heavily powdered face, I know I look more presentable than usual. Even so, I am not looking forward to tonight and wait by the front door, hoping that something will prevent my participation in the evening's events.

Mrs Ponsonby glides down the stairs dressed in an elegant ankle-length evening gown with her hair swept behind her ears. I stare at her face, surprised to see a smudge of rouge on her cheeks and a slick of pale pink lipstick. It takes ten years off her age, and I glimpse the person she was in her youth. Mrs Ponsonby is tall, but her waist has expanded in recent years. She must have been sporty in her earlier life, judging by the items stashed in the woodshed, including a tennis racket, a javelin, and a pair of skis. I wonder why she swapped that life for this one of servitude.

"You look nice, Connie," she says.

I want to tell her that she does too, but something stops me. It feels wrong to offer a compliment after her heavy handling of my life. "Let's get it over with," I say instead.

Her face falls. "You will enjoy it," she says. "There will be other young people there."

Her words don't improve my mood. Anyone wasting their time at the Pottses' boring supper party isn't worth getting to know.

"The car's here," says Elys, as she twitches the curtains. She helps me into my coat and passes my stick, then accompanies us to the car. Mrs Ponsonby has pushed the boat out. She has booked a driver from Newquay, and the vehicle is a cut above Jory's cart. Elys opens the door, and I slide into the back seat, where Mrs Ponsonby joins me.

"Have a lovely time," says Elys, forlornly waving as if she wished she could come too. I would swap places with her in a heartbeat, even if it meant cleaning for the rest of the evening.

We arrive at the Pottses' home in Tregurrian, and Hannah, their maid, admits us. She guides us into the orangery, where Clementine Potts is waiting to greet us. I gaze around the room in horror. It is full of people. I was expecting half a dozen guests to be seated around the table drinking tea and eating cake with a few games of canasta later. This supper party is a full-blown gathering, and there must be thirty people in the room. It is as well that the Pottses extended their property last year, and I cynically decide that the purpose of tonight is to show off the results. Mrs Ponsonby presents our plum cake, and Hannah places it on the sideboard to join the other mismatched dishes of food. Everyone has brought something with them, and we will dine buffet-style tonight, an arrangement that does not suit me at all. It's tricky using my stick while helping myself to food, and the thought of anyone offering to help makes me feel nauseous. People are well-meaning for the most, but the constant mollycoddling is more than I can bear. I could have coped better with a sit-down meal, which would have put me on equal terms with everybody else, but not this.

"How are you, Connie?" asks Clementine Potts.

I stand quietly fuming until Mrs Ponsonby interrupts.

"Connie," she barks. "Answer Mrs Potts' question."

"Sorry," I say, shaking my head. "I was miles away."

"I asked how you were, my dear," says Mrs Potts condescendingly. I don't like the tone of her voice. She seems to think she is speaking to an imbecile.

"Perfectly well," I say. "How are you?"

"Likewise," says Clementine Potts. "Excuse me. I must mingle."

I scowl. I must mingle, is code for I don't know what to say next. Of course, she doesn't know what to ask me. I don't work or socialise and consequently have nothing interesting to say.

"That was rude," says Mrs Ponsonby.

"What did I say?"

"It wasn't what you said. It was the snappish way you said it. Mrs Potts was trying to be kind."

I think about the impending trip to Plymouth. Nothing must stop it, and I decide to be all sweetness and light for the rest of the evening. I see Edgar Sutton chatting to Samuel Potts.

"Shall we say hello?" I ask, nodding towards them.

"Yes, let's," says Mrs Ponsonby, and we approach the two men.

"Welcome, welcome," says Mr Potts, beaming from ear to ear. Samuel Potts earned his fortune from a rolling mill. He has since retired and is making the most of his wealth and enjoying life to the full. "Glad you could join us," he continues. "You know Edgar, don't you?"

"I do. How are you, Edgar," I say, in my friendliest voice.

"Jolly good," he replies, "although it's quiet here, but what can you expect?"

Compared to what? I think, but I don't say it. I must be on my best behaviour. "When are you going back to the City?" I ask. Edgar spends most of his time in London but takes regular breaks in Cornwall with his relatives. I wait for him to reply as I plan my escape. I have approached him and been friendly, and that should be enough to please Mrs Ponsonby. But when I turn away, she's walking towards the door with Mr Potts. He has offered her a tour of the extension, and now I'm alone with Edgar.

"Not for another month," he says. "I am spending the festive season in Cornwall this year. How about you?"

"Here, I suppose," I say.

"We are hosting a New Year's dance. You should come along."

My brow furrows as I try to work out whether he is goading me. But when I look into his eyes, it's clear that he hasn't given my condition a thought. He mistakes my glance for interest.

"I'll make sure you're on the guest list," he says. "I say, I've got a new motor outside. A brand-new Morris Major, hot off the factory floor. It cost me over two hundred pounds, and it takes five passengers."

What a show-off, I think. "How lovely," I say. "What colour is it?"

"Burgundy," he replies proudly, "with a fifteen horsepower engine. Would you like to see it?" I open my mouth to say a firm no, but a slender woman weaves her way through the crowd and touches Edgar's elbow.

"Charlotte, you're here. How lovely to see you," says Edgar, enthusiastically.

I cringe inside. Charlotte Napier is her usual glamourous self, and I pale in comparison. If she is around, then so is Kit Maltravers, and I turn into a dithering idiot in his presence. I hope she will go away, but Edgar encourages her.

"You know Connie, don't you?" he asks.

She presses my hand and smiles. "Peter talks about you often," she says.

I am shocked. I didn't know Peter was friendly with Charlotte Napier, and I rack my brain trying to remember whether I have said anything I shouldn't have.

"How do you know him?" I ask, grasping for something to say.

"Kitty is a member of his acting group," she replies.

I don't know who Kitty is, and I don't ask. For once in my life, I am desperate to see Mrs Ponsonby's familiar form. There are too many people in the room. The heat rises in my chest, and my face flushes beetroot red.

"Do you need to sit down?" asks Charlotte.

"Here." Edgar pulls a chair from a nearby table.

It is too much. One minute I am chatting like a grown-up, and the next, I am relegated to a seat behind everyone else like a naughty child. Charlotte and Edgar carry on talking in front of me, flashing concerned glances every so often. I stare at the enormous pork pie on the buffet table, wishing I could push her perfect face into it. Then I take stock. I am thinking like a child, and it's no wonder that people treat me like one. I am still considering my behaviour when a shadow looms beside me as a man pulls another chair from the table and sits down. "I thought you'd like to hear about Dolly," he says. I look across to see Doctor Kit Maltravers and am overwhelmed with gratitude that he is sitting at my level and hasn't once asked if I am feeling alright.

"Yes. How is she?" I ask.

"Dolly is very unwell. Her respiratory infection has improved," says Kit Maltravers," but she can't keep any food down and is consequently very weak. I can't account for it, so I've sent her to the convalescent home for some rest. I would have called in to tell you, but Peter said you'd be here tonight."

"Thank you," I say. "Can I visit her?"

"Give it a day or two," he replies, as an announcement interrupts us. The Pottses' housemaid bangs the dinner gong twice, and Mr Potts stands up to speak.

"Thank you all for coming," he says. "Clementine and I are delighted to have you. I won't bore you with a speech, but please help yourself to the buffet."

There is a polite silence for a moment, then a scramble for the food. I stay where I am. Charlotte reaches for Kit's hand and draws him away, but Mrs Ponsonby occupies his chair almost immediately.

"Are you hungry?" she asks.

"Not particularly," I say.

"Why don't I fetch you a plate of food? You can pick out what you want, and I'll eat the rest."

I would have declined if anyone else had offered, but I don't mind Mrs Ponsonby looking after me on this occasion. I'm sure it will be less humiliating than a public struggle at the sideboard.

We eat, chat for a while, and the evening zips along. When everyone has finished, Mr Potts and his family arrange chairs along the outside of the room, and Beatrice Potts sits at the piano. I expect the worst, but Beatrice is a talented musician. She plays a mix of classic melodies followed by some of the latest dance tunes and before long, the younger members of the party have taken to the floor. I watch entranced as Charlotte and Kit perform the Charleston, legs moving backwards and forwards in perfect harmony. Where on earth did a rural doctor learn these skills? It must have been in London while he was training. The room is buzzing. Edgar has grabbed the hand of a girl I don't recognise. His loose-limbed dancing looks effortless as he whirls around, legs bobbing up and down as if made of jelly. She copies him, but less confidently, as if in the presence of a master. She might be right. To my untrained eye, he is an excellent dancer. The atmosphere is electric, frenetic – all business and bustle. Mrs Ponsonby watches with a smile on her face, and the Pottses look on benevolently. Everyone belongs there – everyone but me. Then Beatrice stops, waits for a moment, and selects a fresh piece of music. It is slow, and only couples remain on the dance floor, swaying together in tight circles. I avert my eyes, almost embarrassed to watch, and feel very alone.

"Are you ready to go?" asks Mrs Ponsonby as Kit Maltravers strides towards us. "Feel free to say no," he says, "but I wondered if you'd like to dance?"

I look up, startled and burning with shame – the absolute humiliation of it. Kit Maltravers feels sorry for me.

Mrs Ponsonby beams. "Go on, Connie," she says.

"I can't dance," I blurt, devastation washing over me in red, angry waves.

"Just doing it is the best way to learn," says Kit, "but I understand if you would rather not." He smiles kindly and prepares to walk away.

"Wait," I say. The word explodes from my mouth. It is bad manners to decline an invitation to dance, and I should know better. I can trust Kit. He won't let me fall. And he will be the one who feels uncomfortable if I publicly turn him down when he was only trying to be kind. Yes, he feels sorry for me, but he's not the first, nor will he be the last. "Thank you, Kit. I'd love to," I say, "but I may need some help."

"My pleasure," he says, taking my arm. I rise with the aid of my stick, then pass it to Mrs Ponsonby in a tremendous leap of faith. I have been reliant on a walking stick all my life, but I do it anyway. He guides me to the centre of the floor with his arm supporting me around my waist. I try not to shuffle and concentrate on picking my feet up. Then, when I am balanced, he removes his arm and holds my hands in his before guiding them to his shoulder as we move slowly to the music. Kit is taller than me. My head tilts naturally upwards as I hold his shoulders and watch his face, searching for signs of boredom. But he smiles down good-naturedly, and after a few moments, I relax and grow in confidence. We do little more than sway. I will not risk putting too much weight on my bad leg in a public place, but I enjoy the sensation of almost dancing. And when the music finishes, I thank Kit and tell him that I am tired, so he doesn't have to feel awkward about terminating the experience. He escorts me to my chair, and I take my stick from Mrs P, who is gazing proudly towards me in a manner that I don't recognise. I suppose she must keep up appearances around other people. But if I've pleased her, then my trip to Plymouth should proceed as planned.

We sit for another ten minutes before the clock chimes and Mrs Ponsonby notices the time.

"The driver will be here in a quarter of an hour," she says. "We must say our goodbyes."

I follow her around the room and join her in thanking the Pottses and their daughters. Then Mrs Ponsonby sees one of her WI friends and parks me in the hallway while she says goodnight. I've had enough of sitting alone and wait until she is out of sight before rising. I claim my coat from the hall stand and make my way into the porch. The night is mild, and fresh air is preferable to sympathetic stares, so I go outside and walk for a few yards down the Pottses' expansive driveway. I meander into a little gated area with a seat nearby and sit down, soon realising that I am not alone. I can hear two voices beyond the neatly trimmed hedge, one male and one female.

"He doesn't appreciate you, darling," says the man, who I immediately recognise as Edgar.

"He adores me, and I adore him." The second voice is Charlotte's. Lovely, perfect Charlotte.

"You would like me more if you would only try," says Edgar.

Charlotte laughs daintily. "I am marrying Kit, and that is the end of it," she says.

I bite my lip, feeling uncomfortable. I shouldn't be listening, but I can't tiptoe away with a stick in tow. And I don't like what I am hearing. Edgar is trying to seduce Kit's fiancée, and she is loyally defending her man. Is there is no end to her perfection? And then she says something that hits me like a train.

"Where is he anyway?" asks Edgar.

"Inside still, I suppose," she says. "Kit was dancing with that poor little crippled girl the last time I saw him."

"That was a decent thing to do," says Edgar.

"Oh, it was my idea," says Charlotte.

"Then, it was very generous of you. Now, are you going to kiss me or not?"

Charlotte Napier laughs. "Not."

They continue joking and flirting, but I have heard enough. I don't care how much noise I make – I need to leave right now. I crunch down the gravel pathway, their laughter ringing in my ears, barely audible above my deafening internal dialogue: poor little cripple, our local charitable case, pity poor Connie, poor, poor Connie. I stifle a sob as I see Mrs Ponsonby emerging from the house. She is looking for me. I fix a smile and join her, resisting her attempts at conversation on the way home. She thinks I am tired, and my silence doesn't offend her. She is right. I am tired. Sick and tired. I undress and hurl my clothes at the wall, letting them stay where they fall. Then I burrow into my bedclothes and sob until sleep takes me.

CHAPTER NINE

Driven to Suicide?

Monday, November 17, 1930

I wake and stare at the open curtains, watching them as they gently sway, and contemplate the day ahead. Then the events of the previous night rush into my memory, swirling out of control until I'm overwhelmed. "Oh God," I say aloud and slide under the bedclothes with my hands over my face. Why did I have to go? Why didn't I tell Mrs Ponsonby that I was sick? It's worked before and could easily have worked again. I should have known better than to socialise with people I don't know. And I can't decide who is worse – slippery Edgar, condescending Kit, or charitable Charlotte. I hope I never see them again.

I lie in bed and watch the clock, my life ticking by one second at a time. Half past seven, quarter past eight, now it's nearly half past nine, and I am still lying there feeling sorry for myself. I consider stretching it out until ten. But at a quarter before the hour, someone knocks on my bedroom door.

"Go away," I say, not knowing or caring who is there.

I wait for a moment and think that I have got away with it, but the door opens, and Elys enters without a second knock.

"I said, go away," I repeat.

She sits on the bottom of my bed.

"Did you hear me?"

"Loud and clear."

"Why are you still here?"

"Why are you in bed? It's almost ten. Are you ill?"

"No. I'm tired, and I can do as I please."

Elys gets to her feet and latches the window wide open. "I thought you'd be in a good mood today," she says. "I hear you had a nice evening."

"Well, I didn't."

"That's not what Mrs Ponsonby says."

"How would she know?" I say, irritated. How dare Elys and Mrs Ponsonby decide whether I enjoyed myself?

"I hear you danced with Dr Kit."

"That's the sanitised version. Charlotte Napier made him. She felt sorry for me."

"Oh, giss on!"

I roll my eyes. "I am not making it up."

"There must be some mistake."

"No mistake," I say coldly. "None whatever."

Elys resumes her seat on my bed and I know she will stay there until I tell her everything that is on my mind, so I do.

"Do you want my opinion?" she asks.

"No," I say. Elys gives it anyway.

"Dr Maltravers did nothing wrong. Not a single thing. You're proper teasy today, Connie, and I expect it's because you are tired. What does it matter if Charlotte suggested it? He could have said no."

"He felt sorry for me," I mutter.

"He's a good man," says Elys. "And as much as you don't want to hear it, Charlotte is a kind young woman."

"She's patronising," I say. "Superior and patronising, and I will never forgive her for calling me a cripple."

"I don't think she meant it the way it sounded. The only person who has misbehaved is Edgar, and that's not much of a surprise."

"How would you feel if she'd said it about you?"

"What? Called me the same thing she called you? That's silly. It wouldn't apply."

"No. If Charlotte called you a poor little housemaid."

"I am a poor little housemaid."

"You know what I mean."

"Yes, I do," says Elys. "And if it was me and I didn't like what she had to say, then I would prove her wrong."

"Right. I'll just stare at my leg for few days, and if I try really hard, I might grow a new one."

"Or you could just stop feeling sorry for yourself."

I stare at Elys aghast. She has never spoken to me quite so bluntly before.

"I'm sorry, Connie, but there's a lot you can do. You walk, you read, you are intelligent, you can be witty. You are better in company than you think you are. You are warm, fed and well looked after. Things could be a lot worse than they are. Look at poor Dolly, sick and alone in the hospital."

"Go away – right now!" I yell, throwing a bolster at Elys in temper. She scowls and leaves the room, closing the door firmly behind her.

I lie there seething with anger, thinking of all the ways I would like to punish her, but it doesn't take long for my nagging conscience to surface. Far from being unfair, every word Elys said is accurate, and I know I'm fortunate. I've always known it. And what's more, I am so much stronger than this. My world is tiny, usually no broader than the distance from one end of the beach to the other. Yet this week, I have been to Newquay and Tregurrian and have an impending visit to Plymouth to look forward to. I have seen more people in the last five days than I usually do in a month. I may not have many friends, but the ones I have are loyal and trustworthy. It shouldn't matter what Doctor and soon to be Mrs Charlotte Maltravers think of me. I cheer up a bit and decide to dress, go downstairs, and apologise to Elys. She deserves better. But as I descend the stairs on my way to look for her, someone raps on the front door. Elys bustles through, shoots me a glare and opens the door, revealing a very animated Peter.

#

"I come bearing information," he says, stepping over the threshold with easy familiarity.

"It's just as well I'm here," I say.

"Why wouldn't you be?"

"I have other friends, you know. If you'd called yesterday, I would have been out."

"Where?" he asks, sounding surprised.

"On the beach with Mary Newson, but never mind that. What information?"

"I'll tell you when you've offered me a seat," he says.

"Is Mrs Ponsonby around?" I ask Elys.

"She's popped to Newquay. Why?"

"Oh good. I'd rather sit in the parlour. Peter, go through. Elys, would you mind bringing some tea?"

"Not at all," she says, good-naturedly.

"And Elys…"

"Yes?"

"You were quite right, and I'm sorry."

She smiles. Elys is a good sort and doesn't hold a grudge, but I feel better for apologising. I join Peter in the parlour.

"It's good of you to call," I say. "How are you?"

"Fine," he says. "I've been speaking to Malcolm."

"About the poisoning case?"

"Exactly," says Peter. "Some more details have come to light. It turns out that the funeral didn't go according to plan. Not for Annie Hearn anyway."

"Do tell," I say, joining Peter on the sofa.

"Well, Alice Thomas's funeral took place last Saturday in Lewannick," said Peter.

"News travels slowly," I say. "That's more than a week ago."

"I know. But news and gossip travel at different rates. Now I know what Malcolm meant when he mentioned hearing rumours at the weekend."

"Gossip," I say, feeling a frisson of excitement. I know I shouldn't but tattling with a friend is unifying – especially when the rumours aren't personal and can't come back and bite.

"As I said, the funeral was in Lewannick, so everyone in the village was there, including Alice's brother, Percy Parsons. From what I hear, Annie Hearn felt uncomfortable throughout the service. Though people were speaking to her, they couldn't quite hide the suspicion in their eyes. After the funeral, William Thomas invited them back to his farmhouse for some refreshments. Well, Annie was still there. She'd been nursing Alice at the farm before she died if you remember, and she'd never gone home."

I stare at Peter, surprised. "I thought she lived nearby?"

"Less than two hundred yards away," he says.

"Then what reason can she have had for staying on?"

Peter raises an eyebrow. "What indeed? But the fact remains that she did. And I suppose it was jolly useful on the day of the funeral, as she probably helped prepare the food."

"I expect there was a lot left," I say. I am still largely sympathetic to Mrs Hearn, but even I would think twice before eating anything she'd made.

"I don't know about that," says Peter, missing the point. "But regardless, they all went back, and within a few moments of Annie Hearn's arrival, Percy Parsons had cornered her. He started asking detailed questions about the food that she had packed for Bude in a loud and overbearing way."

"Ouch," I say. "That must have been awkward."

"It was. Parsons asked what else she'd put in the sandwiches and told her the police would have to investigate."

"That's almost an outright accusation."

"Yes, and she certainly took it that way. Look at this," he says, producing a folded piece of paper. "Annie Hearn fled the farmhouse almost immediately after he made the remarks. Two days later, she disappeared, and the day after that, William Thomas received a letter in the post. It's in all the newspapers, but I haven't picked one up in days. Malcolm has, and he read it out to me, so I copied it for you. I assume you're still not allowed a paper?"

"Elys is working on it," I say. "And this is exactly the sort of thing Mrs Ponsonby objects to. It's a good thing that your mother was so convincing. If she had the slightest idea that I was going to an inquest, she'd self-combust."

"Well, read it then," says Peter, pushing his notes towards me.

Dear Mr Thomas

Goodbye. I am going out if I can. I cannot forget that awful man and the things he said. I am innocent, innocent, but she is dead, and it was my lunch she ate. I cannot stay. When I am dead, they will be sure I am guilty, and you, at least, will be clear. May your dear wife's presence guard and comfort you still.

Yours A.H.

PS My life isn't a great thing anyhow, now dear Minnie is gone. I should be glad if you'd send my love to Betsy and tell her not to worry about me. I will be all right. My conscience is clear, so I am not afraid of the afterwards. I am giving instructions to Webb about selling the things and hope you will be paid in full. It is all I can do now.

I whistle. "Poor thing," I say. "Annie must have felt utterly persecuted."

"Are we reading the same words?" asks Peter.

"Why?"

"I see it as an admission of guilt," he says.

"But she says she's innocent several times."

"She has to if she doesn't want to hang."

I shudder. This crime is already so uncertain that capital punishment should not be under consideration. "Who are Minnie and Betsy anyway," I ask.

Peter takes out his notebook. "Minnie is a deceased sister, and Betsy is a living one," he says.

"How devastating for Betsy," I say. "With one sister dead and one under suspicion. Do we know when Minnie died?"

"Not yet," says Peter. "I wouldn't mind betting they'll check, though."

"Have they located Annie Hearn's body yet?" I ask, assuming the worst.

He shakes his head. "No, but they found her coat and hat on the clifftop at Looe a few days ago."

"Then it's all over, and she was right. They'll find her guilty for sure," I say. Then a momentary, selfish panic overtakes me. Will there still be an inquest?"

Peter nods. "Definitely," he says. "It's a week tomorrow. We'll go down the night before and stay for a few days. And I wouldn't assume too much about Annie Hearn in the meantime. I have a feeling that she's alive and well. That note begs more questions than it answers."

I am about to argue with Peter but swallow the words down, determined to do better than I did with Elys earlier. But a flash of irritation still burns inside me at the obvious partiality Peter has for William Thomas. Man supporting man against a feeble and friendless woman. I don't like it. But my annoyance doesn't last long, and Peter has already moved on to another topic.

"Who is Mary Newson?" he asks.

"My artist friend," I reply proudly.

"Do I know her?"

"Not as far as I know. Mary lives in Bosula."

"I say, she's not a relative of Crawford Newson, is she?"

"Yes. Crawford was her brother."

"Was? What do you mean?"

I explain.

"Damned fine writer," says Peter. "I don't know how I missed his death in the papers. I'll watch out for some of his books and bring them with me tomorrow. You should read them."

And on that note, Peter departs. I sit for a while contemplating the Lewannick poisoning case. I can't shake off the feeling that all is not as it seems. Everything looks black for Annie Hearn, but surely she's the victim? Though who's to say that I'm not suffering from prejudice. After all, Annie is the underdog; middle-aged, dowdy, widowed and short of money. She has lost a sister, a friend and what's left of her family live some distance away. She must feel isolated and friendless. Our situations are not dissimilar. Perhaps that is why I sympathise and dearly wish I could help if she's still alive. And suddenly, I am filled with an earnest desire to do so. I am alone, and she is alone, but perhaps I can do something for her. I dream walked my way to the hotel library a few nights ago. Might I be able to use the same technique to find Annie? I don't know how dream travel works or how long it will take. My skills may not be good enough, but I could try one more time and see if I can get past Mawgan Porth cliffs. I'll take baby steps and try going a little further to see how it works out. But if I can use my abilities to help this poor woman in her hour of need, then there is a point and purpose to my life. I glance at the clock. I'll go to bed early tonight and see what I can do.

CHAPTER TEN

Losing Control

The afternoon drags after Peter leaves, and supper is late because Mrs Ponsonby is late. I am starving by the time we sit down to mutton pie at seven o'clock. Elys and I eat with gusto, but Mrs Ponsonby is subdued and does not finish. After supper, we sit in the parlour. I read while Mrs Ponsonby knits and listens to a boring radio show. By nine o'clock, I am restless, and even the book doesn't grip me. I wait for night to fall, providing cover for another dream walk. But then I wonder why I feel the need to go to my bedroom. What would happen if I tried to dream walk downstairs and succeeded? Would Mrs Ponsonby notice? I don't know what happens to my physical being and feel a surge of embarrassment at the prospect of someone seeing me outside my body. It would be like being in company and finding myself unexpectedly naked. I shake my head at my silly musings. Yesterday, I was too frightened to contemplate dream walking again. Yet today, filled with the zealous expectation of being Annie Hearn's saviour, it's a different matter. My safety has slipped further down the list than my outward appearance. And so it should. My fear at the prospect of encountering my reflection is already so far in the past that I can't remember why it upset me. But I am still ignorant of the scope of my abilities and wish I had paid more heed to Oliver Fox.

"Are you well, dear?" asks Mrs Ponsonby, watching as I shake my head from side to side in full inward rebuke. She's only started calling me dear in the last few weeks, and I don't know why. I don't like it, and apart from making me feel ancient, it's insincere.

"I'm tired," I say. "I think I'll go up now."

"I won't be far behind you," she says. "See you in the morning."

"Goodnight," I say, hooking my stick over my arm and picking up my book. I take a few steps towards the door and reach for the handle. Since last night's dance, when I moved with only a little help from Kit Maltravers, I try to take a few stick-free steps at every opportunity. It is tiring and uncomfortable, but it can only help strengthen me. Mrs Ponsonby's eyes burn into my back, and I wonder if she's noticed, but I don't ask. Instead, I open the door and use my stick to climb the stairs. I reach my room and rest on top of my bed, once again reluctant to fall asleep in my nightclothes.

I occupy my time fantasising about Charlotte Napier and her permanent removal from my life. In my imagination, she lives in New Zealand and is the frumpy mother of seven children – Kit Maltravers is *not* their father. I wait for the household to settle and am glad that I didn't get straight into bed when there is a tap at my door.

"Come in," I whisper, wondering what Mrs Ponsonby wants this late at night, but it is Elys, and she is carrying a bag.

"Try this on for size," she says, thrusting what looks like a yard of material towards me.

I pick it up and shake it out.

"It's your dress," she says, unnecessarily. "Tell me what you think?"

I think it's rather late at night to be trying on dresses, but I have learned from my earlier outburst and say nothing.

"Go on," says Elys. "I'll turn the other way."

I shed the black woollen horror I've been wearing all day and slide into the proffered dress. It is calf length, slim-fitting, and navy blue with pretty white flowers. I stare at myself in the mirror, but all I can see are the ugly boots that I didn't remove while lounging on my bed.

"Don't worry about those," says Ellis, watching my face fall. "I have a plan. What do you think about the dress? It needs taking up an inch, but I'll see to that now."

She crouches and pins the hem.

"Not too high," I say, alarmed at the amount of leg showing. Elys ignores me and carries on with her task.

"Well?"

"It's beautiful," I say. And it is. I mean it. If only I could find suitable footwear, I might carry it off.

"Good." Elys grins as best she can with a mouthful of pins.

"I can't thank you enough," I say. The more I look at the girl in the mirror, the less it looks like me. This girl is shapely and confident. She doesn't carry a stick, and while Elys crouches in front of her, she doesn't wear a built-up boot either. This girl compares favourably with Charlotte Napier.

"Away with you," says Elys, flushing with pleasure. "Right. Take it off. I'll make the adjustments as soon as possible, and you can have it in plenty of time for your trip."

I smile, thrilled at the prospect, and make a mental note to find something nice for Elys in Plymouth. That is if Mrs Ponsonby gives me an allowance. But I see no reason why she shouldn't when I'm not here, and she is saving money on food.

I pull my old dress over my head and look in the mirror again. Plain, dowdy Connie is back. Elys leaves the room, and I lie on the bed and wait until I hear Mrs Ponsonby in her room.

It is a short wait, and I am soon ready. I move the candle to the dresser and concentrate on the flame as I did before, watching until my eyes grow drowsy.

#

I wake. Something has gone wrong, and I have fallen asleep, my task unfulfilled. I shouldn't be surprised. It would be unusual to succeed twice running with no previous experience. I don't have the energy to try again and decide to get a good night's sleep instead. But as I roll over, I see a furious flapping at the window. A bird, as black as night, is hovering, wings outstretched. At first, it looks like a hummingbird, but it can't be. They are not native to this country. And then I realise my mistake. It is a bat. The poor thing must be trying to get in – except that it is already here, hovering on the inside of the windowpane. I watch it, torn between curiosity and fear. But then I remember what Oliver Fox said about false awakening. If something happens that doesn't occur in reality, then the chances are I'm dreaming.

I test my theory and reach for my water glass. My hand glides straight through it. I sit up, then walk towards the window. As I approach, the bat vanishes before my eyes. I look towards the bed and see my sleeping form. I am not afraid and feel comfortable at the sight of it. Tonight is just another night like the many I had experienced before when I ran along the pathway to Mawgan Porth. And no sooner do I visualise the cliffs than I am on top of them, watching the waves crash into Beacon Cove, white horses thundering onto the sandy bay. I watch entranced. I have seen it many times before, but I have never been so aware, so in control. The moon is high, but the night is overcast, and heavy raindrops dance beneath my feet. I cannot feel the rain or the cold, but it doesn't disturb me as it did before. I am glad to be immune from the weather.

I consider my next move and navigate my thoughts carefully. My ability to move between locations depends on how I contemplate getting there. I am confident about Mawgan Porth. I have been here often, though I have never appreciated that I can both walk from the house and think myself there. I wonder what will happen if I try to go somewhere I haven't been before? I would like to see Annie Hearn, but I don't know where she is. They found her clothes on the cliffs at Looe. Though I've never visited, I know it isn't far from Plymouth. I could find my way there and get a feel for the place. I close my eyes and think of Annie, and the horrible reception she had from Percy Parsons on the day of the funeral. My skin tingles, I sense a whirr, a tiny vibration, and I know I am somewhere else. I open my eyes, expecting to see the sea and hear the crash of waves breaking against the cliffs, but instead, I find myself in front of a wall.

I recoil in surprise, immediately feeling a pulling sensation in the back of my head. I screw up my eyes and fight the urge to retreat. My head thumps with the pain of it, and my scalp is on fire. But I persevere and wobble forwards, eyes open and ready to learn more about my surroundings. I am near the entrance to a dark room. I would ordinarily feel cold in such conditions, but my senses don't work the same way when I'm dreaming. In the distance, I can just make out the glowing embers of a dying fire. There is a window to one side, and I peer out, catching sight of the moon, low and half-hidden behind clouds. The sparsely furnished room contains a threadbare rug covering dark and ancient floorboards, which look as if they would squeak if there were any weight to my form. Next to the fireplace is a carved bureau, squat and weighty over spindly legs. On top is a sequence of silver-framed photographs depicting a couple in their fifties. Next is an older woman, then a group at the seaside and finally, a man standing proudly by his automobile.

I try to touch the photograph, forgetting the limitation of my abilities, but my hand slips through the frame. I peer closer, but I don't recognise anyone, then I marshal my thoughts and wonder what to do next. I don't know where I am, and I had better go outside and try to orientate myself. But before I can act on my decision, I hear someone coming down the stairs. He is walking with a heavy tread, and he pushes the door open with no care. And then, to my horror, he walks straight through me. I don't feel a thing, and it's more unnerving than if I had. The man advances to the first photograph and clutches it to his heart. He throws himself onto a nearby chair, where he sobs with deep guttural gulps as if his heart would break. I cannot watch this profoundly personal display of grief, and I flee through the wall by the window and find myself outside.

I am in a field. It is dark, and the pale moon casts the merest trace of light, yet I know I am deep in the countryside with little around save for livestock. I still don't know where I am, and it is time to go home. I must return. I haven't been away from my body for this long before, and it's making me feel uneasy. But when I imagine home, nothing happens. I close my eyes and visualise my cosy bed, but I am still outside and staring at the same rickety fence when I open them again. Butterflies flit through my chest; savage giant-winged flying beasts drawing terror in their wake. I cannot feel in this environment, but I'm mindful of what, under normal circumstances, would be a racing heart and jagged breathlessness. What if I can't get home? What if I am stuck here? I turn towards the building, seeing it properly for the first time. It is a farmhouse, clad in cold stone. Panicking, I spin around and dart across the field. I run and run, thinking of home, and wishing for the pull in the back of my head. Nothing – endless nothing. Ahead of me is an open entrance, the great yawning maw of an ancient barn.

I go inside. I don't know what else to do, so I fall to my knees in the corner, put my head in my hands and close my eyes. It is pitch black with not a chink of light. And finally, surrounded by darkness, my skin tingles, a frisson of pain tugs at my scalp and I am pulled backwards, hurtling through the astral realm. I know I am closing in on my physical body when everything slows and grinds to a halt. I am suspended in time and find myself face to face with a person – a man. He is portly and balding, and around his neck is a silver chain bearing a strange symbol. I stare into his eyes. They are black, pupils dilated and burning with intensity. He looks directly at me, an eyebrow raised in puzzlement. He reaches out and touches my hand. I recoil, feeling sensation for the first time. Goosebumps shiver down my arms, and my heart lurches with sudden dread. One edge of his mouth quivers upwards in a sly smile, but at that moment, something draws me back again to the safety of my bed.

I sit up, hands flying to my temples. They are wet with perspiration, and I am trembling. I settle down to sleep exhausted, with the image of the man indelibly printed on my memory. I don't know who he was or even what he was, but as time pulled us apart, I glimpsed a final gesture. He pointed to me as if in recognition, leaving me in no doubt that he knew exactly who I was.

CHAPTER ELEVEN

Calicem Aureum

Tuesday, November 18, 1930

I make my way to the hotel lobby, gritting my teeth and pushing through the pain. I am exhausted by the time I arrive, and thoughts of last night's travel swirl through my mind. My heart still thuds when I remember how difficult it was to return to my body. It beats harder still when I think about the man I met on the astral plane. His eyes were dark, almost hypnotic, with bottomless pupils. He looked half-crazed yet wise and all-knowing, and I swear he recognised me. But I don't know this man. I have never seen him before.

I enter the reception hall, my heart fluttering with nerves. I want to see Oliver Fox, but he might not be there, and I couldn't bear it. My questions might remain unanswered, and I cannot hold on to them for much longer.

I see Roxy Templeton out of the corner of my eye as I pass by and ignore her as per our unstated arrangement, but surprisingly she calls out. "Miss Maxwell!"

"Yes."

"This is for you." She holds a brown envelope towards me. I approach her, and instead of handing it over, she places it on the desk and slides it towards me as if disgusted at the thought of getting too close. I snatch the envelope, nod an undeserved thank you and continue to the library where I hope to find Mr Fox. I open the library door to find it empty. A library without people would ordinarily please me, but under these circumstances, it's inconvenient. I don't know which room Mr Fox occupies, and Dolly's sour-faced replacement is unlikely to help me find it. I sigh, sit beside the fireplace, then notice a box of books by the far shelves. Oh, good – it looks like Peter is re-stocking the library. . He must be outside unloading the van.

Though tempted to rifle through the books, the urge to open the brown envelope is more pressing. I untuck the flap and slide out a small, lined sheet of paper before glancing at the page. It is from Dolly. I smile and read her note. She's still ill, she says, and the doctors are no further forward in diagnosing her problem. But Dolly feels up to visitors and asks if I can come and see her soon. She is in a ward at the rear of the convalescent home with no prospects of leaving within the week and is finding life very dull. I glance at the library clock, wondering if I can find Jory and arrange a lift to Newquay this afternoon, assuming Mrs Ponsonby will allow it. I am considering the best way to approach her when the door opens, and Peter arrives carrying a wooden box.

"Ah," he says. "Come over here."

I do as he asks, and he turns his back and rummages through the container. "Look," he says, thrusting a pile of books towards me.

I take them and scrutinise the top one. It is the first in a trilogy written by Mary's deceased brother, Crawford Newson.

"Can I take them all?" I ask.

"Greedy," says Peter. "I would usually say no, but we haven't had them out for a while, and nobody will want the second without having read the first. "

I grin. That suits me down to the ground and will give me something pleasant to do for the rest of the week.

Peter swaps the books over and speaks to me over his shoulder. He is waxing lyrical about his latest role in a forthcoming musical when the library door opens. Several hotel residents enter, one of whom is Oliver Fox.

"I have to go," I say to Peter, halfway through his story. He raises a curious eyebrow as I turn away.

"Can I speak to you?" I ask as I approach Mr Fox.

"Of course," he says. "How can I help?"

"Not here. Somewhere private," I mutter, trying not to draw attention to our conversation. I don't want anyone else to hear what I've got to say. It will be hard enough telling Oliver Fox.

"We can try the snug," he says and, balancing the books under one arm, I follow him through the door.

"This way," he says, relieving me of the books. "I'll take these."

I don't argue, and we cross the corridor, enter the dining room, and make for the side door. Mr Fox opens it and peers inside.

"All clear," he says. He pulls out a chair, and I sit down while he perches on the end of the sofa.

"What's troubling you?" he asks.

I swallow, not knowing how to start. But then I describe my journey along the cliffs and my sudden appearance in the farmhouse. Before long, the words come tumbling out, and I shake as I tell Fox how scared I was when I struggled so hard to return to my body.

He strokes his chin. "Where do you think you were?" he asks.

"In a farmhouse," I say. "Fields and livestock surrounded the property."

"And you were trying to get where?"

"I don't know. As I said, I hoped to find the missing woman, Annie Hearn."

"Could she be in a farmhouse?"

"I suppose so," I say doubtfully. "She's more likely dead."

He considers the matter. "No," he says, eventually. "If Annie were dead, you'd be more likely to linger on the astral plane. It sounds as if you arrived at a destination that would have been familiar to her. Did she live near a farm?"

"No," I say. "Annie lived in a cottage, but – oh! I know. She was staying with Alice Thomas before she died. Of course – I must have been at their farmhouse. It was William Thomas that I saw last night crying over his wife's death. I must have been on Annie's trail, after all."

Oliver Fox nods. "It sounds like it. Your abilities are astounding, yet you struggled to get home. How do you think you managed it, in the end?"

"Only by blocking out every trace of light," I say as I recall crouching in the dark barn with my hands over my eyes.

"Yes. That makes sense. Did you resist returning to your body at any point in your travels?"

"I did. I had to fight hard to stay where I was when I arrived at the farmhouse."

"You shouldn't have done that. Resistance is not without risk – great risk, in fact."

"But I'd only been away for five minutes," I say. "I couldn't have achieved anything in so short a time."

"You closed the pineal door," says Fox. I am surprised it wasn't painful."

"It was, a little," I admit. "But no worse than a headache."

"You are fortunate," he says. "The same thing has happened to me several times, and the pain was excruciating. It took days to recover."

"I need to ask you something else," I say.

"Go ahead."

"Do you know anyone else capable of dream walking?"

He winces. "Astral projection," he says. "Yes. I know others."

"Have you ever met anyone on your travels?"

"Frequently," he says. "I see them as I move around, but they don't see me."

"I don't mean people you pass in the street," I say. "I mean people like us who are journeying."

"Once or twice," he says. "But never anyone I recognised."

I draw a deep breath, suddenly reluctant to speak further. Then I pull myself together. "I saw a man last night as I returned to my body. It was the strangest thing. Time slowed and I unexpectedly found myself face to face with him. He seemed to recognise me."

Oliver Fox stares at me. He cocks his head to one side as if he is thinking. "What did he look like?"

"Balding, overweight, and he was wearing a silver chain with a strange symbol on it."

"Describe the symbol." The words shoot from his mouth, staccato.

"I can't remember," I say, screwing my eyes up tightly. "It was like a squashed star, I suppose."

Fox reaches into his jacket pocket and pulls out a notebook and pen. "Like this?" he asks, drawing a squat hexagram with one fluid motion.

"Well, yes. Very similar. But there was something underneath."

Fox pushes the notepad away and gazes at me. His face is pale, and his eyes skitter over my face as if he doesn't know quite where to look.

"This," he says, pointing to the symbol, "is a unicursal hexagram. And I expect the other thing you saw looked something like this." He picks up the pencil and draws a rudimentary wine glass shape below.

I nod. "Yes," I whisper. Fox's face sets in grimly determined concentration as he considers his words, and I can tell from his demeanour that they won't be words of comfort.

"This symbol represents Calicem Aureum," he says, steepling his hands. "Which means you likely crossed paths with its figurehead, Felix Crossley."

"I've never heard of him!"

"I'm not surprised," says Oliver Fox. "Fortunately, he is abroad now, which is a good thing. He is a very unpleasant man."

"Tell me more," I ask.

He nods. "This may take some time."

#

"Have you ever heard of the Hellfire Club?" asks Fox, leaning back in his chair.

"Not really," I say. The name is vaguely familiar, but I don't know why.

"It was an infamous eighteenth-century gentleman's club full of young rakes with too much time on their hands. They were utterly selfish, living their lives as they pleased with no care for the consequences, and the more offensive their actions, the better they liked it. Hellfire Club members were notorious for attacks on religion and morality. They mocked Christianity by conducting pagan rituals of a most unsavoury nature."

"Did they use black magic?" I ask.

Fox nods. "Yes. But fortunately, the organisation faded away, and I doubt any remnants of the Hellfire Club exist. But people are still interested in the occult. Magic and esoteric matters have always fascinated man, and I am a prime example of someone who spends too much time learning about it. It's why I have devoted considerable energy to the study of astral travel."

"But not black magic?" I ask, suppressing a shudder. Things are strange enough as they are, without confiding in someone actively involved with dubious cults.

"Certainly not," Fox says, looking hurt. "I deplore the very idea. But I have some experience in the matter, and given what you saw, I should warn you about Calicem Aureum. Now, as I've said, interest in occult matters has waned somewhat in recent years, but a few societies still exist, though others did not survive. One such defunct organisation is the Order of the Crescent Moon. They were not dissimilar to the Freemasons, except they admitted both men and women. Initiates learned various magical practices, rituals, and meditations aiming to progress further in the order. It was hierarchical, you see, and they increased their grades by improving their knowledge of esoteric matters."

"Did they do anything apart from learning?"

"Such as?"

"I don't know," I mutter, suddenly feeling embarrassed. I was about to ask whether there was any purpose to the rituals, something tangible, like becoming invisible or walking on water. I realise, just in time, the childishness of such questions and swallow them down. "Why did it die away?" I ask, instead.

"I was coming to that. Two men and a woman founded the Order of the Crescent Moon. One was a public figure who occupied a parliamentary position. When a colleague mislaid a membership list while travelling by train, his name came to public attention. The press published details, embarrassing the government who gave him an ultimatum – the order or the cabinet. He chose the latter, leaving Gregory Carmichael and Stella McGregor in charge."

I stifle a yawn. Oliver Fox's account sounds like a history lesson, a subject I had no love for as a child.

"For some years, they rubbed along well enough," Fox continues. "But then a young man, Felix Crossley, joined the organisation and rocketed through the ranks."

"The man you think I saw last night?" I ask, my interest renewed.

Fox nods. "Exactly. Crossley's progress within the organisation was nothing short of remarkable," he continues. "As was his fierce intellect and energy. His interest in magic and all things occult was unrivalled. He tried everything in his power to expedite his knowledge, going well beyond the order's teachings. But that included certain rituals and ceremonies frowned upon by the order."

"Such as?"

Fox's face reddens as he looks up, unwilling to meet my eyes. "Sexmagic, drugs and devilry. Much of what you refer to as black magic."

His evident embarrassment makes me feel awkward, but I want to know more. "Did he stay with the Crescent Moon?"

"He did not," says Fox. "Carmichael was in thrall to Crossley, but Stella McGregor saw danger in the man and his practices. She did everything in her power to convince Carmichael to drop him, but he remained blind to the risk. Crossley was remarkably persuasive. He was not a likeable man, but his self-confidence was powerful and charismatic. And Crossley had invested time in mastering the art of psychological manipulation, which he used in abundance. It reached the point where the lodge found themselves hopelessly divided. Some were loyal to Carmichael and Crossley, and others to Stella McGregor. And in 1920, the inevitable schism occurred. The order divided in two. McGregor's followers joined the Cult of the Shining Path. And Carmichael's formed Calicem Aureum, otherwise known as the Golden Chalice."

I stare ahead, lost in last night's memory of Crossley's malevolent eyes. But the image of people fighting like cats in a sack over leadership of this strange esoteric cult dilutes my fear. Oliver Fox watches me.

"They are more dangerous than they sound," he says. I don't know what I did to betray my inner thoughts, but Fox has detected my cynicism.

"I don't see any danger if they possess only knowledge," I reply.

"Don't you? Both groups are adept at astral travel, and some practise spiritualism and levitation," he continues. "They may have other powers of which I am not aware."

"But it shouldn't matter," I say. "Crossley couldn't harm me even if he pulled out a gun. The bullet would travel straight through when I'm in my dream state."

"Perhaps," says Fox. "But let me tell you a little more. No sooner had Carmichael founded Calicem Aureum than Crossley betrayed him. He rallied his supporters within the organisation, hoping to remove Carmichael from office. How he achieved this is still unknown, but it involved a ceremony. When the ritual was over, they found Carmichael in a state of abject terror, and medics removed him from the cult headquarters for his safety. His hair had turned white overnight, and he was a gibbering wreck. He has not spoken from that day to this, and he currently resides in Coney Hill asylum."

My hand flies to my mouth as I gasp aloud. Fox has recounted a story of a tangible threat. I involuntarily shiver at the thought of Carmichael living the rest of his life in a mental institution.

Oliver Fox pats my hand. "I don't mean to frighten you," he says. "I wouldn't have mentioned any of this were it not for your vision of Crossley last night. And there's always the chance that it wasn't Felix Crossley who passed you, after all."

But as I return his stare, I see the fear in his eyes, and I know he believes the worst.

"What happened to the others?"

"The Cult of the Shining Path? They are still around," he says. "Stella McGregor occupies premises in London and a lodge in Bristol. Their members actively study astral travel. But they also learn about trance, automatic writing, and ceremonial magic. And there is one other practice into which they've put considerable effort," he says. "It is now their primary focus, and that is psychic defence."

"What do you mean?" I ask.

"Calicem Aureum and the Cult of the Shining Path are at war," says Fox. "They have been since 1925. But it is not a war in the physical sense of the word. Much of it is psychological, although I have heard some disturbing rumours about Calicem Aureum. There are reports of them using physical manifestations to induce terror. Psychic defence is the strategy used by the Shining Path to keep them at bay."

A shiver of fear traverses my body. I remember the bat in my bedroom before my dream walk and consider the prospect that it might have been real.

"How would I know if a manifestation was attacking me?" I ask.

"My dear girl," says Fox paternally. "There is no reason either organisation should have the smallest interest in you. Their issues are with each other."

"But the way he looked at me…" I say, my words trailing away as I try not to disclose my fears.

"If it was Crossley, he might have an idle interest in the presence of another astral traveller," says Fox. "But that is the extent of it."

He is right. It's silly, and my imagination is running riot. "Is there anything else I ought to know?" I ask, ready to bring the conversation to a close.

"I don't think so. I doubt you will ever see or hear of Crossley again. If it were not for the symbols, I wouldn't have mentioned him at all. Now, Miss Maxwell, I leave on Saturday. Please don't hesitate to contact me at any time if you need my help. I am on the telephone, and you can speak to me day or night."

"I will," I say solemnly. My feelings towards Mr Fox have transformed over the last day. Far from wanting nothing more to do with him, I now regret his imminent departure. I wonder how much I should tell Peter. Part of me wants to talk openly about my astral travel experiences. But I still can't shake off the awkward embarrassment of leaving my body. And I couldn't bear for him to humour me in sympathetic disbelief.

A man of impeccable manners, Oliver Fox holds the door open as I leave the snug. I wander slowly back to the library, deciding en route that if Peter is still there, I will tell him everything, and if he has left, I will hold my silence. When I open the library door, there is not a soul in sight.

CHAPTER TWELVE

Secrets of the Shed

I see Elys on my way home. She is outside the cottage, leaning into the front window of Jory's cart, and I hear peals of laughter as I pass. Elys teases him good-naturedly, and they barely notice me until I reach the door. Elys hears the door creak and spins around.

"Mrs Ponsonby's gone out again," she calls. "I'll make a pot of tea in a moment."

"No rush," I say, waving at Jory. He pays me no heed, seeing nothing beyond Elys. I wish someone would look at me that way.

I sigh as I pass through the door and kick off my boots in favour of a pair of fluffy slippers. They make my limp more pronounced, but they are comfortable, and now that I'm feeling fretful, comfort matters more than ever. I cannot erase the image of Felix Crossley, and it is preying on my mind.

I head towards the stairs, intending to go to my room, but as I pass the dining room, a large box on the table catches my eye. I go inside to investigate. The package, addressed to Mrs Coralie Pennington in Mrs Ponsonby's spiky writing, is wrapped in brown paper, and tied up with string. I don't recall seeing the Pennington name before, and I wonder what is inside. Curiosity gets the better of me, and I take a chance I wouldn't dare contemplate if Mrs P were in the house. As she is not, it is an opportunity too good to miss. I untie the first knot, which secures the vertical string, but she's bound the second so tightly that I can't undo it. The string is loose enough to ease from the parcel, and I unwrap the paper and look inside. Mrs Ponsonby has wrapped the contents in layers of tissue paper and secured them with tape, much to my annoyance. I can't open it any further without tearing the delicate paper. Scowling, I re-wrap it and am working the string back around the box when it suddenly snaps.

"Damn." The word explodes from my mouth, and I am glad Mrs Ponsonby isn't around. It is bad enough that I broke into her parcel, but she hates blasphemy, and it would earn me a frosty stare or worse. My heart beats faster as I gaze at the now useless frayed string. I will need to find some more if I want to conceal my crime. I examine the drawers on the sideboard, pulling them out in quick succession. Mrs Ponsonby has stored stationery there in the past, but she's rearranged them, and they are now full of cutlery and silverware. I'll have to hope Elys has some in the kitchen.

I take the package and tuck it under the table in case Elys sees it when she comes back in. I don't want to have to explain my nosiness to her. She's already under orders to keep me out of Mrs Ponsonby's room. I will never catch her out unless she drops her guard, which is not likely to happen if she thinks I've been poking around.

I perform the same drawer opening ritual in the kitchen. Almost everything I could ever need is in the drawers and cupboards except for string. I slam the pantry door shut in a fit of temper at the failure of my search. How Elys trusses a joint without something to tie it with, I don't know. But if she has anything, she doesn't keep it anywhere conspicuous, and now I am stuck. At this rate, I will have to throw the package away and feign ignorance about its existence. But that's a risky move. I can't carry the parcel from the cottage, and there's nowhere to hide it on the premises that Mrs Ponsonby wouldn't check.

As I gaze out of the window in frustration, I see the trellis has come loose from the wall, and a solution pops into my head. There's bound to be a ball of string in the shed. No respectable gardener could get through the year without it, and Mrs Ponsonby enjoys pottering around in the summer. Regretting my choice of footwear, I shuffle outside, leaning heavily on my stick. I advance along the path, picking up decomposing leaves on the soles of my slippers as I walk. By the time I reach the stone-built shed, my slippers are filthy. I slide them over the path, dislodging the unwanted mulch, then yank the bolt across, open the door, and go inside. The air smells musty, and I shiver as I try to remember the last time I was here.

The damp shed, built in the same stone as the cottage, is at least as old. It must have been a stall or outhouse in the past, and its spacious interior is useful for storing unwanted furniture and gardening tools. An old wooden cupboard with half a dozen drawers nestling below rickety shelves lurks against the far wall. I fling open the left-hand door and immediately find a ball of string. It is almost the same colour as the original, and I am sure it will be an adequate substitute. "Good work," I say to myself, relieved.

I take the string, close the cupboard and am about to leave when I see an old tennis racket from the corner of my eye. I smile in recognition. It belongs to Mrs Ponsonby, who let me borrow it occasionally when Kate Lewis was still here. Kate left us when I was about fourteen, but I still fondly remember her. I never understood why she went away, but it was a terrible wrench. She was kind to me and made light of my limp, insisting I could do anything I wanted if I put my mind to it. We would play in front of the cottage, Kate patiently hitting the ball close to me, enabling an easy return with little more than a stretch of my arm. She took me fishing once in a nearby river, never fussing when I slid from the bank.

I take the racket and feel the weight of it in my hand, closing my eyes as I remember the last time I held it. I see Kate in my mind's eye and remember that free and easy summer. My world seemed larger then, with lots to see and plenty to do, and I am sure we went further afield than Porth Tregoryan despite my injury. I swish the racket back and forth. It feels good, and I wonder if I could still hit a ball with any degree of accuracy. But then I remember the package and the urgency of righting my mistake before Mrs Ponsonby reappears.

I lean the racket back against an open shelf at the back of the shed and glimpse an old kitbag behind. I don't remember seeing it before, and nobody has used it for a while, judging by the thick layer of dust. A label hangs from the handle, and I turn it over to see two letters, V.P. It must belong to Mrs Ponsonby. I reach for the handle, haul it out, then blow the dust away, choking as it billows in my face. One easy slide of the zip and the bag is open. Inside are clothing items of a sporting nature. I am not surprised as I already knew that Mrs Ponsonby was the athletic type in her youth. But to my astonishment, I find a pair of women's trousers and smirk at the thought of her wearing them now. Mrs Ponsonby has become matronly with the passing of the years, and her days of wearing trousers are behind her. The bag yields little else of interest except for a few bits of card. My excitement at finding this paperwork vanishes when I examine it further. The document is a wartime ration book, and someone has written Miss Vera Ponsonby in neat capitals across the top. The second item is a postcard from Margate addressed to Miss Vera Ponsonby from Miss Coralie Cream. And unless it's a coincidence, Cream must be the unmarried name of Coralie Pennington, the intended recipient of the parcel in the dining room. Thoughts of the package prompt me to stop fussing around the shed and start securing it before someone catches me out.

I close the door and make my way to the dining room while Elys is still gossiping with Jory. For once, I am grateful to be an afterthought. I fasten the parcel and slip the damaged string in my pocket for disposal elsewhere. Then I try to remember which way the package faced when I first saw it. I arrange it accordingly and regard my work with satisfaction. Nobody would ever know. It isn't until I am re-reading Coralie Pennington's married name that the penny finally drops, and I understand the true nature of what I saw in the shed. The ration book and postcard both bore the salutation of Miss Vera Ponsonby. Miss, not Mrs. I sit heavily on the dining room chair and absorb this new information. Why has Mrs Ponsonby spent the last twenty-five years pretending to be married?

CHAPTER THIRTEEN

Dolly Grey

Wednesday, November 19, 1930

The next day I wake early and immediately think of Peter. He has known Mrs Ponsonby for years, and his mother may have been her confidant. I wish I had found the kitbag yesterday. Tuesdays are the new book changing day, and Peter is usually accessible at the hotel. It might be another week now before I see him, and I cannot wait that long. It's not only a matter of passing on salacious gossip about Mrs P – my thoughts have dwelled on something far worse.

I woke suddenly in the small hours to a niggling doubt that soon burst into a fully-fledged panic. And having mulled it over for a few more hours, I cannot banish it away. My concerns may be groundless and make no logical sense, but the issue of my background has raised its ugly head again. I don't know who my parents are or whether they're alive. Mrs Ponsonby has inferred that I'm an orphan, but I don't know whether to believe her. And now, alarmingly, I've discovered that Mrs Ponsonby is not a widow and is, in fact, unmarried, which brings me to a horrifying conclusion. Could she be my mother, and did she create the whole orphan/guardian story as a ruse to conceal her shame? But it doesn't seem likely given her unsuitability for child-rearing and lack of maternal instinct. Mrs Ponsonby doesn't like me, and the servants have shown me greater kindness over the years. But now the cat is out of the bag about her marital status, my worries won't go away, and I'm queasy at the thought that she might be my kin.

I've always wondered about my family. For years I accepted my life as it was. But as I grew up and saw other children with their parents, I realised I was different and began asking why. Mrs Ponsonby had no tolerance for it and either ignored my questions or diverted my attention to other things. With no choice in the matter, I forgot all about it, but coming of age on my twenty-first birthday set in motion a deep desire to know more about my life. I didn't want to spoil the day's celebrations, such as they were, but the next day I begged Mrs Ponsonby to tell me more about my background. After trying her hardest to avoid talking about it, she finally capitulated and said that I came to her from an orphanage in my fifth year. She couldn't tell me which orphanageand she did not know my parents or anything about them. I listened and thanked her, but her story was full of holes. I did not believe a word of it, and I still don't. And keeping her bedroom door locked, and me a virtual prisoner, has done nothing to change my mind, which is why I poke and pry at any opportunity. So far, Mrs Ponsonby is always one step ahead of me. But one day, she will forget, and I will know. And when that happens, what will I find out? That we are flesh and blood, or that perhaps she has stolen me? And what of the allowance? Someone somewhere has made provision for me, which does not fit with the idea of Mrs Ponsonby as my mother. Unless, of course, the money comes to her from my father. I groan and put my head in my hands as I contemplate this logical solution, explaining everything.

I distract myself by rising and dressing before creeping downstairs, hoping to leave before anyone notices. I haven't had breakfast yet and decide it's worth the sacrifice if I can escape undetected. But it is not to be. Elys sees me pass the dining room door where is she is sitting at the table drinking tea with Mrs Ponsonby.

"Connie, come here. I've got something for you."

I sigh and walk into the dining room, flushing as Mrs Ponsonby smiles at me. I cannot meet her gaze and turn quickly towards Elys.

"What is it?" I ask.

"They're ready," she says, pointing to a hanger on the back of the door.

"Oh, my goodness. Two dresses," I say.

"Not only dresses. Open this." Elys picks a box off the floor and thrusts it towards me."

I stare for a moment, not sure what to make of it.

"Sit down, and I'll pour you a cup of tea," Elys commands.

I take a seat and remove the lid from the box. Inside is a pair of beige Mary Jane's. I take them out and examine them. They have sweet little straps and perforated detail, and someone has subtly built up the heel of the left shoe to accommodate my uneven leg. The box contains further surprises – two pairs of Celta stockings thick enough to hide my scars but not so much that they look like woollens.

"Thank you so much," I say, almost on the verge of tears at her kindness.

"You can thank me for the dresses," says Elys. "But Mrs Ponsonby organised the shoes."

"Thank you," I mutter. It is kind of Elys to credit Mrs P, who no doubt arranged payment. But so much thought has gone into the colour of the shoes and the delicate composition of the stockings that it must be Elys.

"Are you going to try them on?" asks Mrs Ponsonby.

"I will do, later," I say. "It's such a pity I've nowhere to go."

"Won't you be off to the hotel as usual?"

"Not today," I say. "I don't feel like it. It's not the same without Dolly. How I wish I could see her."

"Yes. It's a terrible shame," says Mrs Ponsonby. "Isla Tremayne tried to visit last week, but Dolly was too ill, and they wouldn't let her in."

"She's asked for me," I say.

"Really?" asks Mrs P, and I feel my hackles rising.

"Yes, really. Dolly sent me a letter. I can fetch it if you don't believe me."

"There's no need, Connie," says Mrs Ponsonby. "Poor Dolly. I would like to see her too. Perhaps we could go together?"

I contemplate her suggestion. I can't think of anything worse than spending time alone with Mrs Ponsonby while the question of my parentage weighs heavily on my mind. Yet there's next to no chance of seeing Dolly any other way. We won't be able to speak freely, but at least I'll get to see her. "I suppose so," I say uncertainly.

"Good," says Mrs Ponsonby. "Well, there's no time like the present. I've nothing else to do today, so why not go now?"

I am taken aback by her enthusiasm, but this is excellent news. Today was looking distinctly uninteresting. Now, at least, I am leaving the confines of Pebble Cottage and going to Newquay for the second time in a week. It is almost unheard of.

"That's settled then," she says. "Go and change, Connie. Let's see what you look like in your finery."

Fifteen minutes later, I return downstairs feeling apprehensive. I barely recognise myself when I see my reflection in the mirror and feel excited on the one hand and embarrassed at the difference on the other.

Elys gasps as I enter the dining room. She approaches me and fusses over the hemline, checking that it's straight. "You look wonderful," she says. "Simply stunning."

"That will do nicely," says Mrs Ponsonby. "Now, are you sure about Jory?"

"I'm sure," says Elys. "It's not necessary."

I raise a curious eyebrow. "What isn't?" I ask.

"Nothing," says Mrs Ponsonby. "I thought we'd go to town on the omnibus."

The omnibus? She has completely taken me aback. It's rare enough to leave the village, much less travel by public transport, and I begin to wonder if Mrs Ponsonby is having a breakdown. If so, I will take full advantage of it.

"That sounds wonderful," I say enthusiastically. I am going to do everything possible to encourage Mrs Ponsonby's new outlook.

Elys smiles. "Look lively," she says. "The next one's due in ten minutes."

Before long, we are on the 'bus and travelling towards Newquay. Mrs Ponsonby takes the window seat and gazes outside as we travel, occasionally flashing a smile and dropping a word of small talk. I am grateful. I don't feel like conversing, and I don't know what to say to her. I wish I had never poked around in her possessions and discovered her secret. It has created an even greater barrier between us.

The omnibus pulls up on the outskirts of town, and we alight and thank the driver. Mrs Ponsonby searches for a shop and finds one close to the convalescent home where she purchases fruit and flowers for Dolly. Then we take a short walk to the unoriginally named 'Sunnyside' and announce ourselves. A young, uniformed nurse greets us and makes us wait outside while she consults a senior colleague. The matron in charge, a stern-looking woman with a nose like an eagle's beak, crisply dressed in starched collars and a headpiece, soon replaces her. Her tightly pinned hair appears as if it's glued down, and not a strand is out of place. The matron fixes us with an intimidating stare. Her overt hostility is discomfiting, but Mrs Ponsonby demands directions to Dolly's room without batting an eyelid.

"Visitor numbers are limited," says the nurse.

"Then it's just as well there are only two of us," replies Mrs P.

"One visitor at a time," says the matron, coldly.

Mrs Ponsonby draws herself to her full height and regards the nurse with a steely stare.

"Constance cannot walk distances alone," she says. "And I will go with her." She takes my hand and enters the establishment. The matron scowls but does not argue.

"Which way?"

"Show them to Miss Grey's room," says the matron through gritted teeth. She has given up in the face of Mrs Ponsonby's dominance. For once, I am glad of her forceful persona.

We weave our way down narrow corridors behind the young nurse. The building is old and was once a large residential property. When the builders converted it into a medical establishment, they must have had a smaller number of rooms in mind. Everything feels squashed together with more patients than the building can comfortably hold. There is no logic to the arrangement of the rooms and passageways, and I feel disorientated by the time we arrive outside Dolly's ward.

"Visitors," says the young nurse cheerfully as she opens the door.

Dolly's room is dark and unprepossessing. Dingy olive curtains cover most of the window even though it's late morning, and the flowers beneath the glass have wilted and seem to have given up on life. There are two beds in the room, and the occupant to Dolly's left stares vacantly at the wall as if she is still alone. Dolly looks wearily towards us and raises half a smile.

"Connie, Mrs Ponsonby. How nice of you to come. And don't you look lovely. Is that a new dress?"

"How are you, my dear?" asks Mrs P before I can reply, then she gestures towards the only chair.

"I can stand," I say.

"Nonsense," says Mrs Ponsonby, perching on the bed beside Dolly. She does not ask, and if Dolly minds, she does not say.

"How are you feeling?"

"Not the best," says Dolly. Her brown eyes are puffy and sunken, her cheeks gaunt.

"What happened?" I ask.

"I fell ill quite suddenly," says Dolly. "I don't know why, and the doctors can't say what's wrong with me. It's been difficult to breathe, and I've hardly kept a thing down."

"Oh, Dolly. We've brought you fruit. Perhaps that wasn't such a good idea."

"I managed an apple yesterday," she says. "I'll try something later. It was a kind thought, and I'm grateful."

"Do you have influenza?" asks Mrs Ponsonby.

Dolly shakes her head. "I've had the flu before. This illness feels quite different. It may be something I've eaten."

"Poor you," I say.

Dolly heaves herself further up the bed, flinching with the effort.

"Let me," says Mrs Ponsonby and plumps the pillows while Dolly sits straighter.

"I want to hear about the hotel," says Dolly. "Are they managing without me?"

"No, it's horrible," I say.

Mrs Ponsonby shoots me a quizzical stare.

"Why?" asks Dolly.

"Your replacement is rather unpleasant," I say.

"My replacement?"

"Roxy Templeton."

"Oh. Roxy's not my replacement. She started last week and is usually in the office. I suppose they put her on reception to cover for my absence."

"In that case, I can't wait for you to come back," I say.

"Don't you like her?"

"It's more that she doesn't like me," I say. "She's so rude."

Dolly smiles. "How odd. She's been charming to me."

"She's pleasant to everyone. Dr Maltravers, Oliver Fox. Everyone except me."

"Oliver Fox?" asks Mrs Ponsonby abruptly, and I inwardly curse my loose tongue. Mrs Ponsonby doesn't like me talking to strangers and going to the library unsupervised is conditional on not bothering the guests.

"He's staying at the hotel," I reply. "I said hello to him once or twice. That's all. He's leaving tomorrow, anyway."

Her eyes narrow, but she doesn't ask any further questions.

"Dr Maltravers was very kind to me," says Dolly.

"He seemed worried," I say.

"And Charlotte visited yesterday," Dolly continues. She brought me this. Dolly picks up a box of stationery from the nightstand. It is a high-quality notelet set, and it takes every ounce of self-control not to roll my eyes at the thought of Charlotte Napier simpering over my friend.

There is so much I want to say to Dolly. I would like to tell her about Mary Newson's visit. If we were alone, I might even talk about Annie Hearn, but I can't speak freely with Mrs Ponsonby listening to every word. We spend a stilted half hour chatting about village and hotel matters, then Mrs Ponsonby stands.

"Time to go," she says. "It's lovely to see you, Dolly, but we mustn't tire you out."

Dolly yawns. "Excuse me," she says, flushing. "I am tired, but you will come again, won't you?"

"Of course," says Mrs Ponsonby.

"Or I could come alone now I know where you are?" I say, hopefully.

Mrs Ponsonby ignores me. "We'll visit in two weeks if you're still here," she replies. "That's if Connie has the energy after her trip to Plymouth."

"You're going away?" Dolly's eyes are wide. She might well look surprised. I never go anywhere.

I nod. "Peter's mother is taking me away for a few days."

Dolly raises an imperceptible eyebrow.

"Isla will be with her," says Mrs Ponsonby. "They're staying with her sister and won't leave the town."

More's the pity, I think. But Mrs Ponsonby is right. We won't be going anywhere other than the court, and I don't care. It is more than enough adventure after a lifetime of restraint and I am eternally grateful that Isla Tremayne is giving me the freedom Mrs Ponsonby denies.

"Come and tell me all about it when you return," says Dolly, and I promise her I will.

We leave the convalescent home, thanking the nice young nurse on our way out. Then Mrs Ponsonby looks at her watch.

"Twenty minutes until the next bus," she says. "Would you like a cup of coffee?"

I shake my head. "There won't be enough time."

"I suppose not. In that case, we'll pop to the ironmongers, if you don't mind. It will save me a job another time."

We walk the short distance into town, and I wait outside while Mrs Ponsonby goes in. Such is her inclination to keep me in close sight that she almost decides against it when I say I don't want to go inside. It's only my heated insistence and the curious stares of passers-by that change her mind. "Stay by the window," she asks. I wait until she's safely out of sight then make my way to the corner of the street for a little freedom.

"Connie," yells a familiar voice, and someone taps me on my shoulder. I turn around. It is Peter, and I am overwhelmed with pleasure at this unexpected and most fortuitous meeting.

"I say, don't you look nice. Have you escaped? You're the last person I expected to see on the way to the fishmongers," he says amiably.

"Never mind that. I need to tell you something, and there isn't much time."

"What's wrong?"

"Does your mother know anything about Mrs Ponsonby's background?" I ask.

"I shouldn't think so," says Peter. "They've known each other for years, but only since you arrived in Cornwall."

"Has she mentioned a husband?" I ask.

"Mrs P? I don't know. She may have. Shall I ask?"

"Yes. But please be careful. Your mother mustn't ask awkward questions that might get back to her."

"Why would she?"

"Because Mrs Ponsonby never married. She's Miss Ponsonby, and I don't know why she implies otherwise."

"Are you sure? She wears a wedding ring."

"I am certain, and I've only just found out. I need to know the truth."

"Nosy," says Peter, with a knowing smile.

"I'm not," I hiss. "It's not gossip. Mrs Ponsonby might be my mother."

He stares at me, open-mouthed. "No," he says." Surely not?"

"I can't be certain, but I intend to find out. I can't go on like this, Peter. Please ask your mother if she knows anything about my background or Mrs Ponsonby's."

"I will," he replies. "But I can't promise Mother will know any more than you. They're friendly and share a lot of mutual respect, but I'm not sure how much further it goes than that."

I am about to reply when the door swings open, and Mrs Ponsonby appears with a brown paper bag in her hand.

"Hello, Peter," she says, striding towards us. "How are you, young man?"

"Running errands for Mother," he says, with a rueful grin.

"Give her my regards," says Mrs Ponsonby. "And tell her I look forward to seeing her on Sunday before you go. We still have a lot to discuss."

"Of course," says Peter. He raises his hand and sets off for the fishmongers, winking as he departs. Thank goodness. At least I got to see him before our impending visit to Plymouth, and he can speak discreetly to his mother ahead of our trip. She might tell him things she wouldn't feel able to discuss in front of me. I am a little more hopeful as we board the omnibus back to Porth Tregoryan.

CHAPTER FOURTEEN

Dark Magic

I am exhausted by eight o'clock and retire early to my room to devour more of Crawford Newson's novel. It is good reading, but my eyes soon grow heavy, and I fall asleep fully clothed. I wake around ten thirty and sleepily undress, donning my nightdress and slipping back under the covers to resume my slumbers. I stay asleep for another few hours, then wake again and cast a bleary eye at the clock. It's three thirty, and I have slept for so long that I'm no longer tired. I rub my eyes. It's too early and too cold to get up, so I stay in bed.

I consider lighting a lamp to read, but I cannot muster the energy, so I stare at the gently swaying curtains and think about my trip into town. It was good to see Peter, and I am satisfied that he will do his best to ask the right questions safely. Then my thoughts slip tangentially to Oliver Fox, and I bite my lip while thinking of Mrs Ponsonby's reaction to his name. Not that it was in any way personal. She doesn't know him, and I've no reason to suppose she wouldn't like him, but the thought of me interacting with a stranger clearly disturbed her. I wish I hadn't mentioned it. I'd told her Mr Fox was leaving tomorrow, but he is still at the hotel for a few more days, to my great relief. The idea of him not being close enough to confide in while memories of Felix Crossley still swirl through my mind is something I don't like to contemplate. I still feel unsettled, but not enough to stop thinking about Crossley as I relax back into my pillow and sink deeper as sleep takes me. The goose down bolster wraps around me like a giant pair of feathery wings. I fall back further until I suddenly realise that the mattress has not impeded my progress.

I am still falling backwards, gently floating through the bed, the floor, the house. I open my eyes, but I can't see my bedroom ceiling. I am in darkness, sprinkled with stars and effervescent light, lying on my back, head a little lower than my body, entranced but unafraid. Above me, I see the ragged edges of an alternate space. I stare curiously, and then, with a vibration that fizzes through my body, I am thrust upwards and shudder through the greying curtain. I find myself upright outside the front door of a terraced house. I can feel the impression of my heartbeat, rapid but faint, almost as if it is coming from elsewhere. I look down and see a pale and disembodied version of myself, and I know that somehow, I am in a dream state. It came from nowhere and not by choice.

I am conscious of a tingling sensation on the back of my head, but I do not feel the pull of return, urgent or otherwise. Instead, I feel drawn towards the black, chipped paintwork of the door ahead, and I lift my hand towards its tarnished knocker. My fingers slip through, and I follow, finding myself inside a long hallway. It was dark when I closed my eyes, but it's dusk here, and I can see the tired decor of a house that was once grander than it is today. Three pairs of shoes sit beneath a dark wooden side table that rests under an ornate mirror. The footwear is askew as is a newspaper, thrust carelessly to one side and upon which is a crystal ashtray still full of cigarette butts. I gaze at the paper, waiting for the familiar smell of stale smoke, but feel nothing. My sense of smell has gone, but not my sight, and I see the words *Der Angriff* written in bold italics across the top of the newspaper. I don't know what it means, and I experience a rush of adrenalin as I consider the implications of the unfamiliar tongue. It sounds Germanic, which means I am far from home. I raise my hands to my face in fear, feeling a strange prickling as the surfaces collide. I am still learning the natural laws in this alien dream state, and it is comforting to know that I can still feel skin against skin.

There are two doors off the hallway but I instinctively know they won't be of interest. I hover nervously by the stairwell, unsure whether to go upstairs or take the narrower steps towards the basement. I decide upon the former and arrive on a landing with four doors and another set of stairs to an attic room. Unlike the dingy hallway, the last rays of a low evening sun bathe the landing in a gentle glow, and I realise the house is more extensive than it first appeared. One door is open, and I go inside to find a large but untidy bedroom with a doorless wardrobe and clothing heaped on a chair. Despite the language barrier, the front covers of the magazines lying on the bedside table suggest they belong to a lady. The ashtray and pipe on the other side indicate a man. I expect this is the main bedroom of a married couple, but the room is uninteresting, and I'm wasting my time here. As I cross through the wall into a smaller back bedroom, I am distracted by the squeak of floorboards in the attic room above. I am not alone and I suppose it shouldn't come as a surprise. I stop and listen. Someone is either singing or reciting poetry. I can't hear the words, but the pattern is rhythmic – almost like our local vicar preaching a sermon. I decide to investigate, but not before I notice the untidy state of the smaller bedroom. It is undoubtedly the domain of a man who has carelessly abandoned a cut-throat razor and shaving strop on one side of the washstand. The single bed takes up most of the long wall, with just enough room remaining for a desk to fit below the sash window. Papers, files, books, and ephemera lie haphazardly across the desk with a page of handwritten poetry on top. I read a few lines. It is good but not great, and it takes a few moments for me to appreciate that it's written in English, not German. There is a small door opposite the bed, which someone has left closed over the corner of a piece of purple silk. It looks like it might be a bathrobe and seems an odd choice of colour for a man.

I hear another noise from above – an odd guttural sound that ends abruptly in a screech. There is a familiarity to it I can't put my finger on, and I decide that it's time to investigate. But as the thought enters my head, I shudder, and a frisson of dread snakes through my soul. What if someone sees me? Is it possible, and does it matter if they do? And why am I casually drifting around a house in another country as if it were an everyday occurrence? Streams of anxious thoughts flood my mind, and I am suddenly terrified. I haven't considered how I'm going to get back to my body or if I'll have the same problems as last time. But this house is unsettling, and I don't know why I'm here. Could Annie Hearn have made it to the continent? But then I wasn't thinking of Annie Hearn when I fell asleep. Perhaps this has nothing to do with her.

I am standing stock still, paralysed with uncertainty and torn between wondering who is walking around upstairs and how I can get home. If I could feel my body, my heart would be racing, my stomach twisting with nerves. I will go. I will stay. I will seek safety. But I am curious while knowing that curiosity is not my friend. I regret poking around the shed and uncovering secrets that were not mine to understand. If I linger here too long, I will regret meddling again. And as I process the logic of these thoughts, I suddenly remember who I was thinking about when I fell asleep. It was Felix Crossley. No sooner does the thought cross my mind than the bedroom walls dissolve around me. I am on the last step of a narrow staircase, standing by an angled door. The noise is louder up here. It's not singing or poetry, but a rhythmical chanting. A single low voice leads, followed by multiple refrains. I listen hard and pick out the odd word of Latin. The gathering inside is like a church service – but what kind of church meets in the top room of a Berlin townhouse? Perhaps they do things differently on the continent.

I stare at the door. Only two inches of wood separate me from the occupants of the room beyond. What I should do is find a nice dark corner, close my eyes, and concentrate on getting home. But I can't help myself. I push a nervous hand through the door and follow to where a scene of nightmarish proportions greets me.

The large, low-ceilinged room stretches the length of the house. Dark wooden beams run from wall to ceiling, each fitted at two-foot intervals with a sconce in which torch-like lamp's glow balefully. A dozen or more people occupy the room, and I shrink back against the far wall, hiding my wraith-like body beside a wooden cabinet in case they see me. The light is low, but not so much that I cannot make out their outfits. They are wearing purple silken gowns, long-sleeved and hooded and with a unicursal hexagram on the back. I remember Fox's words. It is the symbol of Calicem Aureum, and the people worshipping in front of me are not the harmless fools I had imagined.

Felix Crossley is standing at the farthest end of the room. Full bellied with quivering jowls, he holds a bowl towards the throng, and they stare in rapt wonder as he chants. Crossley speaks, and they repeat the last sentence of his proclamation while kneeling yet moving in small circles. They gyrate as if hypnotised by this large lump of a man, his voice mellow, controlled and commanding. Men and women prostrate themselves before him. Some are tearing their clothes, others reach out to their closest neighbour. I close my eyes and open them again, willing the sight away. But the scene hasn't changed.

A woman in the middle of the room has pulled her gown over her shoulders, her sagging breasts heaving as she rocks backwards and forwards. And when I think it cannot get any worse, Crossley bellows "*Silentium*", and the room falls deathly quiet. I crouch and try to hold my breath, but in my ethereal state, it doesn't work that way, and I can't take comfort in normal bodily functions. As much as I want to look away, I can't. Crossley points to a dark-haired man on all fours at the front of the room, crooks his finger and beckons him over. A thin, cruel half-smile settles over the man's face as he stands and approaches Crossley, who clicks his fingers and points down. The man kneels, face tipped upwards until he is looking straight into Crossley's eyes. Crossley turns and raises the metal bowl towards a painting behind him, and it's too far away to make out the detail. He waits as if expecting an acknowledgement, but there is only silence. Then he spins around and, with one fluid motion, pours the contents of the bowl into a goblet which he thrusts towards the waiting man. "*In nomine asmodeus*", he says.

The man lowers his head and mutters, "I will serve only you" then downs the contents in one gulp, wiping his hand over moist lips. He stands and strides towards a crimson covered sideboard that looks like an altar. Then the man upends the goblet on the white runner in the middle and delivers it to Crossley. He takes the cup and glances at the red ring, satisfied. One by one, Crossley calls the worshippers over, and they each drink a crimson substance from the goblet that I can only hope contains red wine. I want to leave, but I am too frightened to move. And in a moment, Crossley will have reached his final supplicant, and I don't know what will happen then. They are still kneeling silently before him, but their eyes are rolling, and they appear half drugged. I close my eyes, knowing I must go now. Whether my thoughts take me downstairs or back home doesn't matter, as long as I get out of this room. I put my head in my hands to initiate my return. But the crowd starts chanting again, and the noise is too distracting to concentrate. I try to imagine returning to my body, to the safety of sleep in my warm and welcoming bed. Nothing happens. I am still in this strange attic room, and now one of them has started to disrobe. If I cannot leave by astral travel, then at the very least, I will walk. I stand and flatten myself against the cupboard, but now that I am no longer crouching, I can see further into the room. Crossley has placed the bowl by the side of the altar next to a feathery mass. I squint, hoping for a clearer view, and when my brain finally catches up with my eyes, I gratefully feel a tug on the back of my head. I am pulled backwards and down, down, down until my head touches the pillow.

I wake with a start. I am back in my bed, and my temples are damp with sweat. I am panting so hard that I raise my fingers to my neck and check my racing pulse. I bite my lip and choke down a scream. I cannot believe what I have seen, and yet I am not altogether surprised. Crossley is real. He is present and evil, and somehow our worlds have collided. Those ignorant men and women who ought to know better were not drinking wine, and Crossley was not conducting a religious service. I wish I could erase the last sight I saw before terror whipped me home. But the broken bodies of the black cockerel and white hen, lifeless and exsanguinated, will haunt me forever.

CHAPTER FIFTEEN

Travels to Plymouth

Sunday, November 23, 1930

Oliver Fox has gone away, and with him, nearby counsel should the need arise. His departure was the first thing I thought of when I woke earlier today, and he was still on my mind while I was packing. I feel his loss acutely and wish I had spent more time getting to know him.

Isla Tremayne will arrive soon, and we will depart for Plymouth. I should be excited. I have waited most of my adult life for an opportunity like this, but I can't forget Felix Crossley and the horrors of that night are clouding my thoughts. I don't know what draws me to him and why our paths keep crossing. Neither does Oliver Fox, who tried, but failed, to conceal his concern for me when I told him. He has asked me to stay in touch, and I will, although it will be harder without Dolly. I cannot imagine the Templeton woman affording me the same kindness if I ask to borrow the hotel telephone.

I look in the mirror again and smudge my eyeliner a little more, trying to make it fade until it isn't so obvious. Dressed in my new clothes and footwear, I don't look like me, and I don't feel right either. It's almost as if I have aged by a decade. I am nervous and unsettled, and far from being keen to leave, I'm unexpectedly worried about being away from my usual surroundings. Mrs Ponsonby has noticed my subdued demeanour. She keeps asking if I am well and evidently suspects I am sickening for something. It would be the easiest thing in the world to give in and stay, easing her mind as well as mine. But I would regret it in a few days when I am feeling better. And what protection can she or anyone else offer from something that isn't physical? Besides, I can't tell anyone other than Fox. They would think I was losing my mind. If I betray my secret, I might end up with Gregory Carmichael in Coney Hill, and I shudder at the thought.

"They're here," says Elys, running in from the parlour. "How exciting. You'll have a lovely time, Connie."

I turn and muster an unenthusiastic smile.

"Cheer up," she says. "I'm fed up seeing all these long faces."

"Hmmm?"

"Mrs Ponsonby looks like she's dropped a shilling and found a penny. You're a pair of worrywarts."

I heave a sigh and walk towards the parlour window. Peter is coming up the pathway with Mrs Tremayne and suddenly my spirits soar. Everything seems so much brighter at the sight of an old and trusted friend. I grin and wave.

"I'm going to Plymouth," I beam. "I'm really going away."

"About time," says Elys, bustling towards the door.

Peter bounds inside. "Where are your bags?" he asks, and I point to the suitcase beside the dining room table.

"Good. You're travelling light. There's not much space. I suppose I should have mentioned it before you packed."

I open my mouth to reply, but he has grabbed my case and is halfway back to the car.

Mrs Ponsonby appears from the kitchen and welcomes Isla Tremayne. "Can we have a few moments?" she asks, taking Mrs Tremayne's arm and guiding her into the parlour.

I glance at Elys. "What's that all about?"

"I don't know," she says. "But you know what Mrs Ponsonby's like. She'll be worrying."

I shake my head. "She'd better not be laying down silly rules. It's so embarrassing. I'm a grown woman, and if I can go to..." The words trail away. I nearly said Berlin, and I cannot believe my loose lips. I am beginning to confuse the dream world with real life. "Never mind," I say.

Peter opens the door and waits in the hallway. "Are you ready?" he asks.

"Yes. But Mrs Ponsonby has corned your mother in the parlour. Hopefully, they won't be too much longer."

"Good. Malcolm is getting impatient."

"Malcolm?"

"My cousin. He's driving."

"I didn't realise."

"No reason why you should. You don't mind, do you?"

"No. Of course not."

The parlour door opens, revealing Mrs Tremayne. She crooks a finger and beckons Peter to come inside. He shrugs his shoulders and follows.

I watch the door close, aghast.

"What now?" I ask Elys. I am close to tears. What is Mrs Ponsonby telling Peter that she can't say in front of me?

Elys takes my hand. "In ten minutes, you'll be away from here and off on your adventures. Just let it wash over you. Whatever she's saying is not worth getting upset over. And anyway, Peter is sure to tell you."

She's right, of course. I don't doubt that Peter will confide in me. He better had, or he'll be in my bad books. We've been friends for a long time, and he knows how I feel about Mrs Ponsonby.

Five more minutes pass, and Peter emerges, face uncharacteristically stern. Isla Tremayne follows, straight-backed and serious.

"Are you ready, Connie?" asks Mrs Ponsonby. Her face is pale, and she has forced a smile that doesn't fool me for a moment.

I smile back. "Yes, thank you," I say. "And I appreciate the opportunity to visit Plymouth." I know little about body language, but Mrs Ponsonby is bristling with concern and could change her mind at any moment. The slightest reason could be enough, and I am determined not to give her any room for further doubt. Being excessively nice is a small price to pay.

"Good. Let's be on our way," says Mrs Tremayne. Peter opens the door and leaves the house, followed by his mother. I fasten my coat, collect my stick and handbag and am about to join them when Mrs Ponsonby grabs my arm.

"Be careful, dear," she says, pecking my cheek. "It's time I let you go a little. Enjoy yourself."

I walk to the car in stunned silence. Peter opens the door and helps me inside. I watch from the window as Elys and Mrs P stand outside Pebble Cottage waving as we pull away, and I feel the shadow of her kiss for a long time after.

#

"Is she dying?" I ask, sitting heavily on the pink counterpane in my bedroom at Smugglers Cottage. It is the first opportunity to speak privately with Peter since leaving Porth Tregoryan that morning. Though Malcolm drove and Mrs Tremayne sat in the front of the car, I didn't dare ask Peter the questions burning in my mind after Mrs Ponsonby's strange behaviour.

"Who?" asks Peter.

"Mrs Ponsonby, of course. First, she dragged you into her parlour to speak about goodness knows what, and then she kissed me. She actually kissed me on the cheek and said she hoped I would enjoy myself. It makes me wonder if she is suffering from a terminal illness."

"Or she might genuinely hope you'll have a good time," says Peter.

"No. Mrs Ponsonby hates me."

"I assure you she does not."

"What did she want?"

Peter bites his lip. "What if I said I'd rather not tell you?"

I clench my fists and try to swallow the burn of anger his words provoke. Peter speaks again before I can reply. "But I will, of course," he continues. Peter is nothing if not perceptive and will have taken seconds to interpret my reaction. "But Mrs Ponsonby asked me not to, so I would appreciate it if you didn't tell her."

"What do you take me for?" I ask. "And you shouldn't have agreed to keep something from me. Don't collude with her."

"I'm not," he says. "But I feel sorry for Vera."

"Vera!" I explode. Then I take a breath and try to calm down. "What did she say?"

"Only that she's worried about you. Mrs Ponsonby knows it's time to give you a little more freedom. She would love to have joined us but understands why it wouldn't be sensible. But she's asked us to promise not to leave you alone for a moment."

I groan. "Please tell me you didn't agree."

"Of course, I did. Mother too," says Peter. "But I suspect she will take a loose approach to that promise. Mother has no intention of coming to court with us. She has better things to do, and if that means putting Malcolm in *loco parentis*, then I'm sure her conscience won't trouble her unduly."

"There you go again," I say, and my lip trembles. "Treating me like a child. I don't need supervision."

Peter perches next to me on the bed and jabs a friendly elbow into my side. "Connie," he says fondly. "We're in Plymouth for a few days – the world is our oyster. We've made a few promises to make your guardian feel better, but that doesn't mean we can't enjoy ourselves. Malcolm will hardly trouble us. He will stay nearby while we are in court, and Mother will watch us from a distance the rest of the time. She is very easy going, and you will hardly notice her."

"We won't be able to talk," I say moodily.

"What are we doing now?" he replies. "It will be much easier to speak privately, and Mother is so pleased to see Aunt Veronica that all she wants to do is gossip. She won't be paying the slightest attention to what we do."

"I like your aunt," I tell him. We'd arrived earlier in the afternoon, and Veronica had greeted me like a long-lost niece, ushering us into her homely cottage in New Street for tea and homemade scones, which she had spent the morning baking. Veronica was widowed a few years ago. Her children have all left home, and she doesn't have a maid. Our rooms are spotless, and she made up the beds herself; that is, Peter's, mine, and Mrs Tremayne's. Malcolm is staying with a friend in town, which will suit him better and me too, if I'm honest. I've always found Malcolm slimy. Being stuck in the car with him for the duration of the journey and a lunch stop has not improved my opinion. Malcolm has an unfortunate sense of humour bordering on the vulgar. I am no prude, but there are limits when you don't know someone very well. He overstepped the boundaries more than once, causing Isla Tremayne to flush with embarrassment. I haven't seen her lost for words before.

"Do you need a hand unpacking?" asks Peter.

I shake my head. "I'll manage."

"Then I'll leave you to it. We're eating out tonight," Peter continues, winking as he leaves the room.

I stand and walk to the window. Smugglers Cottage nestles among a range of eclectic properties, from grand timbered Tudor buildings to rough-hewn stone cottages. It is too narrow to drive down, and Malcolm had to park the car some distance away. Peter took two trips to carry our bags while I struggled to negotiate the cobbles with my stick. All this activity has made me tired. I glance at the clock. There are two hours until supper time, and I decide to spend them wisely by taking a nap.

CHAPTER SIXTEEN

The Inquest

Monday, November 24, 1930

We meet Malcolm outside the Plymouth Guildhall, having eaten a hearty breakfast at Smuggler's Cottage. We are too early to go in and spend ten minutes chatting outside. Malcolm listens enviously to our account of the laden breakfast table we feasted from that morning. Peter's aunt Veronica had excelled herself and spoiled us for choice.

"Norman burned the sausages," Malcolm complains. "He nearly burned the bloody toast as well. I'm eating with you tomorrow."

Peter anxiously paces while we wait for the doors to open and moves so far away that I am left alone with Malcolm, who is still protesting about his paltry meal. One by one, a small crowd gathers around us, mainly composed of journalists and photographers. Two arrange their tripods and start discussing the witnesses whose pictures they hope to take. Malcolm spots a journalist he knows and calls out his name, then walks towards him with his hand outstretched. I listen to them discussing the impending trial before glancing towards Peter, who is close to the main door of the

Guildhall. I am standing alone. Neither man is watching, and even at my sluggish pace, I could walk away, and nobody would see me go until it was too late. I am free – free of Mrs Ponsonby's eagle eyes and no longer a prisoner. It feels good. But I don't flee because I am keen to watch the proceedings. I had hoped they would have found Annie Hearn by now. As much as I'm looking forward to attending the inquest, watching Annie getting a fair hearing in court would improve things further still. Peter thinks she's dead, but I'm not sure. I still hope she's alive, though she's probably frightened and lying low until she can prove her innocence. I want to help her, and I hope this inquest will not leave me thinking otherwise.

The doors to the Guildhall open with a creak. Peter turns and looks for me, then smiles in relief as I wave. He strolls towards me.

"Where's Malcolm?" he asks.

"Over there." I gesture towards Malcolm and his friend.

"So much for keeping an eye on you," he says.

"I thought we agreed it wasn't necessary."

"I know," says Peter. "I don't like to break promises, but I won't stick to you like glue. They're going in now. Come on."

He takes my arm and guides me into the public gallery, where we perch on hard wooden seats. The case is attracting a great deal of interest and before long, there is standing room only. The court orderlies turn several latecomers away, and Peter and I exchange glances.

"It's a good thing we were near the front," he says. "We'd better stand close to the door tomorrow if the inquest runs over."

"Do you think it will?"

"It depends how many witnesses there are. I say, can you see Malcolm?"

We scan the room looking for him and hope that he got through. Peter spies him first, sitting with his friend diagonally opposite.

"Good," he says. "That would have been a disaster."

The coroner's assistant enters the room, followed by two middle-aged men. He waits while they sit behind a long wooden table at the head of the room, then coughs and states that the proceedings are now open. "The Plymouth city coroner, Mr J.A. Pearce, will conduct the inquest," he announces. "And Sir Hugh Protheroe-Smith, the chief constable of Cornwall and Superintendent Pill of Launceston, are also in attendance." The assistant sits as the coroner rises and begins to speak. His summary of the case is slow and rambling, and I find myself becoming irritable and wish he'd get on with it. Then he reads aloud the letter from Annie Hearn written to William Thomas. I recollect the differing conclusions Peter and I came to when we first became aware of it, and Peter does too. He raises his eyebrow and grins smugly, still adamant that the letter points to Annie's guilt, but on hearing the words again, I am more confident than ever of her innocence. Then the coroner calls Dr Saunders to the stand, who transfixes us with his account of Alice Thomas's final illness.

"It was short and painful," the doctor says. "At first, I thought it was food poisoning. Mrs Thomas seemed to improve but suddenly became worse, and I sent her to Plymouth hospital under the care of Dr Lister."

"Did you suspect anything other than food poisoning?" asks the coroner.

"Initially, no. But following her unexpected decline, I became suspicious."

The coroner asks what symptoms Alice Thomas displayed. Dr Saunders lists them and tells the coroner that some were common in both ptomaine and arsenic poisoning. There being no further questions, the clerk dismisses Dr Saunders and William Thomas takes the stand.

I sit up and watch as he walks in, back straight, and eyes fixed ahead. Thomas wears a moustache, and, for a farmer, he dresses smartly, even down to his polished shoes.

"Name?" asks the coroner.

"William Thomas," he growls. His accent is broad but pleasant, and his voice is strong. He looks uncomfortable yet far from defeated.

The coroner asks him about their meal in Bude on the day Alice Thomas became unwell, and William gives a comprehensive answer, omitting no detail. I am impressed by his seemingly honest account while finding it a little too slick – too rehearsed.

"I also ate the sandwiches, although not as many as Alice," he says. "Later, I felt nauseous but banished the worst of it away with the aid of a little whisky." Several men titter as Thomas describes the healing effects of the spirit, and the coroner fixes them with a steely glare. He doesn't have to admonish the men publicly for the laughing to stop as his disappointed demeanour yields immediate results. I wait with bated breath for more questions, and the coroner continues.

"What happened when you arrived home?" he asks.

"I sent for Mrs Parsons, Alice's mother," says Thomas. "She prepared our food for the next few days."

"And where was Mrs Hearn?"

"With us, at the farmhouse."

"Did she prepare any food?"

"The Sunday dinner, I believe," he says.

Peter glances at me in an 'I told you so' sort of way.

"Did your wife take any medicine?" asks the coroner.

Thomas nods. "Yes. Two aspirins from a bottle which Mrs Hearn brought from her house."

I hear a gasp from the crowd and realise that the sound also came from me, as I wonder whether he somehow doctored the pills. I expect the coroner to ask for further details, but he does not. He passes over the matter and asks what happened next.

"My wife became very unwell," says Thomas. "Her mother, Mrs Parsons, worried about her too and thought the aspirins might have upset her. Alice was sleeping in a different room as she was so unwell. And in the early hours of the morning, I heard her cry out and went to her. 'Carry me back to your room,' she said. 'The bed is streaming wet, and the bedclothes torn to pieces.' I did as she asked, but she did not improve, and when Dr Saunders saw her, he sent her to Plymouth."

"Was your wife insured?" asks the coroner.

Several journalists stop writing and stare at Thomas. His eyes flash, and his face reddens. Whether in guilt or fury, I cannot tell. "No. She was not insured," he says in a low, calm voice.

"And do you keep arsenic on the premises?"

"I have never purchased arsenic," he replies. "I bought some sheep dip, but I do not know its composition, and I keep some rat poison under lock and key in my desk."

The coroner regards William Thomas sympathetically then takes a deep breath as if he is about to apologise for his next question. But the thought disappears before he opens his mouth, and instead, he curtly asks if his wife was jealous of Mrs Hearn.

Mr Thomas narrows his eyes and does not hesitate. "No," he says. "She had no reason to be."

"Did she mind Mrs Hearn coming to your house so often?"

"They were friends. Why would she?"

"And have you ever lent Mrs Hearn any money?"

Thomas chews his lip and seems uncertain whether to answer. "I did, sir," he says.

"When?"

"In December 1928. I gave her a cheque to repay a debt owed by a relative who died in Canada."

"Did you ask her to repay the money?"

"Not until my wife died."

"Why then?"

"Because I had a lot of worry and expense."

The coroner seems satisfied. He nods to his clerk, who scribbles a note, then the coroner tells William Thomas that he is free to go, and I watch as he walks stiffly away.

By now it's nearly midday and the coroner's party whisper among themselves and decide to break for lunch. I am reluctant to leave in case we can't get back in again, but Peter insists. He is starving. We buy pasties from a nearby baker and eat them shivering on a bench a few hundred yards away. And though I am tired and walking is painful today, we return as speedily as I can manage and are soon in the Guildhall again. We are much earlier than necessary and loiter inside the hallway as they've locked the inquest room over lunch. Peter finds me a seat and chats to Malcolm as I take the weight off my feet. Nobody else is back yet, and we are alone until a middle-aged man enters from an inside room and makes his way to the main door. I recognise him at once. It is William Thomas, and he is oblivious to the presence of a woman striding behind him and keen to catch up.

"Excuse me," she says breathlessly, tapping him on the shoulder. He turns around.

"Elizabeth," he says, doffing his hat.

"Mrs Uglow to you."

William Thomas wears a pained expression and visibly shrinks.

"How can I help you, Mrs Uglow," he says.

"By giving this box of junk to your fancy woman."

She thrusts a shoebox towards him and catches him off guard. He reaches out, but it is too late, and the box falls to the floor with a crash. A white lace handkerchief drifts towards my chair.

"I don't understand," says Mr Thomas.

"That woman left it behind on the day of the funeral."

"Where?"

"In your kitchen. Mrs Hearn couldn't get out of the door quickly enough once Percy challenged her. She put the box down and forgot to pick it up again. Percy gave it to me for some unfathomable reason. It's bad enough having to come here as a witness without holding onto her nasty things."

"I don't know where Mrs Hearn is," says William Thomas, eyeing the mess on the floor.

"Well, I'm sure she'll get in touch," says Mrs Uglow.

"I doubt it, and I don't want these items."

Mrs Uglow draws herself to her full height. "I certainly don't," she says. "And if you hadn't encouraged that woman into your house, poor dear Alice might still be alive."

"She was Alice's friend more than mine."

"So, you say," says Mrs Uglow, raising an unforgiving eyebrow.

A red flush travels across his cheek. "I'll bid you a good day, madam," he says, doffing his hat again.

I reach towards the handkerchief. "Don't you want this?" I ask, but he has already left the room, striding away from the embarrassing spectacle.

Mrs Uglow sighs and squats down, scooping the items from the floor. "I suppose I'll have to take them back," she mutters. "Insufferable man."

"Here, let me," says Peter, rushing to her aid. She smiles disingenuously, replaces the lid, and walks away with her nose in the air.

"She's left the handkerchief," I say before leaning forward and picking it up. My fingers go numb as I touch the lace, and a spark of energy flashes up my arm. I see Annie Hearn getting into a car; the vision fades. Now she's standing on the cliff, carefully dropping a coat. It must be a spare because she is wearing another. The image disappears with a static-like buzz, and I see her once more, dressed in a uniform. She is working as a domestic and seems confident and secure. A flash and she's gone, then one last sighting. Annie Hearn is sitting on the edge of a bed, sobbing into a handkerchief like this one. She picks up a pencil and scribbles in a journal. 'My life is worthless,' she writes.

"What is it?" asks Peter. "You look like you've seen a ghost."

"She's alive," I say. "Annie Hearn is alive."

#

"How do you know?" asks Peter.

"Not now," I say. I don't know how to explain my vision to Peter or even whether I should. I don't understand it myself. But I am certain beyond all doubt that I saw Annie when I touched her handkerchief, and I know she is alive. Alive and frightened.

"Are you alright?" asks Peter, eyeing me with concern.

"Fine," I say, casting a sideways glance towards Malcolm. Finally, Peter understands that I can't speak while in his company.

The reception hall fills with people returning after the recess. They mill around, murmuring about their expectations for the afternoon. It's not long before the inner door opens, and the clerk beckons us inside. We try to sit where we were before, but someone has beaten us to it and forced us into chairs closer to the door. There is no significant difference in our view, but I am disorientated by the different angle, especially with visions of Annie preying on my mind.

"Penny for them?" whisperers Peter, and I realise I am frowning. I am about to respond when the coroner stands and addresses the room again before calling on another witness.

"Name?" he asks, without preamble.

"Claud Mathew."

"Where do you work, Mr Mathew?"

"At Shuker and Reed."

"What is the nature of the business?"

"Shuker and Reed is a grocer and chemist shop in Launceston."

"Have you ever sold poison to Mr or Mrs Thomas?"

"No," says Mr Mathew, with conviction.

"Are you certain?"

"Quite certain. I have examined the poison register for the last ten years. Neither Mr nor Mrs Thomas appears."

"And Mrs Annie Hearn – is her name in the register?"

Claud Mathew nods. "It is."

We gasp at the news, and I want to cry. Surely it must be a mistake.

"Did she purchase the poison in person?"

"No," says Mr Mathew. "She wrote to me asking for some powdered weed killer for a neglected part of her garden."

"What was the date of the letter?"

"Thirtieth July 1926."

"And are you sure she wrote that letter?"

"Oh, yes. I prepared a one-pound tin of Cooper's powders early in August, and she came to the shop to collect it. We provided the registers for inspection, and the police have confirmed that it is her signature."

"And what is the primary ingredient in Cooper's Powders?"

"Arsenic."

"I have no further questions, Mr Mathew. Please sit down. Now, Superintendent Pill. Have you examined the poison register?"

The tall policeman stands facing the crowd, hands clasped in front. "I have," he says. "I personally examined it, and the signature does indeed belong to Mrs Hearn."

"Have you examined any other registers?"

"Yes. We checked all known poison registers from the chemists in Stratton, Holsworthy, Liskeard and Camelford. There were no sales of poison directly tied to Mrs Hearn, William Thomas, or any member of the Parsons family in those locations. But Mrs Elizabeth Uglow purchased poison at Shuker and Read's some eight years ago."

The coroner raised a curious eyebrow. "Go on?"

"She made this purchase at Mrs Thomas's suggestion. We do not attach any significance to it."

"Have you searched the farmhouse for poison?"

"Yes, we have. We made a thorough search of Trenhorne House on the twentieth of November. There was no trace of poison except for a small packet of worming tablets on the mantlepiece. They contained nought point two seven of a gram of arsenic, precisely what one would expect to find on a farm."

"One last question, Superintendent. Was a search made of Mrs Hearn's house?"

"No. We had no right to make such a search."

I watch Peter as he exchanges glances with Malcolm, now sitting close beside us. Neither seems impressed with the superintendent's words. I can almost hear their thoughts condemning Annie Hearn long before the inquest concludes.

The clerk invites Mr Tickle, the Plymouth city analyst, to the stand, and he submits his evidence quickly. I am relieved at the speed of his delivery as my leg has gone to sleep, and I am worried about what will happen when I try to stand. Though succinct, Mr Tickle's evidence is not for the faint-hearted. He describes the removal of Alice Thomas's bodily organs and the tests he undertook to establish the presence of arsenic. And then it is over. The coroner thanks the witnesses, sending them on their way with instructions to return at nine o'clock the following day.

Peter stands, and I grab his arm and ask him to wait. My leg still feels numb, and if I'm going to fall, it won't be in front of a crowd. I attempt to stand once the last group of people reaches the door and lean heavily on my stick as I negotiate my way across the room. I feel better for moving, and my leg is stronger than I thought.

"What do you think about that then?" asks Peter. "You can't still believe in her innocence?"

It is a long time until I get the chance for a detailed reply – some six hours later, in fact. We return home from the Guildhall and enjoy a delicious meal of lamb stew and dumplings followed by treacle tart. Then we listen to the radio and chat about the day. Isla Tremayne and Veronica Davies have spent time shopping in Launceston, where they bumped into an old school friend. After a day of treats and reminiscing, they are in excellent spirits, and though tired, I do not want to interrupt the evening too early. But at ten o'clock and with no sign of the chatter slowing, I make my excuses and go to my room. Within minutes, I hear a tap at the door.

"Can I come in?" Peter whispers.

"Briefly," I say. I am shattered and need to conserve my energy for tomorrow.

"What happened earlier?" asks Peter, coming straight to the point.

It is the last thing I want to hear. I hoped he would forget about the handkerchief. There is no quick way to explain what I saw, and the last time I attempted to tell him about my dream walking, he was sceptical.

"I don't know where to start," I say candidly.

"I'd like to know," he says.

"You won't believe me."

"Try me."

I sigh, knowing that I'm not going to get away with it and start by telling Peter about Oliver Fox, the dreams, Felix Crossley, and Annie Hearn's handkerchief. The words stream from my mouth as relief at unburdening myself replaces my initial reluctance to tell him. Whether he believes me is almost immaterial. The fact that I have disclosed it and someone close to me knows brings a sense of peace.

"Well?" I say when I have finished.

"Now I'm lost for words," says Peter.

"I'm not making it up."

"I know. You were as white as a sheet earlier," Peter says. "I could see straight away that something had happened. But how do you know that it wasn't your imagination and that any of it really happened?"

"I just do," I say.

"Will I offend you if I ask you to prove your abilities?"

"No," I say. "But I don't know how I can."

"The same way you did for Oliver Fox."

"What – meet you in a dream?"

"No, silly. I don't have a clue how to dream walk. I mean something a little more scientific."

"Such as?"

"Come to my room tonight. I'll leave something on my bedside table. Then you can tell me what it is."

"I see. You doubt me, after all."

"You said you wouldn't get upset."

"I'm not, but…"

"I'm sorry. I'm a natural cynic," says Peter. "I can't help myself. But I'm willing to let you prove me wrong."

"Do it then," I say, laying down the gauntlet. It's a risk. So far, I have got into the dream state when I need to, but it's not a foregone conclusion.

Peter talks for a few more moments, but I'm not listening. He's annoyed me and hasn't understood that I have bared my soul to him. There is nobody else, other than Mr Fox, who is almost a stranger, to whom I would consider telling my secret. I've unburdened myself to Peter against my better judgement, and it's been a disaster. He won't believe me without proof, and a churlish part of me contemplates dropping the subject altogether and telling him I made it up. But that wouldn't be of any use to Annie. If I can convince Peter, then he might understand why I want to save her. He might even help me do it. There is nothing for it. My eyes flutter, heavy with sleep, but I will have to force myself to stay awake until Peter is asleep himself. Peter leaves the room, and I remain dressed and read for an hour before tiptoeing into the corridor to see if there is a chink of light under his door. It is dark in his room, and for one moment, I consider opening the door and looking at the bedside table the old-fashioned way. But Peter, being Peter, will have thought of this, I know. So, I return to my room and light a candle, ready to sink into a waking dream.

I recline on my pillow and stare at the candle, waiting for the usual signs. No time seems to pass, then I wake with a start, shivering with cold. I search for the candle, and it takes a few moments for my eyes to grow accustomed to the dark. And when they do, I realise, of course, that it's dark because the candle has burned down to a stump. I gaze at the wall clock. It is three in the morning. I touch the nightstand to prove I haven't somehow settled into a waking dream, but my fingers graze hard wood, and I know that I simply fell asleep.

I see the hazy shape of a spare candle lying on its side across the room and consider getting up to light it. But fatigue makes me immobile, and I can't summon the strength to do it. Instead, I wriggle under the bedspread fully clothed, intending to snatch a few hours' rest and resume my quest at dawn. But I have been hopelessly optimistic. I miss sunrise altogether, and the next thing I hear is Peter banging on the door and telling me to hurry if I want breakfast before we leave. I rise quickly, wash and put on my spare dress before heading downstairs.

CHAPTER SEVENTEEN

Last Night at Smuggler's Cottage

Tuesday, November 25, 1930

"Well?" We sit in the Guildhall waiting for the coroner to begin when Peter breaks his silence on the subject of my midnight dream walk or lack thereof. I raise my finger to my lips and point towards the seated jury, hoping he will hush at the thought of the imminent proceedings. He sees straight through my ruse.

"We've got a few minutes," he whispers. "Did you see it?"

"What?" I ask.

"You know. The thing on my bedside table."

"I fell asleep," I say.

"Oh." Peter shuffles his feet as he looks towards the floor, and I grit my teeth at his evident embarrassment for me.

"I didn't make it up," I hiss. "I was tired, and I couldn't keep my eyes open."

"Another time," Peter says.

"Tonight."

"Whatever you say."

I turn my back to him before glaring at Mr Pearce, the coroner, who has finally stood.

He makes a brief address and tells us that there is a lot to get through, and there will be no morning break today. Then he calls on his first witness, Mrs Tryphena Parsons, mother of Alice Thomas.

Mrs Parsons is a stout, redoubtable lady, square chinned, stoic, and still dressed in black mourning garb. Mr Pearce introduces her gently, reminding the jury that she came to Lewannick to care for her daughter when she learned of her ill health. Mrs Parsons stayed at the farmhouse until they removed Alice to Plymouth Hospital and witnessed her daughter's terrible suffering. Mr Pearce softens his voice as he speaks, but Tryphena Parsons answers brusquely, suppressing her emotions. She tells him that Annie Hearn was present at the farm for the duration of her visit.

"What were you told was wrong with your daughter?" asks the coroner.

"Food poisoning," says Mrs Parsons.

"And who cooked while you were at the house?"

"Mrs Hearn."

"The previous witness said that Mrs Thomas had special food and that you prepared it yourself?"

"That's not entirely correct. I did cook for Alice once or twice, though Mrs Hearn still brought her drinks and cooked the rest of the time."

Mr Pearce cocks his head to one side. "What happened on Sunday, November second?"

"The day started well," says Mrs Parsons. "Alice seemed to be getting better, and I thought she was over the worst of it. Mrs Hearn brought us both a cup of tea, and Alice kept it down. She seemed so well and, encouragingly, asked for some lunch. Mrs Hearn had cooked a meal of roast mutton and vegetables. She carved a portion for Alice, and I collected it and took it to her, then returned the half-empty plate to the kitchen. Later on that day, William, Mr Thomas, that is, took the leftover part back to Alice. He came back with an empty plate and joked that he had made her eat it. Alice seemed all right after the meal, but after a few hours, she asked for some lemon juice as her mouth was dry and her throat burning. Then she started vomiting."

"How was her health in general while you were with her?"

"Alice was never strong," says Mrs Parsons. "But at no time during my stay did she have any strength whatsoever. She couldn't even feed herself. I was so worried about her I slept in the same bed."

"And how did her illness progress?"

"She took some pills after she began feeling unwell, then became very restless. At about four o'clock in the morning, my daughter started shouting for her husband. He came in and carried her into his bedroom, where she stayed. By mid-morning, her nose started bleeding heavily and did not stop until the doctor arrived at two o'clock."

"Excuse me. A question, please." A tall, straight-backed man stands from within the jury box and raises his hand.

"Admiral Moorshed. Go ahead," says the coroner.

"Mrs Parsons, what effect did the mutton meal have on your daughter?" he asks, with an air of authority. I presume he is the foreman and glance at Peter to see if he is as taken aback by the interruption as I am. Peter's features are impassive and not in the least perturbed.

"Alice was perfectly well immediately after the meal," says Mrs Parsons. "She did not get worse until the evening."

Mr Thomas is sitting quietly near the jury box next to his representative. His head jerks up as he listens to Mrs Parsons, and he points to a piece of paper. His solicitor coughs.

"Yes, Mr Wilson?" asks the coroner.

"How long was the lemon juice made before Mrs Thomas consumed it?" he asks.

Mrs Parsons looks thoughtfully into the distance. "About two hours before," she says. "It sat on the dressing table for some time."

Finally, Mrs Parsons recounts the moment the ambulance left with her daughter, and the coroner releases her. I watch her face crumple as she leaves the stand, and my heart aches for her. It does not ache for her obnoxious son Percy, who is up next.

Percy Parsons strides purposefully towards the witness stand and faces the jury, black eyes boring like gimlets. He stands, shoulders back, and his neat moustache can't conceal lips trembling with anger.

"Name?" asks the coroner.

"Percy Roy Parsons."

"Occupation?"

"Farmer, living and working at Tremaine Farm."

"November eighth," says the coroner, steepling his fingers. "Tell me about it."

"It was the day of Alice's funeral," says Percy Parsons. "I was introduced to Mrs Hearn, who I had not previously met. I asked a few questions about the day at Bude, and the answers she gave me were not satisfactory."

"What did you ask her?"

"I wanted to know what they had to eat that day. She replied, 'Tea, cake, bread and butter, and sandwiches."

"Why was that unsatisfactory?"

"She left a gap after bread and butter as if she was reluctant to mention the sandwiches."

The coroner leans forward. "I understood she made no secret about including sandwiches in the meal."

"She paused," repeats Percy Parsons, confrontationally. "And what is more, my wife asked Mrs Hearn where the sandwiches came from, and Mrs Hearn replied they came from Bude. Then she changed her mind and said they had taken the sandwiches with them. I asked her which of the statements was true, and my mother interrupted and said that Mrs Hearn had made the sandwiches. Well, all that subterfuge raised my suspicions, and I told her so."

"Told her what, exactly?"

"That I suspected there had been foul play."

I imagine the scene in my mind's eye, Annie Hearn timidly trying to explain the situation in front of three hostile members of the Parsons family. From what I now knew of her quiet demeanour, the confrontation would have terrified her. And Percy Parsons was bristling with anger in the jury box, glowering at William Thomas like a school bully. No wonder Annie fled.

The coroner interrupts my musings. "What made you suspicious of foul play?"

"The fact that my sister had been ill for ten days before anyone informed my mother or me."

"Any other reason?"

"Isn't that enough?" Parsons does not wait for an answer before continuing. "I found it puzzling that Mrs Hearn had been the only woman in the house practically the entire time to do the housework and attend to my sister."

"And you found that odd?"

"Well, to put it plainly, I heard a report that Mr Thomas and Mrs Hearn were too friendly."

"But that is hearsay?"

"Maybe, but it's what they told me."

"What was your relationship with Mr Thomas?"

"We didn't speak, nor did he approve of Annie visiting her family."

"Did your sister get on with her husband?"

"No," says Percy Parsons.

"How many times did you see them when they were not getting on well together?"

Parsons gives the coroner a withering stare. "As I said, they didn't visit."

"How many times?"

"Once."

Percy Parsons leaves the stand, and I am glad to see him go. I rarely dislike anyone on first acquaintance, but Parsons is an exception. I stare at his chair, half expecting to see a puddle of slime, but it is empty until the clerk calls Mrs Tucker, William

Thomas's neighbour. She occupies the chair just long enough to contradict Percy Parsons. Mrs Tucker smiles as she says that to her knowledge, the marriage was a happy one. I like Mrs Tucker much better than Parsons, but the chair takes on merry-go-round proportions as another witness takes the stand.

The following three witnesses are doctors. I listen intently as their factual evidence contrasts with Mrs Parsons' emotion and her son Percy's anger. I expect the doctors to spend a long time on the stand, but the coroner ushers them through with unseemly haste. Dr Saunders gives a brief account of his diagnosis of arsenic poisoning. Then Dr Millicent Fox, resident medical officer, tells of her encounter with William Thomas. She says that she told him that his wife was not suffering from food poisoning but had ingested arsenic and that the news shocked Thomas, who suffered the further indignity of being asked to keep away. They did not permit him to attend her bedside, and he could only see Alice through the window. According to the doctor, Thomas displayed genuine distress and seemed overwhelmed with concern for his wife. Finally, Dr Eric Wordley, pathologist, describes his post-mortem examination. It is no less gruesome than Mr Tickle's evidence yesterday, and I fan my face with my hand to fend off the red flush of revulsion that threatens to engulf me. Finally, it is time for the coroner to sum up, and a hush falls across the Guildhall as we listen to his words.

Dr Pearce clears his throat. "Mr Thomas was undoubtedly indiscreet," he says. "But I can find no evidence of a guilty association with Mrs Hearn. It was unwise for him to lend money to Mrs Hearn without telling his wife. And Mrs Hearn's frequent visits to the house would naturally give rise to gossip among the neighbours. I must now deal with four circumstances in connection with Mrs Hearn," he continues. "She undoubtedly prepared the sandwiches and did the cooking, as you have heard. Undeniably, she bought some weedkiller in 1926, principally comprising arsenic. If she had formed one, a plausible motive might be that if

Mr Thomas were a widower, there would be more chance of becoming his wife."

"On the other hand, you must consider that you have heard no evidence that Mrs Hearn wanted to marry Mr Thomas. Regarding the sandwiches, she did not express a desire for any particular sandwich herself. Mrs Hearn ate from the same plate as Mrs Thomas and suffered no ill effects. There was no evidence of arsenic in the sandwiches nor the cooked food. True, the opportunity was there, but did Mrs Hearn take advantage of it?"

I hear a sound to my left. Peter is nodding his head vigorously as if agreeing that she did. His lack of impartiality is annoying, and I am cross that he has distracted me from listening to every word the coroner says. I want to form an unbiased view, and so far, I've heard nothing to convince me of Annie Hearn's guilt. The coroner sips from a glass of water before resuming.

"The letter which Mrs Hearn sent to Mr Thomas," he says, "is capable of two constructions. One could ask why Mrs Hearn jumped to the conclusion that someone poisoned Mrs Thomas, especially as nobody considered the possibility until Mr Percy Parsons intervened. And he said he knew nothing other than what Mrs Hearn said herself. Was it a guilty conscience that struck her when Mr Parsons made the remark? But there is another construction, emphatically asserted in Mrs Hearn's letter. She said she was innocent of the cause of the death of Mrs Thomas. And even more remarkably, that her own passing would clear Mr Thomas. What did she mean by that?"

This time, it's my turn to nod, and I cast a smirk at Peter, who raises his eyes heavenward.

"But she is not here to defend herself," says the coroner. "And in her absence, we must not forget to give due weight to interpreting evidence in her favour as well as the other way."

His summing up concluded, the coroner sits, and a short time later, Admiral Moorshed stands and delivers the jury's conclusion. The coroner makes a formal announcement of the verdict. "Mrs Alice Thomas of Lewannick near Launceston," he says, "was murdered by arsenic poisoning. But there is no evidence to show who administered it."

And that is that. The coroner thanks the jury, the policemen and the public before dismissing us for the final time.

"She's as guilty as sin," says Malcolm, grinning as he approaches Peter. He has spent the second day of the inquest sitting with his journalist friend. I open my mouth to argue but find I don't care enough. Malcolm is boorish, and reasoning with him is pointless. "Get outside quickly," says Malcolm.

"Why?" asks Peter in a muffled voice. He is trying to find my stick, which has rolled under the seat.

"Come on – sharpish. The pressmen are trying to get an interview with Thomas."

"You go," says Peter, ever the gentleman, and Malcolm doesn't argue. He disappears apace while Peter locates my stick. We wait for the room to empty, then make our way outside. But when we leave the Guildhall, we soon realise that we have missed nothing at all. We almost walk straight into a pack of reporters who have corralled William Thomas by the side of the building. Peter raises an arm, and we retreat while staying close enough to listen.

"A few words," Mr Thomas," says a young man, scribbling furiously in a notebook. His colleague stands beside him, clutching a copy of the *Sheffield Telegraph.*

"Very well," sighs William Thomas with an air of inevitability. "This has been a terrible ordeal," he says, and his voice wobbles. Thomas licks his lips, chokes down a sob, and I dig my fingers into my palms. His misery looks like an act and not a particularly good one.

"I am not in good health," he says. "And not only have I suffered the loss of my wife, but it's amid all this mystery and suspicion. I would be happy if they found Mrs Hearn so she could throw some light on my wife's death. The jury did not name the perpetrator in the verdict, and although I am innocent, they've left me under a cloud. I have lost my wife, and now I am plunged into all this. I know I'm innocent and can face my neighbours, but I shall have to work hard to live this down and forget the terrible ordeal. I think the inquest has been fair, and I have nothing to fear, for I have told my story faithfully."

"That's all," says Mr Thomas's solicitor, raising a hand in the air. He reaches for his client and guides him away by the elbow while waiting for photographers to snap pictures of his retreating form.

"That's that," says Peter, "all done. What did you think?"

"That Thomas has got away with murder," I say.

Peter raises an eyebrow. "I can't believe you still feel that way. It's hard to credit that we were in the same inquest."

#

We are still bickering about the verdict when we get back to Smuggler's Cottage. It is our last night in Plymouth, and Peter's aunt has pushed the boat out once again, and invited Malcolm and his friend for tea. To his credit, Malcolm moderates his behaviour in front of his aunt and fills our last evening with good humour. Once again, I retire early, but Peter is enjoying himself and stays downstairs. I pass Peter's room on the way to mine and eye his door as I contemplate whether to bother attempting a dream walk tonight. I'm still tired, annoyed at the way Peter has taken against Annie Hearn, and past the point at which I care whether he believes me. I could enter his room the traditional way, take a casual glance at his bedside table and save enough time for half an hour's reading followed by the luxury of a good night's sleep. And although part of me wants to prove a point, I give in and push the door. To my disappointment, it stays shut. I turn the round black handle and try harder – nothing. Peter has locked the door and taken the key. Not only does he not believe me, but he has made sure that I won't discover the hidden object by nefarious means.

I walk to my room, stick clattering against the floorboards louder than is necessary, still furious that Peter doesn't trust me. I prop my stick against the wardrobe and dress for bed, unwilling to stay awake to prove I'm not lying. If Peter can't take me at my word, then he can forget it. I sink back into my pillows as I grab the Crawford Newson book. It's a thrilling story but I haven't spent half as much time as I expected reading lately as long days in the Guildhall have left me weary. No sooner do my eyes focus on the pages than the letters disappear in a blur as my eyelids flutter closed. Seconds later, I wake again, hands still clutching the open pages. I try but fail to fight sleep, and the book falls from my grasp and slides face up on the bedspread. I watch the words half-heartedly, too tired to summon the energy to read the book or put it back on my nightstand. I'm happy to take a lingering glance before slipping into a restful sleep. I watch the words, beautiful lines of text, small, symmetrical, and meaningful as they lay regimented on the page. But my eye turns to an undisciplined line in the middle, which throbs and pulses alarmingly among its well-behaved neighbours. And as the vowels disappear with a pop, I raise my finger and push it into the writhing text. My fingernail vanishes as I somehow knew it would. I have entered the dream state without trying. Feeling a clarity of thought at odds with my usual out-of-body consciousness, I decide to take advantage of the situation and deal with Peter's scepticism once and for all. I jump from my bed and spin around my room like a dainty ballerina, light and free, and then I explode through the door in a flurry of energy.

I stop dead in my tracks. The light is on, and someone is coming up the stairs. I fade into the wall and watch as Peter's mother ascends, still close enough to my body to feel my heart fluttering in the distance. It is the strangest thing to feel connected with remote bodily functions, and stranger still to be hiding in a landing wall. But I would die of embarrassment if Isla saw me. I stay there as she passes, and she doesn't seem to notice. Once I am alone again, I proceed towards Peter's room, wondering if the bedroom will be empty. I can't hear anything downstairs, so Malcolm must have gone, and I am paralysed into inaction while I decide whether to risk Peter seeing me. Then memories of his lack of trust spike my thoughts, and my coyness evaporates. I don't care whether I'm visible and it will serve him right if he thinks I'm a ghost. As soon as this crosses my mind, something pulls against the back of my head, and I experience an existential dread again. "No, no, no," I say, trying to direct my inner voice towards safer ground, and I slip inside Peter's room before fear overtakes me.

It is empty. Peter is not there, but he has left a night light glowing on top of the dressing table. It radiates a beam sufficient to illuminate the nightstand, upon which is a piece of paper. I make my way towards it and look down on the jagged-edged document which Peter must have torn from a jotter. He has drawn a right-facing arrow, and I follow the direction with my eyes. It points to a door, presumably a cupboard with a substantial bolt drawn across and a lock without a key. I examine the width of the wall and roll my eyes. If this is a closet, I don't know what Peter expects me to see, but I try anyway. I reach towards the door and find myself in an unlit cupboard. I can just make out the edges of a piece of paper tacked to the sidewall, and only because there is a sizeable wormhole in the door. Doubtless, it contains a written message or even another drawing for all I know. But because of Peter's cynicism, I have yet to explain the mechanics of dream walking, and he won't know how much darkness inhibits me. I can only see as much as Peter could see if he were in the room. I can't make out detail in an unlit area, nor can I snap my fingers and create light. Far from proving myself, I am no better able to solve Peter's puzzle than I would have been if I'd let myself into his room in the usual manner. Quite the contrary. At least I could have rummaged around in search of the key, which I couldn't now use, even if I found it. I flounce from the closet and swipe the arrowed paper in disgust, but it doesn't move an inch. It is a great pity because Peter has left his water glass on the nightstand and if I could, I would spill it on the bed. I blow as hard as I can, but there isn't so much as a ripple. A nebulous, unfamiliar ache pulses in the centre of my forehead as my frustration takes shape in a rare physical feeling. I am still concentrating on the glass when I hear the door handle turn and immediately flee back into the cupboard. It must be Peter, and he is talking to someone on the stairs. I listen intently.

"Yes, a wonderful time. We've been thoroughly spoiled," Peter says.

A woman's voice replies, but I can't hear her words.

"Oh, I should think so," says Peter. "She'd be pleased."

There is another muffled sentence.

"Yes, I'm sure," Peter replies. "Connie has a very vivid imagination."

I gasp so loudly that I worry he might hear me. What does he mean by vivid imagination? Is he calling me a liar? My mouth hangs open at the unfairness of his words. I am stuck in a cupboard in the middle of the night trying to solve his silly puzzle because he can't trust me. I know it is a leap of faith to believe in something that doesn't seem possible, but Peter knows me. I don't think I've ever lied to him or even in front of him. He should have made some effort to take my word at face value, but he didn't. And now he's telling someone, who by process of elimination must be his aunt, that I have an overactive imagination. It is only a short step away from calling me a liar.

As the anger builds inside me, there is a tugging at the back of my head. I want to burst from the door and scream in Peter's face, but the pull is painful, and I feel friendless and disappointed. I give in to it, and within seconds, I am back in bed, eyes brimming with unshed tears. I sleep, but it is fitful, and I wake up longing for home.

CHAPTER EIGHTEEN

Coralie Pennington

Tuesday, December 2, 1930

I am sitting in the dining room, glumly stirring a cup of tea. It has stewed for too long and is dark and unappetising, a bit like my life. I haven't seen or spoken to Peter for over a week, and I did not go to the library this morning. Peter called at the house when he finished sorting books. I watched him from the upstairs window while Elys told him I was out, as we'd agreed. Peter waited at the top of the path for a few moments, staring bemusedly at the cottage as if unsure what to make of it. He must have known something was awry. I don't go anywhere, and I never miss book changing day. It was and is the highlight of my week and it took all the self-control I possessed to stay away. But Peter has hurt me, and though I know I will get over it, I can't face him right now and need time apart.

The return journey from Plymouth was uncomfortable. I made polite conversation, but Peter had sensed my change of mood. Our usual easy chatter vanished, and the silences grew more prolonged and awkward. Fortunately, Malcolm and Mrs Tremayne were so deep in conversation that they didn't notice. And when the car pulled up, and Peter took my bag to the door, I watched his retreating form with relief. But it was short-lived. Now that I've been back in Pebble Cottage for a few days, I am as frustrated as ever, and my small world feels claustrophobic. Mrs Ponsonby was tolerable for a day, but she is once again clucking around me, checking on my every move like a broody mother hen.

Mrs Ponsonby questioned every detail of my time in Plymouth, which was difficult because I couldn't tell her about the trial. So everything she heard was a product of my imagination, though it has eased her mind. In my fictional account, Mrs Tremayne was with me every second of every day, and I comfort myself knowing that she was hardly there at all. But nothing dire occurred. I did not explode in flames or pass out from exposure to other people, so whatever fears Mrs Ponsonby had came to nothing. At least this means I can escape again in future should the possibility arise. My safely conducted visit has greatly relieved my guardian.

I check the clock. Time has inched forward a little, but the sacrifice I made in not going to the library has left me with a lot of day and not much with which to fill it. I could go for a walk, but it's blowy outside, and I'm not in the right frame of mind. I've finished the three Crawford Newson books, and I should have returned them. I'm halfway through my last library book and now must eke it out over a week, so I can't read either. I am so bored that I contemplate helping Elys in the kitchen.

I am preparing to rise and take my teacup through when I hear a loud rap at the door. I wait for Elys to answer but she must be elsewhere, and someone is impatiently hammering the door with the flat of their hand. It is an unexpected noise, and so soon after the first knock, that I jump and almost drop the cup. Where is Elys? Where, for that matter, is Mrs Ponsonby? I deposit the cup on the sideboard and pick my way down the hallway, calling "Wait a moment," as I peer into the parlour, hoping Mrs Ponsonby is around. She is not and would have to be deaf to have missed the commotion. There is nothing else for it. I'll have to answer the door myself. I inch it open and peer cautiously around the side.

"Well, look at you," says an unfamiliar voice. "You must be little Connie, though you're not so little now."

I appraise the woman in the doorway. She is in her mid-fifties and is slender and exquisitely dressed in a tailored coat. Her sleekly coiffured hair is brunette without a trace of grey. I stare in baffled amazement.

"Close your mouth, my dear. You'll catch flies," the woman says. "Can I come in?"

"No," I say. "I don't know who you are. Is Mrs Ponsonby expecting you?"

"Not exactly," she says. "Where is Vera then?"

"I don't know," I say. "She was here."

"Well, I'm not made of money," says the woman. "I can't keep the driver waiting any longer. I'll have to get my bags and hope for the best."

She disappears in a flurry of fur stole and high heels and makes towards a smart Bentley parked to the left of Pebble Cottage. Moments later, she returns with a uniformed driver, puffing as he carries two heavy suitcases with a carpetbag tucked under his arm.

"Pop them inside," commands the woman.

"You can't," I say. "What will I tell Mrs Ponsonby? And who are you?"

"Don't you recognise me?"

"No," I say emphatically.

"Well, it's been a good few years," she says. "Probably the best part of twenty."

"No wonder I don't know you," I say, feeling a surge of irritation now that I am less surprised.

"Coralie Pennington," she says, thrusting a well-manicured hand towards me. I lightly shake it, unable to overcome habit even though she is not welcome, and I'm not at all sure I believe her. "Now, are you going to invite me in?"

"I don't know," I say. Then the kitchen door opens, and Mrs Ponsonby appears, followed by Elys.

"Ah, Vera. There you are."

Mrs Ponsonby looks up and stops motionless in the hallway. For a few moments, she stares in shocked silence, then speaks with a tremble in her voice. "What are you doing here?"

"What sort of greeting is that to an old friend," says Coralie.

"I'm sorry. I didn't mean to be rude. This is so unexpected," says Mrs Ponsonby.

"Well, I received your parcel and then had a bit of trouble, and I thought, I know, I'll visit Vera. She'll know what to do."

"But I thought we'd agreed never to…" Mrs Ponsonby's words trail away.

"It's been twenty years, Vee," says Coralie, as I stop myself sniggering at her pet name. "Nothing has happened, nor will it. I'm tired and cold. Now, can I please come in?"

Mrs Ponsonby beckons her inside.

"I'll see to your bags," says Elys.

"But where will she sleep?" asks Mrs Ponsonby.

"She can take my room. I'll go to my mum's for a few nights. Don't worry. She's only a mile away, and I can be back here in time for breakfast."

"Or she could stay at the hotel?" I offer, outraged at the suggestion that Elys should make way for the uninvited visitor.

"No," says Mrs Ponsonby.

"I could if it's too much trouble," says Coralie. "But it would be better if I stayed somewhere less public."

Mrs Ponsonby raises an eyebrow. "Could you fetch some tea, Elys," she asks, then directs Coralie Pennington into the parlour. I follow, but Mrs Ponsonby holds her hand across the door. "We'd like a little privacy," she says before shutting the door in my face.

I hobble up the stairs and find Elys on the landing. She has deposited the suitcases in her room, and her face is puffy and red with exertion from carrying the weighty luggage.

"Who does she think she is?" I ask angrily.

"Oh, I don't mind," says Elys.

"Well, you should. How dare she. What gives her the right?"

"They are old friends," says Elys.

"How do you know?"

"Mrs Ponsonby has mentioned her once or twice. They used to work together."

"Where?"

"I don't know. Mrs Ponsonby didn't say."

"Well, I don't like it."

"That's up to you, Connie," she says. "But I can't stay here gossiping. I must make tea."

I slump on the bed, contemplating how badly the day is going. I have nothing to do, and now I am banished from the parlour. I may as well go to sleep. Sleep – I wonder? I have never tried dream walking in daylight hours. Not once, not ever. But if I could, then I might find out what they are talking about downstairs without me. I light the candle and stare.

#

Only seconds pass before I feel a frisson of goosebumps followed by a vibration that tingles from forehead to feet. I know at once that my plan has worked, and I have attained my goal quicker than ever before. I rise quickly, conscious of the conversation going on downstairs. I want to hear every word, and I lose no time in making for the door. Instinctively, I reach for the door handle, but it evades my grasp, and just before I pass through, I look back at my sleeping body. That one glance is enough to feel the now familiar pull in the back of my head, but it isn't as painful as before, and I find it easy to ignore.

Seconds later, I am outside the parlour listening to Mrs Ponsonby's voice growing shriller. I can't quite hear what she's saying and decide to risk entering in the hope that they won't see me. I slip through the door, but Mrs Ponsonby stops and looks around as I arrive. I quickly duck behind the sofa, feeling foolish.

"What was that?" asks Mrs Ponsonby.

"What, Vee?" asks Coralie.

"I don't know. Something's wrong. I haven't felt like this since…"

"Since Operation Calico."

I wonder what has triggered this memory. Surely, they can't see me. Yet Mrs Ponsonby's disquiet coincided with my entry into the room. The two women have fallen into silence and quietly examine their surroundings, eyes darting from wall to ceiling.

"Wait a moment," says Coralie as she stands, places her hands on the windowsill and leans forward, scrutinising the outside. "There's nothing out there."

"What did you expect to see?" asks Mrs Ponsonby. "It doesn't work that way."

"I know. I thought it might be Robert."

"Your husband? Why would he come here?"

Coralie sighs and closes her eyes as if in pain.

"He shouldn't turn up," she says. "He doesn't know where you live."

"Quite right too," says Mrs Ponsonby curtly. "But that doesn't explain why you think he might appear."

"I don't think he will, but it depends."

"On what?"

"On whether he comes looking for me."

"You haven't?" Mrs Ponsonby stares, open-mouthed, at her friend.

"I didn't intend to. It just happened."

"I will never forgive you if you bring trouble to my door after all this time and the sacrifices I've made."

"It's not a risk unless he's followed me, and I'm sure he hasn't. I left without notice. He wasn't there, and he didn't see me pack."

"But he's a bloody politician, Cora. With friends in high places."

"And low ones," Coralie says, shaking her head. I barely notice her in my shock at Mrs Ponsonby's language. She hasn't sworn in all the years I have known her. Judging by the state of her clenched hands and pale cheeks, she is seething with barely controlled anger.

"Does he know who I am?" hisses Mrs Ponsonby. "Does he?"

"Only that you're an old friend. He thinks you live abroad."

"Unless he saw the parcel with the Cornish postmark."

"Good Lord, no," says Coralie, lightening the mood with a soft laugh. "The butler brings our post separately."

"So, the butler will have seen the postmark."

"He won't say anything," says Coralie, shaking her head. She is wearing a pair of drop earrings covered in sparkling stones, which twinkle with every movement. When I first noticed the earrings, I assumed they were costume jewellery, but now I am not sure, given this talk of butlers. If they are real diamonds, then Coralie Pennington is a wealthy woman, but this does not accord with someone who baulks at the idea of staying in a hotel. I stare, entranced, as Mrs Ponsonby gets to her feet and starts pacing the room.

"I wish I'd never sent the bloody thing," she says. "I thought it would be safe after twenty years, and it was your birthday, and I was feeling nostalgic. Haven't you got any other friends to go to?"

Coralie swallows. "Not real friends, no," she says. "I thought I had, but when the scandal broke – well, they all took Robert's side."

"I am surprised you remember where we live after all this time," says Mrs Ponsonby.

"It hasn't changed since the day we found it," says Coralie. "It's lovely and homely."

"Don't patronise me," says Mrs Ponsonby bitterly. She's clenching her jaw, and a flush of red has settled over her pale cheeks.

"That's not my intention," says Coralie. "I know you had the rough end of the deal."

Mrs Ponsonby shoots her a withering glare. "I'm not going to dignify that with a reply. Why are you here, Coralie? What do you want from me that's worth the risk?"

"I don't think there is a risk – truly, I don't. I just need somewhere to stay for a few weeks until the furore has died down."

I hear a cough, and the door opens to reveal Elys carrying a tray. If I am visible, then she will see me. There is nowhere to hide from her viewpoint. But she says nothing and deposits the tray on the coffee table before retreating. Mrs Ponsonby coughs, and I crane my neck before realising to my horror that she has perched on the arm of the sofa, and I have brushed my head through her leg. She flinches as if burned.

"What is it, Vee?"

Mrs Ponsonby shudders. "A goose walked over my grave," she says. I shrink back into the sofa. She definitely feels my presence. Yet Elys didn't.

"Come here, Vera," says Coralie Pennington, patting the seat beside her. This won't be easy, but I'll tell you what happened, and you might feel able to help."

Mrs Ponsonby takes the offered seat and perches on its edge, legs facing towards the door as if she would rather be anywhere else than here. "Is it another man?"

"How well you know me," says Coralie, sarcastically.

"I didn't mean to imply…"

"I think you did. There was a time when you respected me."

"I do," says Mrs Ponsonby. "It's a shock after all these years. I trust you as well as I ever did."

"Good," says Coralie. "It's not a man. She's a woman – Robert's fancy woman. He's been seeing her for years, and everyone knew but me."

Mrs Ponsonby gasps. "I don't know what to say. I'm shocked and saddened for you."

"And you're no doubt wondering how I missed it after the heady days of our youth. How many husbands did we catch at it?"

"More than I can remember. I'm so sorry."

"It gets worse," says Coralie. "He has a child. A six-year-old son."

Mrs Ponsonby's face crumples. "Oh, my dear," she says, patting Coralie's hand as a tear trickles down her face.

"Don't. You'll make me start."

"He's a rat. I never liked him," says Mrs Ponsonby, wiping her face. She pulls a handkerchief from her sleeve and blows loudly.

"I can't say you didn't warm me."

"Your marriage lasted two decades. Long enough to prove me wrong."

"No. You were right," says Coralie. "My marriage has been a sham for the last ten years, at least. But the humiliation of finding out about Rory was the final straw. Trudie Farquharson let it slip at a dinner party, and I made a terrible scene. Robert was furious, and because I humiliated him in front of his friends, he saw no reason for any further subterfuge. Robert has openly walked out with this woman in public, and I found out last week that they'd spent a fortnight at his mother's house. Robert is powerful, and his lady friend has money. They want to marry, but I won't give him the satisfaction of a divorce."

"Wouldn't it be easier to let go?" asks Mrs Ponsonby.

"Perhaps, but I need time to think. It is too much to bear."

"You can stay here for as long as you need to," says Mrs Ponsonby.

Coralie bites her lip, and the tears she has held in for so long start to flow. She puts her head in her hands and wails, guttural sobs wracking her slender body. Mrs Ponsonby puts her arm around her friend and buries her nose in her hair. It is time to go. I slide through the door, make my way to the bedroom, walk inside, and stand in front of my sleeping body, feeling awkward. I don't know what comes next, and it hasn't happened for a long time. Not since the early days when I didn't know what dream walking was, let alone how unusual. I struggle to remember how I used to return to my body without the prompting tug. I stare at myself, feeling adrift, and wonder what to do next. Then, perhaps from some forgotten memory, or primal instinct, I reach to touch my arm. And at once, I am absorbed back inside myself, melded and complete. I wake and sit up, brain banging with all I have seen and heard. Who is Vera Ponsonby? Who is she? This woman who has guarded me wolflike for all these years is a stranger. I don't know her at all. I pull my legs up and hunch over, hugging my knees as I stare at the sea beyond. I am still staring when Elys calls me for supper.

CHAPTER NINETEEN

Peter's House

Friday, December 12, 1930

It is seventeen days and four hours since I last spoke to Peter, and I miss him so much that I can't remember why I was cross with him in the first place. I haven't been to the hotel for ages and have resorted to reading old copies of *Women's Own* to get through the day. Elys smuggled newspapers in for a while until Mrs Ponsonby found out, and I am now cut off from the outside world with no books or visits. I am so miserable that I haven't been for a walk since Monday and feel weaker than ever. The only light in an otherwise tedious existence is Coralie Pennington's presence. She is currently installed in Elys' bedroom and not at all what I expected. Though stuffy to start with, Coralie has a wicked sense of humour that grows bolder the longer she's here. She spends the evenings in the parlour with Mrs Ponsonby while I keep to my bedroom or the dining room. But whenever Mrs Ponsonby leaves the house, Coralie seeks me out, befriending me and telling me about her glamorous life married to a politician.

"Call me Cora," she said, the day after she arrived, and I have done so ever since, even though Mrs Ponsonby purses her lips whenever she hears it. But though Cora Pennington tells me all the exciting details about her former life, she has not mentioned the separation. And I am careful not to let the cat out of the bag. But she is good fun, and the house knows more laughter, and we play the occasional card game now she is here. And when we talk, it is as if I am chatting to a woman of my own age. I want to tell her about my quarrel with Peter, but I haven't had a chance yet. And if I do, it won't be for a while as she has popped out with Mrs P, and I am alone. Even Elys is too busy to talk.

I adjust my position on the couch and stare outside as I slouch over the windowsill, chin in hand. I can see the rear of the hotel, and it is busy with delivery drivers and hotel staff crisscrossing the snow-laden lane as they stock up for Christmas. The big day is only two weeks away, and things are getting busy. Dolly, who is now back at the hotel, will be rushed off her feet. I wonder if Peter has seen her yet, and I feel crushed at the thought of them talking together without me.

I didn't realise how much I missed Peter until a few nights ago. He was not in the flesh as usual, but I saw him suddenly and unexpectedly in the middle of the night in a waking dream. That dream was another first. I did not instigate it, nor did I wake in my bed to find myself detached from my body. One moment I was asleep, and the next, I was conscious in a completely different place, wandering around as if in a daze. That moment between the soundness of sleep and the disorientation of being somewhere unknown filled me with blind panic. I was so frightened that I almost allowed the tug on my head to take me home. Had I not recognised one of the fishermen's cottages by the chandlers, I would have allowed the pull to take me. But I resisted because I knew that I wasn't far from Peter's house if I was near the harbour.

The lanes were dark, and an early morning haze drifted through the silent streets. Here and there, a door opened, and a bleary-eyed worker emerged to begin the day. It must have been four thirty, maybe five o'clock, as I drifted towards Peter's house with little effort.

I hesitated for a moment outside the pathway that led to his familiar red door. I wanted to see him so badly that I went in, not knowing if he would even be there. But Peter was in his bedroom and sleeping soundly, snoring as the sheets rose and fell to the sound of his breathing. His room was unlit, but dawn was breaking, and I smiled at the sight of piles of books over his chest of drawers. They were on the floor by the bed, on the nightstand and hanging out of an open cupboard. The thought of a usually organised Peter being untidy in his natural surroundings made me giggle, and I watched over his sleeping form, half wishing he would wake, though he wouldn't see me if he did, so I took a look at a sheaf of papers carelessly strewn across Peter's washstand. He appeared to be reading for the part of Cayley Drummle in *The Second Mrs Tanqueray* and had asterisked the relevant pages.

I am still thinking of that night in Peter's bedroom when there is a knock at the door. I must have been deep in my reverie to have missed someone coming to the cottage. They knock again, and I peer through the window to see the postman carrying a heavy bag over his shoulder, huffing a cold plume into the frosty air. It is warm inside, and I wait to see if Elys will hurry up the hallway and collect the post as usual, but she doesn't, so I make my way to the door. The postman nods as he hands me a small parcel and three envelopes. I take them and put them on the sideboard without looking, then retreat into the parlour. I am comfortable again when the door opens, and Mrs Ponsonby and Cora bustle through, letting in a draught. I listen while they discuss their coffee morning at St Columb Church and their near-miss as the coach slid on some compacted snow. I wonder why they didn't invite me. I'm not religious; none of us is, but it's a pretty church, and I would like to have gone with them, despite the snowfall. They are still chatting when Elys opens the door and gives the parcel to Cora before extracting two letters which she thrusts towards me. My heart skips a beat when I see one envelope addressed to me in Peter's scratchy hand, but I save it and open the second letter instead. It is from Mary Newson and contains a formal invitation to Bosula for Christmas and an accompanying note for Mrs Ponsonby. I pass it to her straight away, knowing that however long I hold on to it, the answer will be a resounding no. She takes it and raises an eyebrow. "What's this?" she asks.

"Open it," I say. There's no point in trying to explain.

She slits the envelope and examines the brief note inside.

"No, dear," she says. "It's impossible."

My heart sinks, but I am not surprised. I knew she would never agree.

"What is it, Vee?" asks Cora. Mrs Ponsonby sighs and hands her the letter.

"I could take her," she says.

"Absolutely not," says Mrs Ponsonby. "It's out of the question." Cora opens her mouth again, but Mrs Ponsonby silences her with a withering stare. I place Mary's letter on the coffee table. I will thank her and reply later. It is a pity but so wholly anticipated that I am not unduly miserable. I open Peter's letter and withdraw the page in gleeful anticipation but stop before unfolding the single piece of paper. It is short, very short, and too concise to be news. I wonder if he is still angry. Perhaps he has written to tell me never to darken his door again. My hands shake as I unfold the note.

I don't know where you've been, Connie, or what's wrong, but this has gone on long enough. I have news about Annie Hearn, and I'm coming to Pebble Cottage on Friday at two o'clock. Don't go anywhere. P.

I smile in relief. Peter is undoubtedly irritated, but he still wants to see me. He is still my friend, and he brings news of Annie. I clutch the letter to my chest, disappointment at Mrs Ponsonby's reaction forgotten at the thought of Peter's impending visit. Lunch cannot come quickly enough, and I wait impatiently for his arrival.

CHAPTER TWENTY

Exhumation

"You'll never guess where I've been?" Peter doesn't waste a moment as he blurts out the sentence while standing on the doorstep.

"Come in," I say, guiding him to the dining room where we can speak undisturbed.

"Go on. Guess."

"Plymouth?" I suggest.

"Don't be silly. We've only just been there."

"Where then?"

"Lewannick."

"Oh, my goodness. To Annie's house?"

"Not exactly. To the graveyard. I suppose you haven't seen the newspapers?"

"Of course not," I say.

"I thought Elys was keeping you supplied."

"She got caught," I reply, squirming with embarrassment. I could understand the problem if Elys was bringing me alcohol or inappropriate reading material. But Mrs Ponsonby's ire at discovering a newspaper in our house went beyond the pale.

"Shame," says Peter. "But worry ye not. That's why I'm here. To bring you news of the exhumation, though I jolly nearly didn't make it with all the snow. I've never seen anything like it."

"What exhumation?" I ask.

Peter sheds his coat, hangs it over a chair and fumbles inside his pocket. He withdraws a crumpled newspaper. "Look at this," he says, pushing it towards me.

I grasp it eagerly. "The *Western Morning News*," I murmur. "The tenth of December. That's two days ago."

"I know," says Peter.

"I can't believe you didn't tell me straight away."

"You've been in a strange mood recently, Connie," says Peter. Besides, we were stranded in the village overnight because the snow was so deep. Malcolm dug our car out of a snowdrift, but it wouldn't start. We were lucky that someone took us in and gave us a bed for the night."

"So, you've only just got back?"

"Not quite, but rest assured, I found my way to you as soon as possible."

"I know. Thank you," I say, poring over the paper again.

"Oh, don't bother," says Peter, snatching it away. "It's more interesting if I tell you what happened, and Mrs Ponsonby might come in."

I nod. "Go ahead," I say, agog with interest.

"Well, it wasn't much of a secret that there was going to be an exhumation. The press has been speculating for a while now. But Malcolm knows a policeman who received a tip-off – an excellent tip-off, as it turns out. Malcolm asked to borrow Mother's vehicle, and I had a quick word with her to ensure that borrowing it was conditional on Malcolm taking me along. Quite a tall order as I was going to work that day, but Mother smoothed it over with Mr Whitstable. She must have done a good job too, as he was all smiles and sympathy this morning."

I think of Peter's capricious employer, who was as likely to be cantankerous as he was to be genial and wonder what Mrs Tremayne said, but I don't mention it. I am all ears for the news. "So, you went straight to Lewannick?" I ask instead.

"Immediately," says Peter. "We arrived mid-afternoon and waited until dusk arrived. I thought there must be a mistake, but Malcolm told me to be patient. Other pressmen had said it would happen under cover of darkness. And sure enough, as night fell, a truck of labourers arrived and set up a rudimentary shelter using tarpaulin and poles."

"Could you see the bodies?" I ask disappointedly.

"No, and I know it sounds macabre, but even though there was little to see, it was still exciting. Snow fell again – fat flakes spun through the air and settled all around us. We stood as close to the graves as possible, and the atmosphere was electric, though eerie. It's hard to imagine without being there, but we were in the middle of a graveyard, in a snowstorm, hypnotised by the swirling wind and falling flakes. All we could hear was the clunk of spades and thuds of soil as the labourers dug ever deeper."

"Why were they digging her body up?"

"Who?"

"Mrs Thomas."

"Not her, Connie. They'd only just buried Alice Thomas, and the police knew full well that she'd been poisoned. No. They exhumed Lydia and Mary Ann Everard."

"Who are they?"

"Annie Hearn's sister and aunt."

"The devils," I breathe. "As if Annie isn't unhappy enough. They've persecuted her so badly, she had no choice but to run away, and now they're wasting time digging up her family. I can't believe it."

"I thought you'd understand," says Peter.

"Why would I? I haven't seen you since Plymouth."

"I'm sure they speculated about this at the inquest."

"I must have missed it," I say. I am shocked and sit back in my chair, feeling close to tears. I don't know why I'm affected by this news, but it's almost as if they had disinterred my kin. My heart breaks for Annie.

"Are you feeling alright?" asks Peter.

I nod. "Yes, I am. I can't explain why this news makes me feel so sad, but it does."

"Perhaps I should leave the rest of the story for another day," says Peter.

"No. Tell me now."

"Well, they dug only partway down that night," says Peter. "And eventually we went back to the car and stayed there until dawn when the sexton arrived, and they started up again. The labourers worked through rain and sleet, and we stood in the shelter of the trees watching as they finally unearthed two coffins. They cleaned off the worst of the soil and took them into the tent."

I shudder. "How horrible," I say.

"It was both horrible and fascinating," says Peter. "The coffins were so far down that we could only see the tips of the labourers' spades appearing above the earth as they tossed out the soil. Then the officials arrived. Do you remember Superintendent Pill?"

I nod. "He was at the inquest."

"And also at the exhumation, together with the coroner and the vicar of Lewannick. The vicar said a few words as they pulled the coffins free. And then, the strangest thing happened, Connie. Two owls were sitting on a low-hanging branch almost immediately above the graves. They were there during the whole exhumation and didn't move. Not once, throughout all the activity. It was as if they were watching and waiting for something to happen, like winged guardians."

"I thought you didn't believe in such things," I say, waspishly. The comment washes over Peter without a reaction.

"Then what happened?"

"Nothing really," he says. "The pathologist arrived, but we couldn't see much after that. We waited for a while and collected as much information as we could."

"You mean you gossiped," I say.

"Fair point. It was, and we did, then we went to start the car, and it wouldn't go."

"Rotten luck," I say sympathetically.

"Connie, we were starving," says Peter. "And nobody was around, only policemen and the press. You would have thought the villagers would have shown some interest, but there was hardly anyone there. Luckily, the village carpenter was nearby."

"I wonder why?"

"He opened the coffins," says Peter. "And presumably had to put them back together again for reinterment. We fell into conversation, and he offered us a room for the night and a very reasonable supper. Malcolm was one of the few pressmen able to witness the reburials. But he was in a filthy mood for the rest of the night."

"Why?"

"Because he couldn't file copy until the next day, which meant some of the other news accounts went to publication first."

"Couldn't he telephone it through?"

"The weather was awful," says Peter. "Nothing worked the way it should."

"Well. There wasn't much to report anyway," I say.

"No, but then fate stepped in. Malcolm woke up in a much better frame of mind and sent for a mechanic to repair the car. While waiting, he decided to make the most of his time in the village and asked questions. Far from being reticent, almost everyone was willing to give their opinion on the exhumations. It took us two hours to finish interviewing, but it was worth every minute."

"Who did you talk to?"

"Who didn't we talk to?" asks Peter, grinning fit to burst. "We started with Elizabeth Spear, Mrs Hearn's next-door neighbour. Mr

Harper, the carpenter, had said something about a will, so Malcolm asked if she knew anything about it. She didn't, and neither did Mrs Tucker at the corner shop. But they said that Mary Ann Everard, Annie Hearn's aunt, had left Annie her entire estate when she died. Quite a motive, don't you think?"

"It depends how much she left her," I say.

Peter ignores me. "By good fortune, the auctioneer was in Lewannick while we were there," says Peter. "Malcolm asked about Trenhorne House, and he said that he had let it to Mrs Hearn about five years before. Then, immediately before she vanished in November, she wrote to him terminating the lease. Annie Hearn said that any monies owed should come from the furniture in the house which she owned. Even you can't say that isn't suspicious."

"It's exactly what I would expect of someone hounded away from their home who was contemplating taking their life," I say indignantly. Peter is so set in his poor opinion of Annie that he cannot see things any way but his.

"I disagree," says Peter. "But let's not argue. Guess who we saw next?"

I raise a sarcastic smile. "I am not playing that game," I say and silently wait for Peter to reply.

He gives up quickly. "William Thomas," he says. "He was in Congdon's shop with Mrs Tucker. She's his cousin."

"Irrelevant," I say in the manner of a high court judge.

Peter smiles. "I suppose it is," he says. "But Malcolm asked him what he thought of the exhumation, and he replied."

"I'm surprised," I say.

"I'm not. Thomas was very cooperative, though I could see the sadness etched across his face. He said that anything concerning his wife was naturally painful. Seeing her photo in the papers now she was no longer alive, had caught him unawares a few times. But he seemed grateful for the conduct of the press. He impressed Malcolm when he said that they'd been civil and gentlemanly when he'd asked for privacy."

"Poor man," I say, before remembering that if Annie hadn't killed Alice, then he almost certainly had.

"Malcolm asked him if Annie Hearn had left a will, and he said that he thought not," continued Peter. "Then Mrs Tucker said that Annie Hearn kept her private life very much to herself and that neither her sister nor her aunt had ever met Annie's husband."

"Well, she was a widow," I say defensively. "And her marriage may have been short." But even as I say the words, something about Annie's marital status feels wrong. I don't tell Peter, though, as he is utterly convinced of Annie's guilt.

"There's quite a lot to think about," Peter says. "Do you still believe she's innocent?"

"I nod. You have said nothing to make me change my mind."

"What if they find arsenic in the bodies?" he asks.

I recoil in surprise. For all the talk of exhumations, it hadn't occurred to me that they might actually find something. "I don't think it's likely," I say, uncertainly.

"But if they do?"

"I'll tell you my opinion then," I say. "This is not one of your plays."

"I have news on that front," says Peter excitedly.

"I know. You're performing *The Second Mrs Tanqueray*, and they've cast you as Cayley Drummle."

Peter stares at me with his mouth hanging open and his eyes wide and round.

"What's wrong?" I ask.

"What did you say?"

I am about to repeat myself when the penny drops, and I realise my mistake. I say nothing but wait for him to speak.

"Nobody's aware yet," says Peter. "Not a single soul. Not even my mother. How could you possibly know?"

I raise an eyebrow, wondering if it's worth trying to explain. Peter won't believe me, and if he's careless of my feelings, we might fall out again. But as sensible as it would be to keep my silence, I can't help myself.

"Try tidying your room occasionally," I say. "It's unbelievably messy, and if you leave your script on the washstand, it won't stay private for long. And while we're on the subject, don't leave silly arrows for people to find that lead straight into dark cupboards. The rules of physics apply in the astral world too, and it's impossible to move physical objects. You're infuriating."

Peter is still catching flies. His eyes dart from side to side, and I detect a faint tic on the top of his cheek. It is a reaction with which I am familiar, and it means that he is processing something. He doesn't speak for several minutes, and when he does, he utters a trivial comment about the weather. He is still making stilted conversation when Elys walks in, followed by Cora and Mrs Ponsonby. Peter flounders in the group of women, seemingly unable to make small talk. His face is pallid, his cheeks scarlet, and he looks distinctly uncomfortable. I am not in the least surprised when he makes his excuses and leaves.

CHAPTER TWENTY-ONE

Bosula

Friday, December 19, 1930

I am writing this journal from my room in the east wing of a large country house set close to the coast near Bosula. My window overlooks the bay, and after only a few hours, life feels as settled as it does at Pebble Cottage. It is blowy today, and dusk is falling as I gaze across the choppy water towards the horizon, and my heart flips with excitement as I contemplate the coming week. I still can't believe I'm here, still don't know the magical, honeyed words that Coralie Pennington employed to convince Mrs Ponsonby to let me join Mary Newson for Christmas. And although her agreement came with an embarrassing condition, it is not onerous. Mrs Ponsonby insisted I must have a chaperone, so Cora volunteered. Mary was more than happy to host her, especially having a widowed mother who enjoys new company, and Cora is nothing if not entertaining.

Still, Mrs Ponsonby was more than a little morose when we left this morning, and she waved us off with her head bowed as if the weight of the world was on her shoulders. She will spend her

Christmas with Isla Tremayne and has nothing to complain about, though whether the same can be said for Peter is a moot point. For a young man to be stuck with two elderly ladies on Christmas Day falls short of desirable, even if Peter is used to spending the festive season with his mother. Perhaps he won't mind. But it's not my problem to ponder, and I am thrilled at the prospect of Christmas at Cormorant House with Mary Newson and her artist friends.

I didn't realise until I arrived that many of them live communally, sharing resources and chores. Most of the artists and their families live in the big house with one or two residing in small cottages within the grounds. Cormorant House is enormous, and I will never get to see all of it, but the spacious accommodation allows plenty of visitors and Cora, and I are not the only guests this yuletide.

I rise, take my stick, and examine my face in the mirror. I have already applied light makeup, and I am dressed for dinner and waiting for Cora to arrive. Though the artists carry out many of the routine daily tasks in their spare time, they employ the services of a cook and a maid. I may not meet them all tonight as they eat dinner in different sittings but that's a good thing as I cannot cope with too many people at once. It makes me feel hideously self-conscious.

I hear a soft tap at the door, which opens to reveal Cora.

"Are you ready?" she asks. I nod, trying to stifle a yawn. I am looking forward to supper, but the journey has caught up with me, and I am beyond tired.

"Come on then," she says, linking her arm through mine, and we make our way along the landing.

"There you are," says Mary, as she spies us descending the stairs. "Come through." She guides us into the dining room, towards a large but shabby area to one side of the table where several battered sofas cluster around a large, stone coffee table strewn with art magazines. "Can I fetch you a drink?"

"Rather," says Cora, and I nod. "Gin, wine or something else?"

"Either will do nicely," says Cora.

"Gin," I mumble, hoping that it's a single measure.

Mary returns in due course carrying three drinks and she is accompanied by an older woman who bears such an obvious familial resemblance she's evidently her mother. Mary introduces us, and we sit on the sofas and chat until a few more people arrive.

"Ah, new blood," says a white-haired man walking briskly towards us. He throws himself into a leather chair by the fireplace, narrowly avoiding spilling his whisky. "Do you paint?" he asks.

I look towards Mary in a blind panic, unsure what to say.

"No, she doesn't. Connie is my guest," says Mary. "As is Coralie. This gentleman is Gulliver Harding, an inspiration to us all. You might say that he's the father of the colony."

"Surely he's not old enough," says Cora, with a slow, deliberate wink. I cringe with embarrassment. She is in her mid-fifties, still married and openly flirting with a much older man. But Gulliver Harding beams at her and they begin a conversation, heads bowed and laughing. With one sentence, she has destroyed the bounds of English reserve, and they are chatting as if they have known each other all their lives. I watch her enviously, only half-hearing Mary's conversation, as I wonder how Cora has the self-confidence to behave with such audacity. There are days when I can't bring myself to look in the mirror, yet here she is glowing with excitement and the love of human company.

Next to join us is a woman in her late thirties, perhaps early forties. It is hard to tell as her slim build defies certainty. She has high cheekbones, arched eyebrows, and a superior catlike smile. "This is my dear friend Boo Lyons," says Mary and Boo watches me through half-closed eyes as if she is sizing me up. For a moment, I sense a frisson of dislike – jealousy perhaps, but by the time we have finished our gins, Mary, Boo, and I have found common ground discussing the works of the Brontë sisters and all awkwardness has vanished. Soon the maid enters and ostentatiously bangs the gong. I wonder at the formality, but it doesn't take long to realise that it is the artist's idea of a joke. There are no butlers or waiting staff. It is all hands on deck. Mary guides us to the table and shows us where to sit while the others head towards the kitchen and return laden with food dishes.

Dinner is a free-for-all, and we help ourselves to whatever is within reach. The food is basic, but the artists have spared no expense on the wine and have liberally scattered bottles across the table. Cora sits to my left and Mary to my right. Opposite me is a young man called Carrington Blake, who bears a passing resemblance to Kit Maltravers. He chats easily with Mary and Boo but largely ignores me, and after a while, the silence becomes uncomfortable. Fortunately, Cora brings me into her conversational orbit. "Have you met Stephan?" she asks, nodding to the man sitting next to Carrington Blake.

"Not yet," I say brightly, trying to mask my social awkwardness.

He leans across and offers his hand, shaking vigorously, and nearly knocking the wine bottle flying. "Stephan St John, painter of seascapes," he announces.

"Like Turner?" I ask.

"Only in terms of subject matter," he replies, pulling a face.

I cringe inwardly, wishing I knew more about art. I thought I was on safe ground comparing him with such a skilful artist but judging by the look on his face, I have fallen short.

"I'm an impressionist," he says, "Turner was a romanticist."

"I see," I reply disingenuously, knowing that I am completely out of my depth. Carrington Blake breaks from his conversation with Boo. "Would you like to know the difference?" he asks, and my cheeks burn red. "Yes," I say, wishing the ground would open up and swallow me. I neither know nor care, but he's forced me into replying in the affirmative because any other response would appear rude. I wish he'd just left me alone in my ignorance. I try to look interested as he explains, and I am no doubt better educated by the time he has finished. I thank him, but neither of us can think of anything else to say, and Stephan St John breaks the silence.

"Have you met the lovely Coralie yet?" he booms at Carrington.

"I'm sorry?"

"I'm trying to introduce you," he continues, and I'm sure I detect a slight slur in his speech. "This is Coralie, er Mrs, or should I say Miss. Dash it, what is your name?"

"Pennington," says Coralie with a self-assured smile.

"God. You're not related to that rotter, Bob Pennington, I hope?"

Coralie purses her lips, and I feel for her. She still hasn't told me about her marital problems and would be mortified if they spilt out publicly over the dinner table. There is only one solution, and I take it. I reach for my wineglass and accidentally knock it, sloshing red wine across the table and splattering Carrington Blake. He jumps back as if scalded.

"Oh no," he says, dabbing at his formerly white shirt with a napkin.

"I'm so sorry, I say."

"Clumsy girl," says St John, shaking his head, thoughts of Robert Pennington forgotten. Coralie glances towards me, her face a mask of restraint. "It was an accident," she says. "I'll sort it out. Go and change," she says to Carrington. "Quick smart if you don't want it to stain."

He does what she says, returning five minutes later clad in a fresh shirt and thrusts the stained one at Cora.

"You don't have to do this," he says as she takes it from him. Cora disappears into the kitchen, leaving me feeling adrift. But Mary steps in and carries the conversation while we pick at platters of fruit. We have moved to the comfortable sofas by the time Coralie returns, with Carrington sitting some distance away. "It's clean now," she says. "Nothing to worry about, and I've told him where to get it in the morning."

I thank her, but she responds with an enigmatic smile. "We'll talk later," she says, and the rest of the evening soon passes as we get to know the other members of the colony. I am too tired to wait up for Coralie and leave her talking to Stephan St John as I return to my room, desperate for a good night's sleep.

CHAPTER TWENTY-TWO

Attack

He comes in the night and tries to possess me. I have fallen asleep on top of my bed but wake on the astral plane. Darkness surrounds me; indigo skies peppered with twinkling stars. I am awake; I am sleeping, but I am not alone. I see his portly form before me, his pale jowly face only inches from mine. If I were in physical form, I could reach out and touch him. I could smell his breath and run my fingers over the embossed silver pendant he wears around his neck. His eyes lock mine, and I am trapped in his gaze like a mongoose in thrall to a cobra. I can't move, yet my mind is active, and somehow I know I must protect myself. He is trying to find me. My presence in the world holds some importance to him. I know this without a spoken word as he probes my mind, his thirst for knowledge projecting like creeping tendrils through my memories. They slide, oily black and insidious as he snuffles my thoughts like a truffle pig. I resist and project an iron shutter. It slams through the tendrils, snapping them clean away, and they skitter along the floor, leaving slimy trails in their wake. Then they vanish into the darkness.

His eyes flicker, and he winces and stares at me as if he cannot comprehend what has happened. My mind is clear. I have successfully blocked him this time. But as I watch his lip curl in disgust, I understand the scope of his power. He has brought me here by means I do not understand, unwilling and afraid. And because I don't know how he did it, I cannot stop him in the future. But he doesn't know where my earthly body lies. What does he want with me? Why the desperate need to find me? I am nothing to him, with no meaning or importance. But I have learned one thing tonight – I have an inherent instinct to protect myself. It is dark, and I know I can flee. So, I close my eyes against the stars, and his bottomless eyes, feel the now-familiar vibration and will myself back to safety.

CHAPTER TWENTY-THREE

Cormorant House

Saturday, December 20, 1930

"I thought we would visit Crawford's house today," says Mary Newson, after breakfast.

I raise an eyebrow, wondering if I have misheard. I am still groggy from my broken night's sleep, but I know Crawford is dead and wonder why she should suggest this.

"It's Laura," says Mary, "Crawford's wife. She's lonely, and I visit her most weekends".

"Will she mind us coming?" asks Coralie.

"Not at all. Laura knows I have guests and has asked me to bring you along."

"Then, that would be lovely," I say, exchanging glances with Coralie, who is smiling at the prospect of another trip.

"Be ready in half an hour," says Mary.

Cora accompanies me back upstairs, but she doesn't go inside when we walk past her room. Instead, she follows me down the corridor.

"Don't you want to freshen up?" I ask.

"Can we talk, dear?" asks Coralie.

We enter my room, and I sit at the dressing table, brushing my hair as Coralie speaks. I think I know what's coming, and it suits me to be facing the other way.

"I wonder if young Mr Blake has collected his shirt yet," she asks.

I bite my lip. The conversation is going in the direction I'd feared.

"I am sorry for being so clumsy."

I see Cora raise an eyebrow as I watch her reflection in the mirror.

"I'd think you deliberately spilt the wine if I didn't know better," she says.

"Why would I make a mess on purpose?" I bluster. "There's no reason to inconvenience a man I have only just met."

"Unless you were protecting a friend," she says.

Damn her percipiency. She has seen right through me.

"You know, don't you," she says. "I'm surprised at Vera."

"She didn't tell me," I blurt out, shocked at my sudden instinct to protect Mrs Ponsonby.

"Then how do you know?"

"I overheard. I was listening at the door."

Cora Pennington rises and touches me on the shoulder, leaving me with no choice but to turn around. She examines my face as if she is searching my soul.

"Do you dream?" she asks.

"No more than anyone else."

"Are you sure, dear? It's important."

"Quite sure," I say, concentrating on maintaining eye contact while my heart is thudding to an almost audible beat.

"Very well. It was good of you to head Mr St John off the track. I have a complicated personal life, and if I'd have thought about it, I wouldn't have used my real name here. I expected to be safely anonymous this far from the capital."

"Does your husband know where you are?"

"No. And I'd prefer it to stay that way for the time being. If anyone asks again, I am unmarried."

I nod. "Of course," I say as Coralie walks towards the door. She reaches for the handle, then pauses.

"And thank you for intervening. It was a useful distraction."

"Talking of which…" I say.

Coralie raises an eyebrow. "Go on."

I take a deep breath. "Thinking about Mrs Ponsonby's husband has left me distracted recently."

Coralie Pennington turns and leaves the room as if I hadn't spoken. And as the door closes, I exhale, not realising I'd been holding my breath, still shaken by what has passed between us. What possessed her to ask me about my dreams? How could she know? Surely, she couldn't have guessed that I was in the room with her when she spoke to Mrs Ponsonby about her husband's affair. Nobody in their right mind would assume that when my confession of eavesdropping at the door was so rational. And having the nerve to ask about Mrs Ponsonby's marital status is something I hope I won't regret. I blame Peter for not approaching the question in the right way when he spoke to his mother. Isla Tremayne clammed up, implying that she knew something. And clearly, Cora Pennington does too, and her reaction indicates that I caught her on the hop without a ready reply.

I grab my stick and walk towards the window, raising the old sash a few inches despite the cold. I sit on the wide window ledge and gaze across the village, towards the harbour and the whitewashed cottages with their mellow brick and lichen-covered rooftops. The view is tranquil, though my stomach is in knots. I knew instinctively not to reveal the truth to Coralie Pennington. As much I like her, I cannot afford to disclose what I'm hiding. I am alone and adrift despite Mary and her kindness. Only Peter knows my secret, and he is still reeling from the shock. I wish he were here, but I pull myself together. Another week will pass before I return home to Porth Tregoryan, and I will make the most of

Bosula no matter what it brings. I collect my coat and hat and make my way downstairs.

#

Penhallow House on the outskirts of St Buryan is a pleasant drive from Bosula, despite the greying clouds and blustery wind. It is a short trip made cheerful by Mary's determination to take us on the most scenic route while passionately relating the area's history. I am in much better spirits by the time we arrive, and Cora is all smiles. We pull up outside the substantial house, and I am almost breathless at the beauty of the surrounding woodland, which seems to go on for miles. I wish I could dream walk through the grounds and run, arms outstretched, among the azaleas and rhododendrons. Spring must bring a profusion of scents and colours, and now that I have seen it, I make a mental note to return one day unencumbered by my broken body.

The front door opens, and Laura bursts out and runs towards Mary with her arms outstretched. She hugs her tightly as if she hadn't seen her for months. They are clearly great friends. "Come inside and get out of the cold," she says. "I've set the fire, and it's cosy."

We enter, and Laura guides us towards a spacious, well-lit living room. The fire is blazing, and colourful paintings adorn the walls. "Sit down," she says, ringing a bell. A middle-aged man appears, carrying a tray of cakes, a teapot, and cups. He arranges it on a large, square coffee table in the middle of the room. "Thank you, Jonathan," says Laura.

Coralie eyes her quizzically.

"I don't know what I'd do without him," says Laura. "He is my man Friday, butler, cook, odd-job man and domestic servant. My friends say it is inappropriate to keep him on, but Crawford relied on Jonathan, and if it was good enough for him, then it's good enough for me."

"Don't listen to them," says Mary. "You do as you see fit."

"That's a wonderful painting," says Coralie, pointing to a scenic harbour with ochre roofs beyond and a low sun dominating the sky.

Mary beams. "It's one of mine. I painted it in Tuscany."

Laura sighs. "I long to go abroad again. I don't think my sadness will ever lift until I am under a Mediterranean sun."

"You must come with me to Gibraltar," says Mary. "I'm going in May, and I would love some company."

Laura beams, and I am pleased for her, yet saddened as I would love to travel, but who wants to take someone with my restrictions?

We spend a pleasant morning with Laura, and after we have eaten, she asks if we would like to walk around the estate. Mary is on the verge of accepting, then changes her mind. I realise at once that she is reluctant to walk, knowing that I cannot keep up.

"Oh, please go," I say. "I will come with you a little way and return to the house if it is too much."

"Are you sure? It's rather cold outside."

"I don't mind," I say, and we don our coats and hats and set off. We stroll along natural pathways that head down towards a stream. Nearby is a wooden building that Laura tells us was Crawford's studio. The paths snake through woodland. I enjoy being outside, but after a while, I tire and lean on my stick.

"Are you alright?" asks Mary. "We should go back."

"There's no need," I say. "But I need to rest a little."

"Would you like to sit in Crawford's studio?" asks Laura. "I keep it unlocked, and there is a little paraffin stove inside. You can sit for a while before you go back to the house."

"That would be lovely," I say. It is only a short distance away and will do very well.

The women wait while I make my way to Crawford's workshop, only resuming their walk when I am safely inside. I unlatch the door and swing it open, expecting to smell damp in my nostrils. Instead, I find a freshly aired hut, which is clean, tidy, and regularly used. Laura must visit often. Mary mentioned Crawford had a study in the house, but he must have used this workshop for his writing too. A wooden desk stands against the back wall of the building with bookshelves on either side. Along the front, a floor to ceiling window allows uninterrupted views across the spectacular grounds. Inspiration would have come easily to Mary's brother in these surroundings. I light the paraffin stove, and instead of sitting on the comfortable sofa nearby, I relax into the chair behind the desk and imagine being a writer.

Five minutes later, I have had my fill of the silence, and boredom is setting in. Curiosity gets the better of me, and I investigate the desk drawers. Someone has cleaned them out as little remains except for a half-empty ink bottle, a paint strewn smock and an old iron key. I touch the key and immediately feel a vibration running up my finger. I pull back and slam the door shut. The only time it's happened before was when I picked up Annie Hearn's handkerchief. I know that if I touch the key again, it will reveal something. I am alone in the hut, and it is so peaceful that I cannot hear a sound from outside. The silence is deafening and makes me fearful of meddling in something I don't understand. But eventually, curiosity outweighs fear, and I reach for the key again. My fingers tingle, and I commit wholeheartedly and grasp it. Newson is alive; Newson is dead. The message vacillates bringing confusion. I see him in my mind's eye, a tall, fair-haired man, confident and prepossessing. The image fades. He is back, this time approaching a sturdy trunk with trepidation in his eyes. A fizz, a blur, and he disappears, and when he returns, Newson hunches as if broken, his red-rimmed eyes staring hazily as if paralysed by an unknown terror. I have never met Crawford Newson, but I know it is his image, and the key conveys terrible suffering, but not death. I don't know what to make of it. When I touched Annie Hearn's handkerchief, I knew she was alive. She is alive. I do not doubt it. On that basis, I should know with certainty if Crawford has drowned. But I don't. Perhaps my newfound skills haven't developed enough to get it right every time.

I look up, still holding the key, and immediately spy a trunk beneath a painting of a windmill on the sidewall. I don't need to compare the key to the lock to know it fits. I walk towards it, casting a glance towards the front of the hut, making sure that the women haven't returned unexpectedly. It is still quiet, so I slide the key inside and open the trunk, delighted to find that it contains a treasure trove of books. Stacks and stacks of books, fiction, and non-fiction alike. Heaven in a box. I busy myself pulling them out, one after another making tidy piles along the floor as I forensically examine each precious tome. I wish I could take them all home with me. I am about to remove the last few books when I realise that I have made a mess and couldn't quickly return the books and cover my tracks if I needed to. Sighing, I replace them, but my butterfingers drop a heavy book in the process and the weight of it dislodges part of the bottom of the trunk, creating a slight gap. I push my fingers in the space and tug a wooden panel towards the other side. It slides into a recess, revealing a shallow hidden compartment containing a shiny purple material. Undeterred by the prospect of being caught in the act, I pick it up and shake it out. It unfolds into a large, hooded robe, and I already know that there will be a unicursal hexagram on the back before I turn it around.

#

We arrive back at the colony mid-afternoon. Coralie is talking nineteen to the dozen about the prehistoric cave in the grounds of Penhallow House that they visited on their walk. It is old hat to Mary and Laura, who have seen it many times before but Laura is proud of the unusual feature on her property. She regaled Coralie with cave related folklore and superstitions during the walk, which Coralie now has a burning need to share. I try to respond as if I am listening, but all I can think about is why Mary's brother owned a Calicem Aureum robe. Was he part of the organisation? I rack my brains, trying to remember what Oliver Fox said. If my memory serves me correctly, he was fearful of Felix Crossley but not necessarily of the order in general. So, it doesn't follow that Crawford Newson was a wicked man just because he was a member. And if the visions I saw were anything to go by, he seemed frightened. I wish I could ask Mary, but I don't know her well enough to risk hurting her feelings. She might not understand and would no doubt take offence at me poking around her brother's studio. I decide it is best to leave well alone, and I try to engage with Cora and Mary, so they don't notice that I'm preoccupied.

When we get to the colony, I prepare to slink off to my room, but Mary has other plans.

"Shall I teach you to drive?" she suggests, and I immediately agree. It is a disaster. My mind is elsewhere. Although we crawl around the country lane at a speed only slightly faster than a brisk walk, I almost hit a passing pedestrian.

"We'll try again tomorrow," says Mary, as we swap seats. "Don't worry," she continues. "It takes a few attempts to get the hang of it, but you did jolly well with that leg of yours. It was strong enough to move the pedal, and we'll make a driver of you yet." I thank her and look forward to a quiet afternoon, but I hadn't reckoned with the vibrant nature of the artist's colony.

"Look lively," says Cora as I walk back through the front door. "The fortune teller will be here shortly."

"The what?"

"It's Boo's birthday," says Cora. "They've arranged tea and cakes, a fire-eater and a fortune teller." I stare, aghast. I am shattered and have done more today than I usually do in a week. I am desperate for a nap and need time to consolidate my thoughts about Crawford Newson's connection to Calicem Aureum. But I don't want to seem ungrateful and stifling a yawn, I sit between Coralie and Carrie Yates, who I only met this morning.

Boo Lyons is sitting with Mary and Mary's mother on the large leather sofa, warming herself by the fire. She is wearing a silk scarf that looks new and is sifting through several sealed envelopes in front of her. Birthday cards, I assume, then immediately feel bad that I haven't given her one. I wish Mary had mentioned her birthday celebrations before we arrived. Though Cora and I have only recently met Boo, we are living with her, if only for a short time and ignoring her birthday seems like bad manners.

I sigh. "I'd have brought Boo a card if I'd known," I say.

"Don't worry. Mary's mother told me yesterday," whispers Cora. "I packed a box of Brazil nuts in case we felt peckish on the journey, so I've wrapped it and given it to Boo. The card is from both of us."

I glance at the table again, and sure enough, there is a box of nuts tied with a red bow. "Well done," I say admiringly.

Teatime is a repeat of last night, announced with a gong and artists trooping through into the kitchen to collect plates of food. As soon as everyone sits down again, we munch cakes and drink tea while watching the fire-eater perform his tricks. It is utterly bizarre and incomprehensively bohemian. I don't know whether to love it or hate it. And I am filled with trepidation when they announce that the fortune teller will see everyone regardless of status. She starts with Boo, who dissolves into peals of laughter at the prospect of becoming famous. Mary appreciates her forecast of increasing riches, and I am cynical when told that I will soon go on a long journey. But things take a darker turn. Carrie Yates learns she will soon meet a tall, handsome stranger, and her granddaughter, Diana, should beware a suitor from afar. Carrie lost her husband a few short months ago, and Diana is only fifteen. Few men take the fortune teller seriously. Gulliver Harding eventually sends her away after rewarding her with a large tip for her services. Before long, they substitute tea for cocktails, and the evening begins to take a riotous turn.

"I am dead on my feet," I say, trying to keep my eyes open as I gaze at Cora.

"Oh, but it's such fun."

"You must stay," I say. "Enjoy yourself. I don't need watching, and I'm going straight to sleep."

"As long as you don't mind," she says. "Best not mention it to Vera."

I nod my agreement, but I am past the point of caring. Tiredness overwhelms me, and it is a struggle to climb the stairs. I cannot summon the energy to get into my nightclothes so shed only my dress before sliding under the sheets in my petticoat and stockings before sleep overtakes me.

CHAPTER TWENTY-FOUR

Warning

June 1948

I am dreaming again, and I have been here before. I am standing outside a red brick terraced house, peering through the dusky dawn at a familiar-looking doorway. In front is a tiny garden, and behind me, a street. The inhabitants are rousing from their slumbers as day breaks. I'm feeling fuzzy and not entirely with it. Something is wrong, something more than the distraction of being in a dimension I still don't understand. I hear the roar of an engine and look behind me to see a car passing by at speed. But what a car. It is terrifyingly modern, and I don't recognise the make at all. A woman walks by with hair piled high in curlers barely contained in a cheap linen scarf. No pride in her appearance, as evidenced by her skirts. Goodness me, but her hemline is only just below her knee. Having only recently abandoned full-length dresses, I am appalled at the sight of her legs. It is too much. I stare at the house, knowing my dream has brought me here for a reason, and that reason is inside. But doubt has paralysed me, and I want to know more about my surroundings. So, I wait, and a paperboy soon arrives and drops his bundle on the mat under the covered porch. I hasten toward it and steal a look. It does not tell me much. He's rolled up the newspaper, and all I can see is half a photograph of a suited man. The headline is on the underside, and as I have no physical presence, I'm unable to move it. Fortunately, a gust of wind does the job for me, and I am astounded to read the date on the *Shrewsbury Chronicle* – Wednesday, June 2, 1948. No wonder I am feeling disorientated. I am out of place *and* out of time. But why?

The door opens, and a woman appears clad in a coat too warm for the season and swamped by an oversized hat. I look and look again. This woman seems familiar, but I can't see her face beneath the hat brim. And in a flash, I remember dream walking to this house, a night memorable because until then, I had never been further than Mawgan Porth. During the dream, I watched someone remove a poisonous liquid from a bottle and mix it into another with clear intent to cause harm, perhaps even death. And now I know why I am here – to warn the victim, whoever she is. I wave my hands and try to call her, try to shout. I hear the shrillness in my voice, high pitched, loud, and increasing in intensity. But the noise is all inside my head. She doesn't see me. In desperation, I glide towards her and hurl myself into her body. She feels nothing, doesn't know I'm there. My job is to save her, but I can't. I'm all that stands between her and her killer, and I have failed. My head jerks violently, and the street becomes blurred, then I sink back into darkness and wake with tears running down my cheeks.

CHAPTER TWENTY-FIVE

Betsy Poskitt's Diary

Wednesday, December 24, 1930

It is Christmas Eve, and we ought to be celebrating, but Alfred is in his workshop mending shoes by gaslight. He will ruin his eyes if he's not careful. He has plucked a fowl, but we cannot raise any enthusiasm for Christmas Day with Annie still missing and under suspicion of such heinous crimes. My heart breaks for her. It was bad enough when Aunt Mary died, but things became worse when our sister, Minnie, faded away into nothing. I remember Annie's letters well. She sent news every week as Minnie was too poorly to write herself. Minnie's illness started with gastric catarrh and colitis, soon accompanied by rheumatic pains in her arms. Annie ministered to her every need and made sure Dr Gibson frequently called to see her. And when Minnie lost a lot of weight, Dr Gibson checked her for signs of cancer. We already had that wicked disease in the family, but there was no sign of any malignancy.

"She'll pull through," I said to Alfred, and he wholeheartedly agreed. But Minnie did not thrive. Quite the reverse. I have kept Annie's letters from that terrible time. Every one of them. They are in the back of my diary for that year, and I read them often as I remember my dear departed sister. By the time Dr Gibson checked

on Minnie two weeks after the cancer examination, she was feeble, emaciated and barely alive. Minnie was so weak that she couldn't turn over in bed without help, and though she moved her lips and tried her best, Annie wrote to say she could hardly talk. My poor sister had winced in pain, raising her head from the pillow in one last heroic attempt to speak. Annie wept as she recalled Minnie's last valiant efforts and her final letter still bears evidence of her distress, tears forming inky furrows down the page. Annie must have posted it in a hurry, for the crooked stamp hung over the edge of the envelope when it arrived. Another letter soon followed, this one scrawled in an unsteady hand only just recognisable as Annie's. It was short and melancholy. Minnie had died the same night. Annie was distraught, and her only consolation was Dr Gibson's kind words. He called her a good nurse and devoted sister. She was all those things and more.

I lower my pen and drift for a moment, thinking about my sisters. We were alike in so many ways, Annie, Minnie, and me. The three eldest Everard girls, of those of us who lived, bound together in an unbreakable sisterly bond. Perhaps it's because we didn't have children. Or maybe because Annie and I married later in life, and Minnie didn't wed at all. Whatever the reason, we relied upon each other, and though I lived away from my sisters, we were as close as sisters could be. I might be the only one left now.

My heart aches when I remember the day I first heard about Annie's disappearance. I'd left my cottage in Long Sandall one November morning to find a grey-suited man standing by the gate, and he caught me unawares. If I'd been expecting him, I'd have thought twice about answering his questions. But he caught me on the hop when he asked what I thought about Annie's disappearance. Well, I did not know she was missing, and his words came as a terrible shock. So, I said I hadn't heard from her for about seven days, which didn't concern me as we write every week and sometimes it goes a little over. But the last letter she sent concerned her friend Alice, who had died. Annie wrote of her devastation at Alice's loss and mentioned the impending funeral.

She did not say that Alice had died by nefarious means. The grey-suited man, who turned out to be a journalist, wanted to know if Annie was on her way to see me. I said that I wasn't expecting my sister, and she hadn't asked to visit. But then the enormity of the situation came over me. I remember sobbing as I listened to his account of my poor bereaved Annie and her flight from Lewannick. He asked about Annie's background and I should have told him to mind his own business but I was so flustered that I talked about her cookery school in Harrogate, which she ran with our deceased aunt, Mary Everard.

I have broken off from my writing because thinking about the three of us, three sisters who will never be a trio again, is too distressing. I have younger sisters, and I love them too, but our bond is more motherly. They could never replace Minnie and Annie.

Over the weeks, I've racked my brains about Annie. I am surprised that she hasn't found her way to me, and her absence makes me fearful that she followed through with her terrible threat. I can't imagine how she felt when she talked about destroying herself, as the newspaperman heavy-handedly informed me. I hear Annie asked Mr Thomas to send me her love in her last letter. That small fact brings me a little cheer. If Annie truly intended to take her life, she would have said goodbye. So, I hope against hope that my sister is alive.

Tomorrow Alfred and I will lay the table for three, though only two will eat Christmas Dinner. We will go to church, pray for Annie's soul and hope they find her soon. My sister is innocent. I do not fear a trial, so Godspeed to those who would locate her and bring her home safely.

CHAPTER TWENTY-SIX

The Mysterious Mrs Faithful

Wednesday, January 14, 1931

Today is a glorious day. Crispy frost shimmers over the sand as the sun hangs low in the sky, casting a warming glow through the sharp winter morn. I am enjoying the view from my favourite cave, where I'm snuggling under a blanket. I am safe and warm. And on my lap is an item of truly magnificent functionality that Coralie Pennington gave me for Christmas. It is an Icy-Hot bottle from America, and its purpose is to keep hot things hot and cold things cold. I am sitting with my legs on a packing crate, enjoying a cup of steaming hot cocoa while reading my newest library book and feeling unusually content.

I returned to Pebble Cottage two weeks ago after a frantic but pleasant trip to Mary Newson's artist colony in Bosula. Coralie and I had a good time, though my break was less carefree than hers because of my preoccupation with Crawford Newson's occult connections. But all visits must end, and I wasn't sorry to return to my natural surroundings. I'd missed my little bedroom and my ready book supply, not to mention Peter and my much-loved cave.

I pull the blanket tightly around my shoulders as I gaze across the bay. The waters are still and unseasonably serene for January. The world is light today; I've left my worries at home and I am happy. If only I could stay here all day. But Peter is coming to the house in half an hour. He wants me to conduct an experimental dream walk, and, filled with joy at seeing him after such a long absence, I foolishly agreed to it. Peter has finally acknowledged the evidence of my nocturnal meanderings and has admitted that I couldn't have invented the description of his bedroom. Not only does he believe me, but he wants to see my powers in action. I have explained to him that dream walking is by no means guaranteed, but Peter says he understands and only wants to see how it looks. The idea has a certain appeal. I don't know how I appear from someone else's perspective, and it will comfort me to have a protector if I encounter any danger. I am doing my best not to enter the waking dream state voluntarily. No good ever comes of it. Sometimes it takes me in my sleep, and I cannot stop it. But the most fearsome of the dream walks happen when I force them, and the obvious solution is not to try so, I expect this will be my last attempt. Although I have dreamed twice since my return to Pebble Cottage, I am not afraid because I have woken near Beacon Cove on each occasion. It is my territory and a place of safety. The cliffs are my domain, and I am midnight monarch of this tiny part of Cornwall.

I close my book and empty the dregs from my cup. My concentration has ebbed away thinking about Peter, and I might as well return to the cottage early. The route was slippery on the way to the cave, and I needed my stick more than I have in a long time. But I must be growing stronger as the outbound walk, usually challenging in extreme weather, was more manageable today. I whistle as I plod home along the sand and ignore the flat rock where I have so often broken my journey. And when I round the lane to see Pebble Cottage nestling behind the hotel, I am pleased with my decision. Isla Tremayne has already parked her car outside the house, so Peter must have arrived early.

I go inside, and before I have time to hang my coat on the hook, Peter has emerged from the kitchen. He clutches a newspaper under his arm, and Elys pulls him back and wags her finger at the offending item before moving it against her lips. He understands and swiftly places the paper into his breast pocket.

"Is your mother here?" I ask.

"Almost," says Peter. "She's popped in to see Dolly but is hoping to have a few words with your, I mean, Vera."

"My nothing," I say, fixing Peter with a stare. "We are not related."

"I thought you said…"

I point to the dining room. "Elys, could we have some tea?"

Elys nods and retreats to the kitchen while I sit at the dining table opposite Peter as we have done so often before.

"Last time we spoke, you said she might be your mother."

"In my worst nightmare. I asked Coralie about it."

"Goodness. What did she say?"

"Nothing. She walked away. And then she asked me about my dreams."

"Odd."

"Isn't it? It's almost as if she knew, though I don't see how she could have. But it made me wonder…"

"Yes?"

"Could Coralie be my mother?"

Peter explodes with laughter and, too late, claps his hand over his mouth.

"What's so funny?"

He rearranges his features in a vain attempt to be serious. "You can't assume everyone is your mother."

"I don't. I just thought it was a possibility. Cora has known Mrs Ponsonby for a long time."

"You don't look the least bit like her."

"So?"

"Look, Connie. You've put me right off the reason I arrived early. Forget Coralie. I come bearing front-page news."

#

"Go on," I say, impressed at his evident enthusiasm.

"They've found Annie Hearn."

"I knew it. I knew she was alive. I'm so pleased. Perhaps they will now let her give her side of the story."

Peter snorts. "Her actions say it well enough."

"What do you mean?"

"Listen to this," he says, "and then tell me you don't think she's as guilty as sin."

He opens the paper and starts reading, initially word for word, but then he can't resist editorialising, and I snatch the paper away.

"Just tell me," I say.

"She faked her suicide," says Peter. "Plain and simple."

"Obviously. The question is why."

"No. The question is how. And the answer is that Annie Hearn planned everything from the moment she left Lewannick. She booked the driver and turned up with all her possessions in one wicker basket. But within half an hour of arriving in Looe, she'd purchased an attaché case, transferred her luggage, and hopped on a train to Torquay. All very calculating."

"No, it isn't. Annie did exactly what you'd expect of a woman fleeing from unwarranted suspicion. She travelled light, with barely any possessions, and sensibly purchased a suitcase for her onward travel. There is nothing sinister about it."

Peter raises an eyebrow and looks down his nose with the air of a man brimming with unspoken information. "She went straight to St Leonard's Hotel and registered as Mrs Ferguson of Heavitree, Exeter."

"She was hardly going to register in her name, was she?" I say.

"Next day," says Peter, peering at the newspaper, "Annie moved to lodgings in Ellacombe Church Road. Once there, she ordered some calling cards in the name of Mrs Faithful while telling everyone that her husband was ill in the local hospital."

I bite my lip, unable to hide my disappointment at this clear evidence of planning.

"Then," says Peter, noting my discomfort, "she answered an advertisement for a cook-housekeeper. She got the job and joined the household of Mr Cecil Powell, a Torquay architect."

"She didn't want them to find her," I say.

"Evidently."

"And did she stay there through the winter?"

"Apparently so. Annie impressed Mr Powell, according to the Gazette. He thought she was intelligent, and it delighted him to see her going to church on Sundays."

"Which must make her a good person," I say cynically.

"Ah. Now you are coming over to my way of thinking."

"Not at all. But the church attendance is neither here nor there. I don't worship, but it wouldn't change my personality if I did."

"Now is not the time for a theological discussion," says Peter. "Now tell me if you still believe she is innocent."

"Look," I say impatiently. "Annie's not perfect, and she's clever, cunning even, but that doesn't mean she killed her friend."

"Do you know that?"

"Of course not."

"I mean in the sense that you knew she was still alive."

"I see." I consider his question for a moment. "No. I can't say that with certainty. It's not the same feeling."

"Then why are you so convinced. It doesn't matter how much evidence I offer you for Annie's guilt. You refuse to consider it."

"But you have said nothing that isn't circumstantial."

"I haven't finished," says Peter. "When they caught Annie, it was very much her own doing."

"Did she give herself up?"

"No. But Annie behaved so strangely that detection was inevitable."

I put my chin on my hands and lean forward, wary of the direction the conversation is taking. "How?"

"She spent a lot of time in her room."

"As I do in mine."

"I daresay. But you don't cut press photographs of yourself from the newspapers and leave them in full view. And especially not next to a clipping of the reward money posted by the *Daily Mail* as an incentive to find her."

"She didn't?"

"She did. And even then, Mr Powell didn't realise for some time. He thought she seemed familiar in a vague sort of way. But he didn't connect the pictures of Annie Hearn with his efficient new housekeeper, Mrs Faithful. Besides, his wife was in poor health, and I doubt he wanted a fuss."

"So, he turned a blind eye?"

"Very much so, until circumstances forced his hand."

"What did she do?"

"She went shopping," says Peter. "She took herself off to the new year sales at Williams and Cox in the Strand where she bought herself a new coat. I expect she needed one, having abandoned hers on the cliff tops at Looe."

I scowl at Peter, and he has the decency to bow his head, knowing that it wasn't necessary to refer to the first part of Annie Hearn's deception yet again.

"Anyway," he continues. "The coat was too long, and Annie had it shortened. For some unfathomable reason, she gave her name as Mrs Dennis when she left the deposit. So, when the errand boy delivered the coat a few days later, he quite naturally asked for Mrs Dennis. Annie couldn't think quickly enough on her feet to provide a reasonable explanation. Her behaviour was so suspicious that Cecil Powell had no choice but to act. He was friendly with the mayor and asked his advice, and he told Powell to inform the Launceston police without delay."

"Poor Annie," I say, without thinking.

Peter shakes his head. "Annie be damned," he says suddenly, and I sit up shocked. Peter is so easy going, amiable, and calm that I cannot believe he has risen to anger.

"You don't like her, do you?" I ask.

"Not at all," says Peter. "She's a wicked woman, Connie."

"She's misunderstood."

"She's sly."

"I think you're wrong," I say with sudden conviction. "Giving all those names isn't sly. It's silly. Annie was bound to get caught. It was utterly inevitable. Everything you have said is evidence of panic."

"Even cutting out her picture?"

"I don't know about that. But it's daft, isn't it? And guileless, too. Anyone else would have steered clear of newspapers at all costs. Yet here is Annie needlessly drawing attention to herself."

"Perhaps she wanted them to catch her."

"Why?"

"Probably a guilty conscience. Don't you want to know how they found Annie?"

"Do tell."

Peter ignores the sarcasm in my voice. "The Launceston police sent one of their men down – one familiar with Annie's appearance. Then Mr Powell sent Annie on an errand so the police sergeant could follow her. He recognised Annie immediately and sent his constable to stop her. She confirmed her name, then they arrested her and took her to the police station."

"And that's it? That's everything?"

"Isn't it enough?"

"I don't know. It doesn't feel right to me."

"Annie Hearn is a liar. A bald-faced liar," says Peter. "There's something else you should know about this latest piece of news."

"Which is?"

"That she isn't a widow. Annie Hearn never married."

"Why would she pretend otherwise?"

"Who knows? Sympathy, I suppose. They've tracked down her sister, Betsy Poskitt, and Betsy told them all about Annie's husband, Leonard Hearn. She even showed them a photograph. But Betsy must be as naïve as her sister. Not only did the reporters look into Annie's marriage, but they studied the likeness as well."

"Lots of women lie about their marital status," I say, thinking about Mrs Ponsonby.

"This is different," says Peter. "It's lies upon lies. Annie Hearn is a fantasist. She asked her sister to publish a marriage announcement in the *Sheffield Daily Telegraph*."

"So?"

"So, she said that she'd married a Doctor Leonard Hearn. Then, only a few days later, Annie posted his death announcement in the same paper. But the only Doctor Leonard Hearn registered in the medical directory is alive and well and enjoying his bachelor lifestyle. And the photograph she said was her husband belongs to a member of one of our most noble and influential families. It's a likeness of Lieutenant Charles Stuart Vane-Tempest, the great-grandson of the third Marquess of Londonderry. What do you make of that?"

"I don't know what to say," I offer, stalling for time while thoughts of Annie Hearn swirl in a maelstrom through my mind. None of what Peter has told me sounds helpful to Annie. I try to reconcile her actions with that of an innocent woman. They fall somewhat short.

"Annie tells lies," repeats Peter.

"Everyone does to one degree or another."

"But the poison in Alice Thomas's body can only have reasonably been administered by Annie Hearn or William Thomas."

"Or Alice's mother," I say, waspishly.

"Be serious."

"Very well. One or the other, then."

"Then think how bad it will be for William Thomas if Annie's lies get him convicted."

"Why would they? Her lies, as you call them, make things worse for her, not for him."

"She's guilty," says Peter.

"No."

"What if you touched her? Would you know then?"

"I don't think so. I knew Annie was alive, but I can't say that I'd be able to get a sense of her guilt or otherwise by laying my hands on her."

"Are you still prepared for this experiment?"

"More than ever. At least I know where Annie is now, and I have a chance of locating her."

"Where can we do it? I can't exactly go to your room."

I point towards the window, and Peter peers outside. Mrs Tremayne is walking back from the hotel, and Mrs Ponsonby is striding purposefully towards her, clad in her hat and coat. "Wait for a moment."

We watch through the dining room window as the two women meet and exchange greetings. Mrs Ponsonby points towards the Newquay cliff walk, and Mrs Tremayne nods her head. Then they make their way towards the stone steps.

"No time like the present," I say, grabbing Peter's hand.

CHAPTER TWENTY-SEVEN

Betsy Poskitt's Diary

Wednesday, January 14, 1931

They've found Annie. She is alive, and I am overjoyed yet brimming with confusion. For as fear departs through one door, trepidation arrives by another. My sister is safe but incarcerated somewhere in Launceston, where she will stand trial for murder. The very idea of it is ridiculous. If they knew Annie, as I do, they wouldn't waste their money on legal affairs. My sweet, good-natured sister couldn't hurt a fly. She is too caring, and it has always been her trouble.

They say Annie lies, and I can't necessarily fault them for coming to this conclusion. It is not so much that she seeks to mislead but sees her life as something relatively worthless. If she can embellish, then she does. Take her marriage, for example. I believed her right up until November when the press hack from the Sheffield Daily Telegraph *started hounding me for information. And I didn't see the wrong in it when I told them about her marriage to Leonard Hearn. But they burrowed into her private doings in a way I didn't expect, and now they know that there never was a wedding, and the short and tragic union was only a product of Annie's imagination. Annie always wanted a husband, but it didn't happen for her. She hoped for so much from life, and by the time she attained forty years, she must have felt that marriage and children were out of reach. It was easier to pretend to be a widow and have a good reason for childlessness. And widowhood brought respectability. I expect that's why she did it.*

Poor Annie. Always the carer and always in demand for the most menial of tasks. Our sister Minnie was never well, and I daresay it would have fallen to me to nurse her had I not married dear Alfred. My husband is or rather was a widower with two grown-up children. His children had already left home, but Alfred still needed me. Annie sought a life of her own, and at Aunt Mary's suggestion, went to Harrogate to run a cookery school. They stayed for several years until Aunt Mary grew frail, and they moved to Cornwall to take advantage of the more temperate weather. Minnie soon joined them, leaving Annie caring for an elderly lady and a sickly sister. I suppose it wasn't fair, and although we were close, I felt guilty for leaving Annie to her quiet ministrations. I still do, although Alfred says there is nothing I can do from afar.

But one thing I shouldn't have done is tattle to the press. Back in November, I was eager to say anything to help Annie. Now, I have learned my lesson. I listen, but I don't speak. And when the pressman told me that Annie lied about her marriage, I nodded my head but did not reply, even though I was thunderstruck at the revelation. I didn't tell them anything after that. I didn't let on that she'd got herself arrested for a bit of bother in Weston-super-Mare, and I certainly didn't reveal the tragic deaths of her two school friends when we lived in Grimsby. They'd have made something of it, and Annie was not to blame. Annie is weak and prone to self-doubt. They could convince her of anything if they persisted.

"We'll go to the trial," said Alfred. It is good of him. He will be laying out money he can ill-afford. But he's always been kind to Annie, and I think it's because I am fond of her, and he is fond of me. But how will she manage until then?

The trial is six months away, and they've locked Annie up like an animal. It shouldn't be allowed, not without proof. And although they have everything they need to show that Mrs Thomas was poisoned, they have no evidence against my sister. Not a shred. I will pray for Annie in church on Sunday. And in the meantime, God bless you, my dear.

CHAPTER TWENTY-EIGHT

Visiting Annie

I lie on the bed feeling foolish while Peter sits in the chair by the dresser, legs crossed and pen hovering over a notebook.

"It's not an interview," I hiss.

Peter grins. "Pretend I'm not here," he says.

"It's not that easy." I sigh and brush a stray hair from my face. The window is ajar, and the curtain swishes as Peter adjusts himself, knocking a cushion to the floor.

"It's too distracting," I complain. I am not enjoying this experience one bit, and the chance of achieving a dream walking state is as likely as running to Truro.

"You're not trying," says Peter. "Concentrate."

"Fat chance." He is starting to annoy me. Peter cannot possibly understand the frustration of trying to do something that doesn't always work. Yet he sits there with a supercilious expression on his face, telling me how to achieve this state he will never know. I clench my fists and try again, but it is no use. "You'll have to move," I say.

"Where?"

"Anywhere, as long as I can't see you."

Peter sighs and drags the chair closer to the window. He is still occupying more of the room than I would like, but he is out of my eye line. I try concentrating on the candle again and peer at the wax stub while chasing the flickering flame with my eyes. They grow heavy and a restful wave settles over me as I drift away. My eyes are tightly closed when the vibration starts at my toes and surges through my torso. By the time it reaches my trembling eyelids, I know I am under. I know I am free. I surreptitiously confirm it by running my little finger against the quilt. It glides across until I plunge it downwards, watching it disappear until my second knuckle is the only visible part. Good, I am there. I sit up and look at Peter, expecting him to notice my movements, but he is still watching me with the same anticipation that he showed a few moments ago. I wave my hand, but he doesn't react. I leap to my feet and touch his face. Not a flicker of recognition. Then I plunge my hand into his heart, and only then do I notice an almost imperceptible shudder. He has felt me, but he does not know it. I turn to face my body and see what Peter sees.

It is unremarkable. I am fast asleep, making little murmurs as I rest, looking for all the world as if my body and soul were one. And before I go looking for Annie, I decide to linger for a while, hoping Peter does something that I can use as evidence of my dream state. I wouldn't believe myself under these circumstances, and I can't expect him to, so I listen to the sound of Peter tapping on the notebook. The noise is so tedious that I fear I will fall asleep standing up and accidentally return to my body. And just as I am about to give up and find Annie, Peter drops the pen, and it rolls under the bed.

"Blast," he whispers, then drops to his knees and feels for the pen. It is not there and has rolled across the floorboards before nestling near the window by an uneven knot. He scrabbles around for a few more seconds, locates it, and returns to his chair before resuming his relentless tapping. But I have seen enough to prove I was watching him. It is time to go.

I think of Annie while I wait for the whoosh of movement as I prepare to travel, but nothing happens. I try again and concentrate. I know Annie is in jail. Why can't I get to her? Is it because I haven't been there before? No. It can't be. I wasn't familiar with the farmhouse, but I found my way through time and space. I raise my hands to my temples and close my eyes, trying to recall the sallow features of the plain, middle-aged widow – middle-aged spinster as it turns out. I see her in my mind's eye, her once dark hair, slaked with grey, full lips showing the first signs of wrinkles, heavy shapeless eyebrows. Her face flashes in front of mine, eyes pleading hopelessly. I open my mouth to tell her I will help, then find myself whipped through space and speeding towards a tunnel of darkness. I am almost giddy with vertigo, sickened by the sudden pull, and then all is quiet and grey. Silent. Or is it?

I open my eyes. It seems dark, and it takes a while for my pupils to adjust. Then I hear a soft pant. No, not a pant, a snore. Someone is near, but they are asleep. I wait as the room takes shape. I am standing in the middle of a narrow, rectangular cell comprising four walls and a metal door with a recess at head height. I turn around. There is a bed against the left-hand wall, and a woman huddled beneath a blanket, her face uncovered. Beside her is the unlit stub of a candle. The only light is coming from a small, barred window high up the wall, and the woman is awake, although she is vainly trying to fall asleep. I drift towards her, and the face I imagined is there before me, thinner, pallid and with a mess of unbrushed hair. It is Annie, and she is not in good shape. Dark bags linger beneath swollen eyes. There is a bruise on her cheek, and I wonder how it happened. I touch her and attempt to rouse her, but she doesn't feel me, as she didn't in my last dream. I wish I could tell her that I haven't forgotten her. And even if nobody else believes her, I do.

The door hatch slams open, and a female wardress peers into the room through the grate. Annie sits bolt upright, clutching her chest. "You frightened me," she whispers.

"What are you doing sitting here in the dark," says a mellow voice with a Cornish twang.

"My candle burned to a stub."

"Why didn't you say?"

"I didn't want to make a fuss."

"Come now, Annie. You are one of the good ones. I'm sure I can find another piece of candle. Won't you want to write in that diary of yours?"

"Yes, please. If I could."

"Give me a moment."

A moment is all it takes, then the warder returns, approaches Annie, and places a brand-new candle and holder in front of her. She lights it with a match.

"Thank you," says Annie as gratefully as if the warder had pardoned her, driven her home, and given her a hundred pounds for her trouble.

"Don't you get fed up with it?" asks the warder, pointing to the journal on the bottom of the bed.

"Never. I've kept a diary all my life," says Annie. "We all did, my sisters and I, that is." She gazes towards the door, eyes soft and sad.

"Well, I won't keep you," says the warder, patting Annie's shoulder sympathetically. I watch, entranced as all the terrible things I have heard about jail melt away at the compassionate gesture. Annie inspires not only trust from me but from everyone. We can't all be wrong.

The door clangs shut, the key turns, and Annie sits quietly in bed with her knees up and the journal resting against her thighs. She scribbles furiously and is still writing ten minutes later when a sudden wave of foreboding floods through me. It creeps up like a dread cloak of terror shrouding me with fear. Something is wrong. If my body were close, every nerve would tingle, every hair would stand on end. And detached as I am, I feel the warning signs. I shouldn't be here. I am shocked and anxious but take comfort that I'll return to my body as soon as I feel the pull on the back of my head. It comes, but it is not powerful enough. I cannot ride the waves, and I cannot leave. Annie's prison is mine. And before the impending spectre of doom completely hypnotises me, I remember that I'm not bound by earthly ties and prise my paralysed body from the cell. I hurl myself through the metal grate and stand cowering on the other side of the door. I watch and wait. And he comes.

Annie sits unknowingly on the bed. She has finished writing, and the diary and pencil lie on the concrete floor. He slinks like an apparition from the dark corner of the cell while Annie reclines, eyes shut. His bulky form hovers beside her, and he turns towards me and sniffs the air, nostrils quivering like a giant snake. I do not move a muscle. Not a single step but watch in horror as he bends over her and touches her forehead, whispering in a language I do not understand. He raises his head and grins, gleaming tombstone teeth set between thin and cruel lips. And then he is gone, and I collapse in a heap by the side of the cell, exhausted. I am drained, fearful, and too weak to return. But I detect a sound, feel a shaking movement, hear my name.

"Connie, for God's sake, wake up."

I try to open my eyes, but I can't. I feel more shaking, and something moist trickles down my cheek. "Connie. Please, please wake up."

I touch my face. My fingers are wet, and I open my eyes to see Peter standing in front of me. I am back. Thank God I am back.

#

"My God, Connie. I thought you were dead." I look up at Peter. His puffy, red-rimmed eyes peer at me from a blotchy face.

I try to speak, but my breath comes in short pants. My heart is beating through my chest, and my temples are moist with perspiration.

"Here, drink this." Peter passes me a glass of water from my bedside jug. I take it with trembling fingers and sip from the chipped glass as water sloshes over the side, dislodged by my shaking hand. Peter cups his hand around mine and steadies the glass. "Drink some more," he says.

I oblige and feel a little calmer as the liquid trickles down my throat, bringing some normality after the terrifying shock.

Peter perches on the side of the bed. "Sit up higher," he says, adjusting my pillow. "Feeling better?"

I nod. My heartbeat is less frantic, and I can hear myself think.

"What happened?" asks Peter.

"I saw him," I say, swallowing at the thought of Crossley's bottomless, all-knowing eyes.

"Who?"

"Felix Crossley."

"Did he see you?"

"No, but he felt my presence. He was suspicious."

"Suspicious?"

"Like he thought someone was there but dismissed the idea."

"Start from the beginning."

I tell Peter everything from the moment I saw Annie to my collapse outside the cell.

"Did you feel faint?" he asks.

"No. Exhausted, as if all my energy had disappeared. I had scarlet fever as a child and was in bed for a month. It felt like that."

"Did it happen suddenly?"

I think about his question. "Yes," I say. "My energy drained away in moments."

Peter shakes his head. "This can't happen again," he says.

"What did you see, Peter? When I left the room, my body looked perfectly normal."

"And so it was for ten minutes, but then you became restless and started thrashing around. You kept touching your head and started sweating. Then suddenly, you stopped, and your face turned grey. You didn't move at all. I couldn't see your chest rise and fall, and I thought you'd stopped breathing and looked for a pulse. There wasn't one. I didn't know what to do, so I threw a tumbler of water in your face and shook you until you woke up."

"Thank goodness you did," I say. "My body is more deeply connected to my mind than I realised. This dream walking is dangerous."

"Extremely," says Peter. "Promise me you will never do it again."

I want to agree. This nightmarish dream walk is by far the most frightening experience of my life. I don't know what Crossley was doing to that poor woman, but I don't doubt his intentions were evil. "Oh, no. Poor Annie," I say.

"What about her?"

"Crossley touched her forehead. What if she's dead?"

"She can't be," says Peter. "She can't feel his touch."

I cast my mind back to the prison cell, trying to recall the look on Annie's face as Crossley's fingers inched towards her. Peter is correct. She didn't flinch, cry out or move a muscle. Crossley's touch was as insubstantial as mine.

"You're right," I say. "Annie didn't feel him. He can't have hurt her, and he left quickly. But I wonder what he wanted. Why go to her? Why visit Annie? I thought he was after me. Have I put her in danger?"

"I haven't got a clue," says Peter. "This is so far removed from anything I have ever experienced. But I'll say this, Connie. You are not to repeat this experiment."

I smile at his obvious concern. "And there was I thinking that you wouldn't believe me. I even lingered in the room long enough to watch you drop the pencil under the window."

Peter flushes. "Were you spying on me?"

"It was more a matter of collecting proof," I say.

"That wasn't necessary, and I am sorry I ever doubted you. But put my mind at rest and say you won't do it again."

"I can't promise you that," I say.

Peter's brows knit together. "Connie. Don't be silly."

"I'm not," I say. "I can't agree because I don't have control."

"You managed it well enough just now," he says.

"Yes. But though I can't always get into the dream state when I want to, I often arrive there when I don't."

"Oh, yes. I remember you saying. But isn't it normally geographically close?"

"Not always," I say, remembering the unexpected visit to the red brick house in Shrewsbury. "And there's something else, Peter. My dreams aren't always in the present."

"What do you mean?"

"I mean, they're not in the here and now. Sometimes I dream myself into the future."

CHAPTER TWENTY-NINE

Betsy Poskitt's Diary

Monday, May 4th, 1931

It's been an entire week since I've written in my diary. Life is an effort now, and I am too tired to go on. Every day is like wading through treacle, buoyed by a piece of good news one minute, and floored by the problems that follow. And people are so unpredictable. Not Alfred, of course, who remains his kind, good-humoured self, eager to help and only wanting what is right for me. But strangers like Mr Cecil Powell, who I despised at first but who has redeemed himself so well that I don't know how to feel about him anymore. Powell was Annie's Torquay employer, and instead of confronting her with his suspicions, he reported her to the police. If he'd only talked to her, she would have been able to convince him of her innocence. But he couldn't bring himself to trust her and gave her up to the authorities. "Bloody grass," Robert called him, but then his language always was a source of embarrassment to our mother. And I took his point. Cecil Powell was a very wicked man until he wasn't, for he did the strangest thing. He took the five hundred pounds reward money from the Daily Mail *and promptly gave it to Annie to use in her defence. His reaction surprised me and quite put me out. When someone makes you seethe with anger, it's confusing when their next act is kindly. "He's not kind but self-serving," said my brother. Robert doesn't believe in charity for its own sake and thinks that people give to feel better. Or, in this case, to present a better account of themselves to the general public. I cannot feel the same way as Robert. In hindsight, it was a charitable act with a hint of remorse. But I digress.*

I have opened this diary after another long absence because there's something worth writing about. Another reporter appeared today, and an important letter arrived too. The guttersnipe from the press wanted to interview me about arsenic found in Minnie's body. He laboured the point, seemingly with access to all sorts of information that he shouldn't know, including precise quantities of the amount of poison in each of the bodies, or so he said. I didn't know whether to believe him or not, so I shut the door in his face. "You shouldn't have done that," said Alfred and I suppose he is right. They might print even worse stories about Annie if they think we are hostile. But it is hard to compare my loving sister to the person they describe in their articles. And I don't see why I should entertain their unfeeling comments to curry favour. So, the reporter left with his tail between his legs and no doubt I will read about it in the Sheffield Telegraph *tomorrow.*

But the post brought better news and lifted me enough that I can now bear to put pen to paper again. The solicitor put Mr Powell's five hundred pounds to good use by securing the services of Mr Norman Birkett, a well-regarded barrister used by the great and good of our land. Without the reward money, we couldn't have afforded such a reputable man. Alfred chuckled at the thought of the press, to all intents and purposes, paying for the defence barrister. I agree with him, and when I first heard about his appointment, I thought it would be enough to guarantee Annie's safe release. But a few weeks ago, a letter arrived from Annie's solicitor Mr Walter West. He was concerned about the amount of arsenic found in each of the bodies, particularly Alice Thomas's. I showed the letter to Alfred.

"He's getting cold feet," Alfred said, and he was right. West's words offered little hope and a lot of warning. We were far from home and dry. But today's letter is a different matter entirely. Mr Birkett, it appears, sent all available evidence to Scotland to eminent forensic pathologist Mr Sydney Smith. Mr Smith has made his analysis and is hopeful of a good outcome. But there is doubt over whether he will present his findings to the court in person. Mr West says his presence will make a significant difference to Annie's chances, and we are waiting with bated breath to find out whether he will come. But finally, there is hope. We have booked accommodation in Cornwall for the trial, and I have already packed a case for Annie. I will bring her back here to stay. Alfred is happy for her to live with us for as long as she wants. At last, things are looking up.

CHAPTER THIRTY

The Trial

Monday, June 15, 1931

The day of Annie's trial is here, and the obstacles Peter and I have negotiated to make it happen, don't bear repeating. Mrs Ponsonby thinks I am staying with Isla Tremayne for a few weeks to help Peter in the reading room. It took a lot of convincing for her to allow this. And when Isla first arranged it, I couldn't sleep for worrying that Mrs Ponsonby would turn up at the house and find out I wasn't there. But against all the odds, Coralie took her for a trip to St Austell with an overnight stay. And they enjoyed themselves so much that they extended the visit for an entire week. I sometimes wonder if Coralie has a sixth sense. She often knows things she shouldn't and has a sensitively honed instinct. Coralie is protective of me in an understated way, not with the savage, overbearing concern of Vera Ponsonby. If Mrs P is a Dobermann, then Cora is a collie, shepherding from a distance with the lightest touch. How I wish that Mrs P would go, and Cora would stay, for the reverse will happen at the end of the month. Cora is returning to London to see her solicitor and will face her husband in the divorce courts. It is now open knowledge, and they are at war.

Things are sure to get nasty, and my heart breaks for her. She takes it pragmatically and is unflappable. I wish more and more that Cora was my mother.

"Penny for them?" asks Peter as the car sweeps into the parking area at the Bodmin Assizes. Malcolm swears as he almost hits a passer-by. People swarm across the front of the building, and press cameras line the entrance. A queue snakes along one side and people of all shapes and sizes jostle for position, hoping to be one of the few admitted to the public gallery. "Thank goodness you've got connections," says Peter, eying the crowd with trepidation. "We'd never get in if we had to queue."

"This is where I leave you," says Isla Tremayne, exiting the car as Malcolm pulls up behind the building. She is going shopping in Bodmin as the trial holds little interest for her. It is uncommon for her to come at all. Though happy to leave me unattended in Plymouth, Isla Tremayne is feeling guilty at this most recent subterfuge. Peter talked her into it. He is good at that, but she is increasingly friendly with Mrs Ponsonby, more so lately than ever, and is getting cold feet at betraying her trust. "But you're not," said Peter last night, when his mother felt so bad that she spoke of it in front of me. "All you are doing is transferring your responsibility to Malcolm. Connie is a grown woman. What do you expect to happen to her?" Isla said nothing. She has always thought that Mrs Ponsonby fusses too much, but it wasn't a surprise when she insisted on accompanying us as far as Bodmin. And if that makes her feel better, then it is fine by me.

"This way," says Malcolm, and we wait while he knocks on the door at the rear of the building. Moments later, a suited gentleman peers through and asks Malcolm what he wants. Malcolm hands him a letter. He nods and admits us before guiding us up a set of wooden stairs. We find ourselves alone in the public gallery, but not for long as, one by one, the lucky spectators at the front of the queue, go inside. I sit with my heart in my mouth at the prospect of watching Annie's fate. Her guilt or innocence is all anyone has spoken about for months. Even in our newspaper-free household, speculation is rife. Every day, Elys gives a running commentary on what everybody thinks of Annie Hearn. They are intolerant, and local opinion finds her guilty. Elys agrees, and so does Jory. They are impatient for the verdict and eager to read all about it in the press. They would be shocked if they knew I was watching proceedings in court, and I doubt Elys could keep it to herself. So, I must keep tight control of my mouth and not relinquish my secret in a future moment of weakness.

I look up and see a woman at the front of the gallery, two rows ahead. There's something about her that catches my eye, and I tug Peter's sleeve. "Who is she?" I whisper.

Peter shrugs, but Malcolm interjects. "That's Betsy Poskitt," he says.

"Who?"

"Annie Hearn's sister."

I crane my neck forward to see the face beneath the hat. It's hard to make out Betsy's features, but I detect a faint resemblance to Annie Hearn. And there's a vague familiarity about the woman that I can't put my finger on. But the trial begins and takes my attention away, at least for a while.

I spend the next two hours in abject boredom. Far from the excitement I anticipated, the witnesses submit a dirge of scientific evidence and legal arguments. The only exciting part of the proceedings is when the Crown asks to introduce Minnie Hearn's diary as evidence. But the judge, Mr Justice Roche, declines and rules it inadmissible.

The trial lasts for eight days. Mrs Tremayne gives up after two, having seen more of Bodmin than a body can take. Her troubled conscience disappears at the thought of another car journey inland, but Malcolm, Peter and I soldier on, determined to be there at the finish. Exhaustion overwhelms us when we get home every night, and though weary to the bone, I sleep fitfully. At least it is not from dream walking. I have not tried since May, and it has been weeks since my last moonlight foray across the cliffs. I wonder if my unwanted ability is waning, and I am filled partly with relief but also sadness. Yet, I accept Peter's advice that it is too risky, and I won't try again.

#

Tuesday, June 23, 1931

Finally, the last day of the trial arrives. I am sitting in my usual place at the back of the gallery, agog with excitement. Peter has long since had enough and is carrying a script from his latest production to learn his lines during the quieter moments. Malcolm's mood is a strange mixture of ebullience and frustration. He is cheerful as we're nearing the end of the trial, cock-a-hoop at the reaction to his reports, yet dismayed at the direction the case is taking. Birkett and Smith have successfully discredited the Crown's attempts to prove that Annie poisoned her relatives. Cornwall is famous for its tin, which contains high degrees of arsenic. And Lewannick churchyard is full of it, thus explaining the arsenic in Minnie Everard's body. Sydney Smith dramatically proved that Annie could not have used her tin of weed killer in the sandwiches. He took a plate of bread and butter and added poison, demonstrating that it turned the bread bright blue. It is a triumph for the defence, and against the odds, it looks as if Annie will soon go free. But nothing is inevitable, and my temples pound with tension as I wait for matters to take their course.

"Cheer up," says Peter, eyeing my pale face. I raise a weak smile and nod to the man on my left-hand side, who is watching with a sympathetic expression. The daily queue to get into the gallery grows ever longer, yet against the odds, a core group gains access every day. We greet each other with friendly camaraderie and an unspoken agreement to keep to our original seats.

The clerk calls the court to order, and Annie is next on the witness stand. She has given hours of testimony already, in a weak but steady voice, never wavering from her story. She is thinner and stoops a little but has suffered no apparent ill effects from Crossley's visit. Norman Birkett approaches her in the dock and asks about her relationship with William Thomas. There have been scurrilous allegations about their friendship, which the Crown has sought to make central to the trial. This disgraceful insinuation is humiliating to Annie, and Mr Birkett gives her an opportunity for a dignified reply.

"Was there ever a time in your mind that you thought to marry Mr Thomas?" he asks.

"Never," says Annie, firmly giving a slight shake of her head.

"Did you ever conceive a passion, guilty or otherwise, for Mr Thomas?"

"No."

"Did you, on eighteenth October, give Mrs Thomas a poisoned sandwich in order to marry Mr Thomas?"

"No. There is not a grain of truth to that statement."

"Have you ever administered or given in any shape or form arsenic to Mrs Thomas, your aunt or your sister?"

"I have not."

Mr Birkett draws himself to his full height. "That," he says," concludes the case for the defence."

"You may leave," says Justice Roche.

Annie stands and flashes a bewildered gaze across the court. She looks towards the public gallery and inexplicably bursts into tears. It is the first time in the eight-day trial that she has broken down, and now she weeps inconsolably with her head in her hands. A uniformed woman rushes towards her, passes a handkerchief, and leads her away.

"Are you alright?" asks Peter, but I can't answer. I can't swallow the lump in my throat, and unshed tears fill my eyes. Annie is so brave against this hostile court in a county of people who condemned her long ago. I shake my head, and Peter wisely turns away.

Justice Roche calls the counsel for the prosecution, and Herbert du Parcq steps forward and embarks on a diatribe against Annie. He talks of Annie's invented husband and her propensity for lies. And then he refers to Mrs Spear's testimony from the week before.

Her unkind words are a pack of lies but would damage Annie's chances if the jury accepts them. Elizabeth Spear sits in the gallery where she has been most of the week when not testifying. She is a sour-faced woman, heavyset and clad head to foot in black as if in mourning. Mrs Spear clutches a Bible, and I cynically think it's a ploy to demonstrate her godliness to the court. She talks about her visits to Minnie Everard, describing how they sat together and prayed. Minnie, she said, had told her that Annie's medicine was too strong and was affecting her hands and legs. Alice Thomas, in a subsequent conversation, had told her the same thing. I watch du Parcq as he recounts the testimony, feeling the jury's sympathy with Annie Hearn slipping away. I clutch my throat and the artery on my neck pounds as I wait with bated breath for him to finish. And then, from nowhere, the back of my head tingles. I look at my fingers, still gripping my stick. But it is like seeing double, my actual fingers and an echo of them inches above. I am half in, half out of my body, and the timing is terrible. I can't fight the pull and look up as the vibration increases to see a dark shape moving towards the box. One second, and it disappears. I am back in my body, wondering if I imagined it. Du Parcq continues for a moment. One more sentence, then another, and he suddenly sinks to his knees and collapses into the arms of his clerk. There is uproar in the court. The judge bangs a gavel, and Norman Birkett rushes towards him, clutching a bottle of smelling salts. Birkett holds his arm and helps him from the court, but he has left it in chaos. The judge adjourns for half an hour while du Parcq recuperates, and we wait in stunned silence for the trial to resume.

"You look terrible," says Peter, patting my hand. "Eight days is too much for you, Connie. There was no need to come every day."

"I wouldn't have missed it for the world," I say. "Annie is close to justice, but this interruption has given them time to reconsider. Have you ever seen such bravery?" My voice trembles as I speak, and I concentrate hard. I don't know why I am so emotional, but I care a great deal, and I don't know what I will do with myself if they convict Annie.

Peter shakes his head and doesn't speak. I watch my friend bemused. He is a compassionate, caring man who appears utterly unaffected by Annie's emotionally charged speech. I thought it might change his mind about her, but it hasn't.

Mr du Parcq re-enters the court and continues his speech without passion. He is unwell and embarrassed at his unexpected collapse. Mr Birkett makes a final address to the jury summoning all the feeling he can muster. "For five months, this woman has lived in Exeter jail during the darkness and dreariness of winter," he says. "She is now before you in the sunshine of summer but still walking in the valley of a great shadow. It is you and you alone that can lead her back again to the road of sunshine and your voice alone that can speak the words of deliverance. I ask you to speak those words to her, to stretch forth that hand that will help her back into the sunlight away from the shadows which have haunted her so long. That is my last appeal to you all."

Birkett bows his head, and silence falls over the court. I hear nothing, not the shuffle of papers or the clearing of a throat until the judge speaks and asks the jury to consider their verdict. Fifty-five minutes later, they are back. And I know because I stayed still and watched the clock while Peter and Malcolm went outside to stretch their legs. I couldn't bring myself to join them, knowing Annie is still a prisoner. But they are back now, and we are all waiting to hear her fate. The foreman stands and faces the judge.

"Not guilty," he says, and a rush of noise fills the court. Women are sobbing, and men shake hands. Annie garnered more sympathy than I realised. I turn to Peter and throw my arms around his neck. Tears wash down my face, but I don't care. They have made the right decision, and I am happier than I ever thought possible. I gave nothing to Annie, offered no hope, help or kindness, yet it still feels like my victory. I am joyous and even more so when the judge instructs the jury to return a second verdict of not guilty in the case of Minnie and Mary Everard. "Sarah Ann Hearn, you are free to leave," says the judge and Annie Hearn leaves the court as if someone has lifted the weight of the world from her shoulders.

I float on air as we make our way downstairs and towards the car park at the rear. Malcolm's connections have given us a private access point not used by the general public. We come and go with ease while they squash into the main staircase like sardines.

I make for a nearby bench as we go outside and sit in the sun for a while, appreciating the quiet, balmy day. All is well with the world, and I am in no hurry to return to Pebble Cottage.

"We need to go, Connie," says Peter. "Malcolm has a report to file."

I sigh, but it is fair enough. I may have all the time in the world, but Peter and Malcolm work for a living. But as we get ready to go, a small group of people emerge from the rear door. Betsy Poskitt, who sat in front of me in the gallery this week, is standing by her husband. She frantically removes her coat and hands it to someone on the other side of the door before taking her hat and shoving it through. I turn to face her, watching the strange behaviour and moments later, a car pulls up to the rear door. A woman wearing Betsy Poskitt's hat and coat steps through the door and enters the vehicle, joined by two men. It is Annie. The car pulls off at speed. Betsy Poskitt waves it away, and they walk towards us, faces wreathed in smiles. Betsy is carrying her spare hat and approaches me with an uncovered face. She is in my direct line of sight, and it's the first time I've seen her clearly. And now I remember where I first saw her. Betsy Poskitt was standing in the kitchen of a terraced house in Shrewsbury, pouring poison into a bottle.

CHAPTER THIRTY-ONE

Return to Shrewsbury

Friday, June 26, 1931

"I have to do it, Peter. I must go."

"You can't," says Peter. "Absolutely not."

"But she's going to kill Annie."

"You don't know that."

"I saw it. I watched Betsy pouring poison into a bottle."

"It was more likely the other way around."

I slam my hand on the dining room table and Elys peers around the door. "Everything alright?" she asks.

"Fine," I say, without explaining. Elys raises an eyebrow and leaves the room.

"I saw Betsy," I say through gritted teeth. "There isn't a doubt in my mind."

"Did you see her give Annie the drink?"

"No, but she put poison into Annie's glass."

Peter sighs. "Perhaps she doesn't drink it."

"It's possible, but I'm not willing to take that chance."

"And I'm not willing to watch you sacrifice yourself."

"I'm going to do it," I say, "with or without you."

"And presumably that's why you asked me to visit today?"

"Yes. Mrs Ponsonby's out for the next hour and a half," I say, checking the clock. "We have plenty of time."

"But, Connie, how can you stop it happening?"

"I don't know. But I must try. I don't even know if I can get back to Shrewsbury. The last time I tried, it was 1936 and someone altogether different was living there."

Peter's eyes narrowed. "What do you mean, last time you tried?"

I sigh, angry at myself for the careless words. "I've tried every night since the trial," I confess. "It depends what I'm thinking about when I leave my body."

"Should be easy then," he says facetiously.

"You try disciplining your thoughts," I snap. "Human minds don't work like that. It's almost impossible to narrow it down to one thing. Anyway, if you help me, I'll tell you what your house looks like in 1948."

Peter raises an eyebrow. "You haven't?"

"Not yet, but I might."

"I don't think I want to know."

"But you'll help me, anyway?"

Peter walks towards the window and stares outside. "I don't suppose I have a choice. What do you want me to do?"

"Two things," I say. "Sit with me and wake me if you think I'm in distress. I won't pretend I'm not afraid because I am. And I regret trying to do it alone last time, which may be the reason I failed."

"And the other?"

"I don't know if my idea will work, but I need to concentrate, and it will be better if I can focus my thoughts. I would like you to repeat the following, 'Annie Hearn, Shrewsbury, 1948.'"

Peter repeats the words.

"Good, now keep saying them softly while I try to detach."

"Very well." Peter's mouth sets in a thin line. He doesn't look happy, and I wonder if I have pushed him too far. Nevertheless, he follows me upstairs, I light the candle, and we settle down in the same positions as before.

Peter chants softly. At first, his words are distracting, but as I stare into the flame, I find myself listening and repeating them in my head. It must have helped. Within a few minutes, the familiar vibration runs swiftly from toe to forehead, and I shift a little knowing that I have achieved my objective. I can still hear Peter as I'm pulled off the bed and into the other world.

#

I recognise the house at once. I am in the right place, but I don't yet know if it's the right time. Darkness surrounds me as I stand outside the red brick terraced home, and I don't waste a moment before gliding through the door to find the kitchen. It is empty, and the house is as still as a mausoleum. I retreat into the hallway and ascend the stairs like a vengeful wraith. I still don't know how to save Annie's life, but one way or another, I mean to try.

Annie's room is easy to find, and she is in bed, asleep, lying on her side with her face away from the door. I navigate the bed to get to the far side and watch for a moment as Annie coughs in her sleep. She has aged well, though she’s a little greyer, and her crow's feet are more pronounced. But Annie's face is plumper than the last time I saw her, and I'm pleased she isn't showing signs of unhappiness.

I leave Annie to her slumbers and examine the other doors leading off the landing before bursting through the closest one. A figure dressed in a shapeless nightdress sits at the dressing table under the window, head bowed and shaking in obvious distress. I inch along the wall before throwing caution to the wind and risk exposing myself fully as I kneel beside her, but she doesn't see or hear me. She is so distracted that I doubt she would if I were in my usual form. Silent sobs rack through her body, and misery consumes her. The woman gulps deep breaths while rivulets of tears splash onto the journal on which she rests her hand. She sniffs and wipes the tears away with arthritic fingers. I gaze at Betsy Poskitt with revulsion. The woman about to betray her sister so vilely bears the face of a person wearing their ugliest thoughts. Betsy looks ill and unhappy with a pallid face, patchy grey hair, and bags so heavy they are visible despite the meagre lighting. And serve her right, too. I have no sympathy, but at least I am here in time.

I watch as she opens the book. There are two, piled one on top of another in matching designs but different colours. Both are weighty tomes, more like journals than diaries and substantial enough to span many years. Betsy turns the pages over until she is about a quarter of the way through, and I crane over her shoulder as she reads.

Thursday, January 1, 1948

My thoughts turn as they so often do at this time of year to Alfred, dear Alfred, who I miss every day. I still don't understand why our loving marriage turned into one of betrayal and distrust. After all, Alfred supported me every step of the way during that terrible court case. His support never wavered during the lonely year when they incarcerated my dear sister in Exeter jail; his commitment to us, absolute. Alfred knew Annie well, and not for a moment did he doubt her veracity. Not once did he ask if she might be guilty. We took her to London as soon as she left Bodmin Assizes and from there back to Long Sandall where she came to live in our house. And we lived contentedly, at least I thought so, for five long years. But Alfred changed, and before long, the affable, loyal husband I knew turned into a scowling, bad-tempered beast. It might have been because of his illness. Alfred ailed for a while and did not cope well with his confinement. Two months of bed rest sent him half round the bend, and though he recovered, he was never the same afterwards.

His subsequent rancour started mildly enough. He said he missed our household when there were only two of us and asked how long Annie would remain. I reminded him that my sister owned nothing and depended on us for shelter. "That's half the trouble," he'd said, and we had words. The argument rumbled on for another year until Alfred gave me an ultimatum. "Her or me," he said, knowing full well that I could never leave my sister. How could I do that when life had treated her so harshly, and she had known so little joy? To cast her out when I was all she had was something neither of us could bear. And Alfred's selfish act of putting me in that position told me everything I needed to know about the depth of his regard.

I packed and left the same month, and Annie came with me. We started a new life, and for Annie that included a new name. She called herself Margaret Day. Day, because it was my mother's maiden name and Margaret because she liked it. We settled in a terraced house in King Street like two elderly spinsters. Only I wasn't a spinster. I was still a married woman with a husband who I missed very much. And I still do. I wonder if Alfred thinks as fondly of me as I do of him. Sometimes, I imagine what our future might have been if they'd let Annie be – if only they hadn't hauled her away to prison. Would I still be with Alfred? Would we have grown old together?

Betsy sighs and turns the page. If I didn't exist in a translucent dream form, she might feel my chin on her shoulder as I lean closer. Betsy skips the following few pages and arrives at an entry in March. She traces the words with her finger, whispering aloud.

Tuesday, March 16, 1948

I have been sick again. Why can't I shift this horrible illness? Dr Niblett says it's gastric flu, but none of his remedies seems to work. Thank goodness for my dear devoted sister who sat reading to me when my sickness was at its worst, and I was too ill to leave my bed. Annie kept me entertained through the worst of it. Dr Bryant attended me at the weekend when Dr Niblett was otherwise occupied. His medicine is better, and though his strict instruction not to take solids was disappointing, my health improved considerably after his visit. I should be well enough to go downstairs tomorrow. Annie says not to do too much until I've completely recovered, but she has errands to run, so I will sit and read downstairs while she's out. I don't want to upset her like I did the other day when I called her Annie in front of the doctor. It was an honest mistake. I wasn't feeling well, and I forgot. But I still think of her as Annie, though I rarely say it out loud.

Thursday, March 18, 1948

I haven't written for two days. I am still reeling with shock at what happened after I left my bedroom when Annie was out. I had felt so much better and made my way downstairs for a cup of Oxo. Several days without eating had left me with a healthy appetite, and food was uppermost in my mind as I descended the stairs. I was still in my nightdress, and it was liberating to move around the house in comfortable garb without fear of visitors. Sharing a home with Annie is no hardship, but I can count the number of days on one hand where I have the place to myself. So, I pottered around, doing a little light tidying until I looked outside and saw a few early blooms. Annie had been so good and kind that I decided to put them into a vase and place them on her bedside table. And while there, I noticed her nightstand drawer was ajar, and I opened it without thinking and extracted her journal. It is similar to mine and retrieving it was an automatic reaction. We purchased our journals on the same occasion many years ago now. All the Everard girls kept diaries – it is a family tradition. I know I shouldn't have, but I opened Annie's journal, wondering if she was still cross with me for calling her Annie in front of the doctor. If she was, she didn't record it, and I was about to put the journal back when I felt the edge of a rough piece of paper. I turned to the back and saw that she'd stuck a little envelope on the rear cover of the diary. Inside was a piece of card that had come loose. I turned it over to find a list of names beginning with two from my childhood – two girls who had died within days of coming over to visit with us. The list continued, but the subsequent entries contained only initials, MAE, LE, AT, AP, BP. With a growing sense of unease, I realised what they represented – Mary Ann Everard, Lydia (Minnie) Everard and Alice Thomas. Well, the women had died in Cornwall, and Annie had likely recorded the deaths for posterity, but who were AP and BP? There haven't been any other deaths. I closed the diary and left it exactly where I had found it, puzzling over the strange list.

Betsy lets out a strangled sob and puts her head on the dressing table. She has covered the journal with her body, and I can't see any more. I sigh in frustration, but of course, she doesn't hear me, and I wait, growing ever more irritable as sobs wrack her body. And with my increased anxiety comes the inevitable tugging at the back of my head. "Go away," I say, determined not to leave before I have read to the end. I don't know if I will ever return, and if I do, at what point in time I might arrive. The tugging is persistent now and painful. It feels as if someone has grasped my hair and is wrenching it away from my scalp. My mind strains against my body, and I wonder if in another place, another time, Peter is screaming my name and begging me to return. It is all I can do to concentrate, and I resign myself to losing the battle with my sleeping form. Then Betsy Poskitt heaves herself up with a sigh, rests her chin on her hand and carries on reading her diary.

It took three hours before I worked out who the last two initials referred to. I would have got there sooner, but I was in denial – denial of the obvious, denial of the impossible, an unnatural act with no apparent benefit. The letters AP represented Alfred and the initials BP belonged to me. Small wonder that Alfred wanted to send Annie away. If he didn't know for sure, then somewhere in his subconscious, he recognised the danger. And that danger was back from the shops and downstairs in the kitchen. I cowered in my bed in abject terror at the thought of seeing my sister now I suspected what she might have done. But I disguised my fear by feigning further sickness, and though she offered to sit with me, I declined, pretending tiredness. Memories flitted through my mind like bats around a steeple, swooping low and out of control. But it did me good to think and by the time evening arrived, I had talked myself into giving Annie the benefit of the doubt. After all, a list of initials is meaningless.

Annie took a bath around eight o'clock. I waited until she had shut the door and the bathwater had finished running. As soon as I heard the slosh of water as Annie lowered herself in, I tiptoed to her room. She'd closed and locked the nightstand, but a search of her underwear drawer soon revealed the key. I opened her diary with shaking hands to find day after tedious day of nothing very much and no one especially interesting. And then I arrived at an entry in February. "It has happened once more – I cannot seem to help myself. It feels like Lewannick all over again. I didn't mean to kill Minnie or Aunt Mary and certainly not Alice, who was my dear friend. They thought the poison was in the salmon sandwiches. Sydney Smith dealt with that so eloquently. And he would have been right if I'd used rat poison which is always stained blue. But I put one of William's white farming powders in the chocolate cake. My actions break my heart when I think of them. I've ruined everything, and soon I will be alone. I know what I'm doing, but I don't know why. A sinister force drives me on, and soon Betsy will be dead." By the time I finished the page, there was no doubt. Annie was deliberately dosing my food with poison and had done for a long time. My sister, my only friend, the woman for whom I sacrificed my home and my husband, is trying to kill me. Whatever shall I do?

I gasp aloud, and I am glad that Betsy can't hear me. It cannot be true. Annie, who I came here to protect tonight, is a killer. Or perhaps Betsy is wrong, and this deed exists only in her imagination. There is no proof but her diary. But even as the thought crosses my mind, I know she is guilty. Only Annie or William Thomas could have poisoned Alice Thomas. And though they acquitted Annie, there was ample proof of arsenic in her aunt's and sister's bodies. Just because the soil in Lewannick churchyard could have contained arsenic doesn't mean the bodies weren't full of it before they went in the ground. Annie has got away with murder.

Betsy turns the page. I can't read the date as her hand is over the entry. She is crying again, and tears drip onto the page, smudging the ink. She picks up a pen and scribbles a few more lines.

Annie means to kill me. She is a broken thing and cannot help herself. I can't stop her, and I can't tell anyone, or she will end up on the gallows. A pigeon flew into the dining room window last week. It lay there, stunned and half alive with a broken wing. I could have left it for the cat to find, but I put it out of its misery and wrung its neck instead. It was a kindness. And that is what I will do to Annie. She will have hidden the poison nearby. Annie does most of the cooking, and I expect to find it in the kitchen somewhere. I will pop it in the bottle of tonic she keeps by her bed, not all at once, but a bit at a time, just like she did. It should be over in a few weeks, and my sister won't suffer. It's the only way I can protect her now.

Betsy stands, walks towards the bedroom door, and puts on her dressing gown. Then she tiptoes downstairs and I follow. I watch as she removes a clothes hanger from the pantry door, searches the cupboard and removes one bottle then another, her bloodshot eyes heavy with desperation. She uncorks the stopper and decants the contents into the brown bottle, which she takes upstairs. I do not need to follow her to know what she's doing with the poison, and I don't try to stop her. Instead, I give way to the pull on the back of my head. Seconds later, with tears streaming down my face, I return to my body, determined never to trust without question again.

THE END

AFTERWORD

Afterword

The 1920s heralded the golden age of poisoning. Though arsenic was regulated, it appeared in everyday products, and a determined poisoner would have no difficulty getting their hands on it. The Lewannick case was one of several murders in this era that went unpunished. And yet, there were only two credible suspects, Annie Hearn and William Thomas. But there was no evidence against William, and that against Annie was largely circumstantial. Case theories often assume that blame lies with William. I am not convinced. Annie was an unstable character who had already been on the wrong side of the law. In 1919, Annie Hearn and her sister Minnie (Lydia) moved from Harrogate to Weston-super-Mare. While there, Annie was charged with the theft of a jewel case, a handbag, a workbox, a writing case, and other sundry items, which she took from the owners of the boarding house in which she was staying. Having removed the items, she posted them to Harrogate. Though committed for trial, Annie was eventually discharged, but this was not her only deception. Annie claimed to be married to Leonard Willmot Hearn MD and posted a marriage announcement to that effect, the marriage allegedly happening in London on June 6, 1929.

A second announcement appeared days later, reporting the death of Willmot Hearn on June 12, 1929. But there was only one Dr Leonard Hearn in the medical directory, a tuberculosis officer for Nottinghamshire who was a bachelor and very much alive at the time of Annie's trial. Furthermore, Leonard Hearn's father, Dr Ethelbert Hearn, was known to the Everard family, and Annie often collected her sister's medication from his practice. Annie must have been dismayed at the dogged determination of police and press to resolve the mystery of her marriage and soon faced further embarrassment. The newspapers published a picture of Leonard Hearn that Annie habitually carried with her. But it was another deception, and they soon identified her 'husband' as the late Lieutenant Charles Stewart Vane-Tempest, great-grandson of the third Marquess of Londonderry. Around the same time, the *Sheffield Daily Telegraph* of November 20, 1930, ran a report about an incident earlier in Annie's life. When the family resided in Grindleford some twenty years before, Annie had invited two girlfriends over from Grimsby, who stayed overnight. Within days of leaving, both girls had died.

Having an interest in family history, I couldn't resist looking for Annie in the 1939 census. After the trial, she accompanied Betsy Poskitt and her husband Alfred to Long Sandall and lived there for a while. But she wasn't there in 1939, and neither was Betsy. I couldn't find Alfred in the census at all, but death records show he died in 1953 and may have been estranged from Betsy at the time. After several abortive attempts, I finally located a record for Betty Poskitt in Shrewsbury. Purporting to be a single woman, she was born in 1878, is the right age to be Annie's sister, and was living with Margaret Day, born June 2, 1885, the year of Annie's birth. Betsy and Annie were daughters of Robert Everard and Betsy Day, and it would be a logical step for Annie to take her mother's maiden name. Having found them in Shrewsbury, I looked at death records. Betsy's (in the name of Betsy, not Betty) showed her dying aged eighty-two in 1960, and if Annie was Margaret Day, she expired in 1948, aged sixty-three. Betsy's 1939 census entry shows her as 'incapacitated', but Margaret died first. I haven't ordered full death certificates, and I could be barking up the wrong tree, but these records were enough to inspire me to write The Cornish Widow.

Still, aspects of this case are far from certain, and naturally, sensational press reports cannot be trusted. Yet, I believe Annie was a fantasist who benefited financially from her aunt's and sister's deaths. She absconded to Looe instead of facing her accusers, pretended to commit suicide, then lied to everyone she encountered until they arrested her. Annie may not have worked alone, and William Thomas might have played a part. Yet, I believe that Annie was justifiably imprisoned and probably got away with murder.

If you have any theories on the Lewannick poisonings, I would love to hear them. You can contact me or find out more about my books on the website below.

Thank you for reading The Cornish Widow. I hope you liked it. If you want to find out more about my books, here are some ways to stay updated:

Join my mailing list or visit my website
https://jacquelinebeardwriter.com/

Like my Facebook page
https://www.facebook.com/LawrenceHarpham/

If you have a moment, I would be grateful if you could leave a quick review of The Cornish Widow online. Honest reviews are very much appreciated and are useful to other readers.

Coming Soon:

The Constance Maxwell Dream Walker Mysteries

The Croydon Enigma

Also, by this author:

Lawrence Harpham Murder Mysteries:

The Fressingfield Witch
The Ripper Deception
The Scole Confession
The Felsham Affair
The Moving Stone

Short Stories featuring Lawrence Harpham:

The Montpellier Mystery

Box Set containing
The Fressingfield Witch, The Ripper Deception & The Scole Confession

Novels:

Vote for Murder

<<<>>>>

Printed in Great Britain
by Amazon

62951138R00142